Where the Bruised Pieces Go

ABOUT THE AUTHOR

Jane Fawley is a psychotherapist and author.
She lives just outside London with her husband
and two neurotic rescue dogs.

Where the Bruised Pieces Go

Jane Fawley

Troubador Publlishing Ltd
Unit E2 Airfield Business Park,
Harrison Road, Market Harborough,
Leicestershire LE16 7UL
Tel: 0116 279 2299
Email: books@troubador.co.uk
Web: www.troubador.co.uk

ISBN 978 1 80514 173 0

British Library Cataloguing in Publication Data.
A catalogue record for this book is available from the British Library.

Printed and bound in Great Britain by 4edge Limited
Typeset in 10.5pt Garamond by Troubador Publishing Ltd, Leicester, UK

Matador is an imprint of Troubador Publishing Ltd

For Tristan, my love.
Everything, always.

"Hell is empty,
And all the devils are here."

William Shakespeare, *The Tempest*, act 1, scene 2

1

Ben spotted her at last, the woman he was going to kill. Just a fleeting glimpse through unmoving London traffic, but enough to make his mouth water. She flowed against the tide of city workers, her red dress a scarlet wound on a sea of grey. Vivid and conspicuous in tones of ripe cherry, a touch gaudy perhaps, but he was stained by her now and couldn't look away. She moved between stationary black taxis, crossing a road thick with belching diesel and dust, trotting when possible to escape a heavy spring shower. Her long, dark hair was damp and plastered across the pale skin of her forehead, tangled across her throat like seaweed, a frond stuck to her bottom lip. Seeing her there, unfazed, not knowing what was about to befall her, made him smile. A secret was such a juicy thing to have. There was something empowering about watching someone who didn't know they were being watched; seeing without being seen made him feel alive and he shuddered as the hair on his arms unfurled.

He imagined lifting the damp hair away from her face and twisting it through his fingers and around his knuckles. Brushing his fingers across her slender neck, caressing and stroking, gently at first, then tightening and pressing until that milky throat was blemished blue with the weight of his passion. He would press his face close to the back of her neck, picking up her scent and breathing it in until she became a part of him. Then perhaps a taste, just a gentle flicker of his tongue behind her ear where the skin was soft and smooth. Maybe then, if he really couldn't resist, he might suck the earlobe into his mouth. Only a nibble, not enough to make her bleed. Not yet.

Love at first sight, perhaps? It was stimulating at the least. She was flirting with his imagination, and he knew how she would taste when she was on the tip of his tongue, her skin damp and salty with the sweat of a humid afternoon, but sweet too, natural sugar and spice leaking from every pore and tempered by warm rain.

Then all too quickly she was gone. An office foyer swallowed her whole and he temporarily doubted her existence, questioned his luck, but then he feels it. Subtle at first, but then surging and consuming, a rising heat throughout his body, a warmth in his thighs pushing up into his chest and spreading across his back as it arches with a brief spasm. A hardening between his legs that exerts and insists, straining against his trousers. The tips of his fingers turn numb, and blisters of sweat form across his top lip. His heart rate increases, and his breathing suddenly feels too shallow and far too urgent, but that is how he knows she is real. He recognises these feelings and is comforted by their familiarity. He is certain of them, guided by them and they hold him steady. He did see her, she showed herself to him, and although the moment was frustratingly brief – just an appetiser – it was pure light and magic. He will look back one day and know this was when it had started with her.

Then the waiting. He shelters from the rain underneath a doorway that reeks so strongly of stale urine it offends him, makes him feel unclean, but she is worth it. The sky is a lilac bruise, but brightening with watery sunlight, the shower moving off. He stares at the office block across the road, hoping to catch a glimpse of her in one of the many windows, but they reveal only the reflection of drifting clouds. The end of the working day is still a few hours away, and impatience is building inside him, but that is part of the routine. If he can slow his breathing and control the excitement fluttering in his stomach, then irritation will give way to anticipation, the in-between moments of wanting and having. Foreplay.

But maybe he has jumped too soon, plunged in with an unbecoming haste because he wants so badly to feel this way about somebody again, to forget how raw the first one left him. He loved her, almost to bursting, but not quite. She lacked the stamina to let it build, she was weak, and she ran dry, but the solitude he craved after her has become stifling and creeps across his skin with insistent fingers, encroaching and suffocating and sticky to the touch.

Perhaps the woman in the red dress is the one he has been waiting for, healing for. The one who will remind him that it's nice to share. Maybe she will see his vulnerability as a gift of trust to hold gently, rather than a sign of weakness to be taken advantage of. Perhaps this one will be kind.

Finally, the hunger for her propels him into the last of the rain, the smell of warm, wet concrete musky and sweet as it dries. She could be special. He wants her to be. He wants so badly to love her all the way down, to the very heart of her.

2

Emma Malone was having trouble focusing on her patient. Simon sat on the edge of his chair, feet firmly planted, hands gripping the armrests as if preparing to launch himself from the room, but Emma knew from experience she wouldn't be that fortunate. His upright position and intensity were born of his own self-fascination. He hung on every word uttered from his own slightly wet lips. Emma was repulsed by Simon's lips, and by much of what came out of them, but she listened to him with tolerance for fifty minutes, just as she did every week.

Goosebumps rose on her arms as the air-conditioning took control of the room temperature and settled on glacial. She glanced out of the window and yearned for the warmth outside almost as much as she yearned for Simon to discover a modicum of self-awareness. Her attention wandered to a book on her shelf by the psychologist, Carl Rogers. He emphasised that therapists should offer their patients an unconditional positive regard, a non-judgemental acceptance to build trust, but Emma couldn't seem to offer Simon that. She wondered, not for the first time, why she found him so offensive. She felt contempt towards him rather than the empathy vital to her work, and she was unsettled by how her feelings were obscuring her process as a therapist for the first time in her seven-year career. She believed wholeheartedly in the process of therapy and its positive effect on people, even the Irish – despite Sigmund Freud's misgivings – but there was something about Simon she found hard to take, and she knew she had to accept some responsibility for his lack of progress.

"I once told her she'd be more attractive with less makeup. She's naturally pretty and doesn't need all that stuff." Simon pushed his hair back from his face leaving a furrow through his hair gel. "She didn't like that, left the table with a mouthful of food. It was a bloody compliment."

Emma felt her eyes aching with the effort of not rolling them. Rogers also recommended therapists be congruent or genuine with their patients, so perhaps it was time Emma dealt bluntly with Simon. If he had such an alienating effect on her, maybe he was also having this effect on others. In fact, this had been the essence of his presenting problem on his first day in therapy. Dismantling him brick by brick wasn't working, she needed a wrecking ball.

When Simon paused to draw breath, she took advantage of the temporary silence.

"Simon." Perhaps she said his name too harshly, but it had the desired effect. He looked at her in surprise, as if he had forgotten her presence in the room. Annoyance twisted his features, interruption had broken his train of thought, which was exactly her intention.

"I'm going to stop you there and ask you to consider something. How would you feel if she said you'd be more attractive if you kept your unsolicited opinions to yourself? Or did you assume her self-esteem would increase under your gaze?" Simon's face sagged, but Emma continued. "You expressed concern in our early sessions about your inability to sustain relationships with women and the long-term implications that may have. I want you to sit back, close your eyes, and think about what you have talked about in this session so far." Emma made sure to emphasise the word *you,* hoping to highlight that, so far, there had been no *we.*

His annoyance morphed to hostility before he turned away. His face creased in concentration, dark eyebrows drooping lower over muddy eyes, but he managed to hold his tongue. He leaned back slowly, looking incredibly uncomfortable in a comfortable chair, the black and white photograph of a stormy beach on the wall behind him shifting slightly as he adjusted his position.

As she witnessed this internal battle, Emma softened towards him. His obvious discomfort in the enforced silence filled the room like rushing water. She felt like she was suffocating but leaned in towards Simon just as he was finally able to lean all the way back. He wriggled back and forth as if trying to bury himself in the chair, perhaps hoping it would allow him to disappear entirely, but then let go of the armrests with a jolt, as if his hands had been freed of invisible constraints, and the stormy beach settled at a crooked angle.

Simon slowly exhaled a jagged breath as Emma deeply inhaled, the scent of sage and lavender from the diffuser reaching her. An exchange of sorts had occurred, an intimacy becoming more powerful than the tension. For the first time, she understood how exhausted her patient must be, holding himself tightly and expressing his emotions in a clumsy way that was causing offence and his own alienation.

At last, as Simon squeezed his eyes shut, Emma saw a vulnerable man tortured by doubt and isolation, struggling under all that was holding him back. She saw a way in beneath all the armour. Sometimes the talking cure benefited from no talking at all.

Emma allowed the silence to build. Apart from the ticking of the clock and the sound of the throbbing air conditioner, the small room was quiet and felt separate from the outside world, but as always, the tightness in her chest was a reminder of the precarious nature of working one-on-one with male patients, even though her chair was always closest to the door and the security office precisely nine steps away.

Emma pushed gently into the silence, as if opening a door that was prone to creaking in a very quiet house.

"Simon," she whispered, "I want you to keep your eyes closed, and when you're ready, sum up today's session so far."

Simon shifted in his seat and licked his lips in preparation, but Emma was expecting his usual launch into rapid dialogue.

"Breathe," she said firmly. "Take your time." She noticed the sweat stains on the armpits of his pale blue shirt increasing despite the frigid air.

After a flutter of his eyelids, he said, "I've been talking about work mostly, about the woman there I like. We used to have lunch a few times a week, until I mentioned her makeup, which apparently, I shouldn't have." He tapped a frantic rhythm with his right foot. "Now she eats at her desk or goes out with the woman she sits next to. She doesn't really talk to me much anymore."

Simon's voice dropped off at the end of his summary, and he folded his arms across his body, a little of the armour back in place. He struggled to keep his eyes closed, but he managed, perhaps understanding the comfort that could come from shutting out all distractions and therefore feeling invisible.

"Now," Emma said, noticing he looked younger somehow, "take some time and try to recall the lunches with your co-worker, think back to the conversations you had and tell me what you learned about her."

There were darting movements under his closed eyelids as

he searched for a response. Then his eyes opened and focused again on her. He wore a stricken look, some of the annoyance from the earlier interruption having dissipated.

"I don't know anything about her," he said in an accusing tone. "She didn't tell me anything about herself." He looked hopefully at Emma, as if wanting her to collude with him in his sense of frustration.

Instead, she asked, "Was there any room in the conversation for her? Did you ask her any questions about herself? Or did you do exactly what you do in this room every week and talk only about yourself? Never pausing for a question from me, never allowing me the space to engage with you in any meaningful way. To really get to know you."

This time when the silence returned, it felt too large to be contained in the small space. It seemed to pulse in time with the palpable anger exuding from Simon like his sweat. Maybe she'd gone too far, and she glanced at the door, at the pen beside her. His cheeks flushed pink, and his hands gripped the armrests once more, knuckles whitening. His mouth opened and closed, and then the anger was gone, replaced by a softness that reassured Emma, soothed the fight or flight response that had clenched her hands into fists.

Calmer now, Emma felt a powerful need to rescue Simon from the anxiety she sensed in him, but she brought herself back under control. Rescuing Simon wouldn't help him, but her counsel would aid him to rescue himself. She watched his expressions ebb and flow and sensed his need to settle. She waited and concentrated on his body language. He reminded her of a novice swimmer about to let go of the side of the pool for the first time.

"Is that what I do?" he asked gently. "I just talk and talk and ignore you?" There was no self-pity in Simon's voice, but instead a dignified concern.

"Yes, that's what you do. I think you resented my interruption earlier in the session. I think it made you feel like I was intruding into a conversation we should have been sharing."

Simon nodded more than once, and to himself rather than to Emma. The sunlight edging into the room glanced across the photograph of the beach, and the final fifteen minutes of therapy slipped by, heavy with all that had taken place but lacking any tension. Emma felt they were sharing something meaningful for the first time. The next session would be important for Simon. He seemed ready to understand his relentless chatter was a disguise for his insecurity.

It was with regret rather than the usual relief that Emma informed Simon the session had come to an end, but he smiled at her, a smile that relaxed his whole face. As he stood, he held out his hand. This uncustomary gesture caught her by surprise. She reached out, and Simon clasped her hand in both of his, and when he thanked her, it felt genuine for the first time.

"I'll see you next week," he said, as he put on his coat and threw his bag across his shoulders. He left the room, ducking under the arched doorway, something Emma hadn't seen him do before, and then she noticed that Simon wasn't hunched over anymore. The therapeutic process was reassuring. She had to trust it, always, even if headway was sometimes a long time coming.

Emma reached for her notepad and sat cross-legged on the armchair to record the session. She allowed herself a moment to savour the pleasure she had experienced as Simon made such a big step. Her pen had leaked ink onto her red dress, but it didn't spoil her mood. It felt enormously rewarding to have finished on such a high note with her last patient of the day.

She checked her diary for the following day's appointments. The first was an introductory session with a new patient, a psychologist in need of some supervision for his own work.

Emma had worked with other counsellors and therapists in a supervisory capacity before. It allowed them a confidential space to bounce ideas off her or to discuss personal issues that prevented them from being at their best for their patients.

Now she had to make her way to the psychiatric hospital wing of the women's prison across town, where she would lead her patients in a weekly group therapy session. This was by far the most challenging part of Emma's week, two hours that always left her exhausted. She had considered giving it up, but therapists for this type of work were in short supply, so her conscience pushed her on, and there was safety in numbers.

She put her diary and the completed notes to one side, stood and stretched, and then removed the band that held her dark hair in a tight bun while it dried from the earlier rain. She moved towards the window. The sun was unfiltered by clouds, the sky a cornflower blue above the roofs of the office blocks opposite.

On the streets below, the bustle increased outside the entrance to Moorgate tube station just down the road. The streets would soon fill with crowds of commuters making their way home or to one of the local bars to await the end of rush hour. Across the street, a man stood in the doorway of a building. He seemed to be staring straight up at her window. She couldn't quite make out his face – it was obscured by the long shadows of late afternoon – but she thought she had seen him there before. Perhaps he was waiting for someone who worked in her building, keeping an eye on the windows for signs of departure.

How long had it been since someone had waited for her? She remembered with a pang of loneliness how lovely that had felt, but she dismissed the thought so that her positive mood wouldn't be tarnished by sadness. She pulled her hair back into a bun, grabbed her bag, and locked the door behind her, preparing for the final journey of her day.

3

In the early hours, just when it should have held him completely, sleep had abandoned Sam Stirling. Case files were spread out on the dark wooden dining table, and he ran his hand across them with both tenderness and a shiver of guilt. All the faces stared up at him. Each woman was different from the last and yet all were somehow the same. Every face was seared into his brain, as familiar to him as his own. He saw them as his mind wandered. He saw them whether awake or asleep. They had all been taken, all murdered, and yet they felt alive to him, present despite their permanent absence. But while they were never far from his thoughts, the meaning behind their deaths remained beyond his reach. The files belonging to the women were his latest case, the one he had been consulting on for over a year now. It had featured in every national newspaper with such regularity, each new edition felt like another accusation sent to wear him down.

"I haven't forgotten you," he told the women, "I won't give up." They looked unconvinced, and his words settled around him like an overcoat a couple of sizes too big.

The dining table was used more for work than eating. The organised mess of paperwork and case files represented the last six years of Sam's work as a psychologist and profiler for the serious crime unit of London's largest police department located near St Bart's hospital in east London. He helped the team with the behavioural patterns or personality traits of dangerous criminals, wading through the minds of abusers, molesters, rapists and killers – the dregs of the London streets, or the "phlegm coughed up by decent society", as his boss had described them not long ago. Sam tried to avoid defeatist labels – they were detrimental to gaining understanding – but lately, after what felt like a lot longer than six years, he appreciated the shorthand they provided.

His eyes felt heavy and sandy. "Coffee and a ciggie," his words nonsensical inside a yawn, but there was nobody to make sense of them anyway. "Breakfast of champions."

Following the routine of the last few weeks, Sam stumbled on heavy legs down the dim hallway and into the bathroom. He squinted as he switched on the lights, then splashed his face with cold water, the remains of sleep disappearing down the plughole. Fatigue had claimed victory over his features once more, adding at least five years to his forty-one-year-old face. The circles under his brown eyes were nearly as dark as his hair, which was flattened on one side and in need of a trim. His hands rasped against a two-day stubble, the odd grey whisker intruding into the brown and settling into the cleft in his chin. He headed into the kitchen in search of coffee and resigned himself to the fact that his days were just longer now. They consumed the nights, leaving sleep like a word on the tip of his tongue.

He carried the coffee back through to the living room and flopped down onto the sofa, the worn brown leather welcoming him back into the indentation he'd made over the years. With well-practised fingers, he rolled a cigarette and inhaled the nicotine. A coughing fit seized him, but the next inhalation went down more easily, and soon the muscles in his

12

neck loosened and his jaw unclenched. As the musky tobacco smoke engulfed him and the steaming coffee took the early morning chill from his body, his mind became still and allowed him to contemplate the childhood nightmare that had woken him again. It always left him gasping until his throat was raw, certain the cloying sweet smell inside the dream clung to his skin, still feeling hands grabbing at him with terrifying strength pulling him under water again and again. Older images from childhood had lately entwined with the faces of the murdered women, the past and present a knot as tangled as the damp sheets he discovered upon waking.

He couldn't remember when his nightmare had first started, but it had been while he was still young enough to call his father to his bedside to soothe him and read to him until he fell asleep once more. The nightmare had been a regular visitor ever since, nagging at him and pushing back into his life like an illness he couldn't quite shake. Carl Jung suggested dreams were a window into the unconscious mind, a way for the brain to work out a solution to a problem the dreamer was having in their waking life. But so far, across all the years that the nightmare had been a lurking presence, a solution hadn't yet presented itself.

Sam rested his head in his hands. "Not now, please not now." The nightmare was often the precursor to a depression capable of plunging him into a deep, dark pit and holding him there with feelings of inadequacy in his job, a sense of failure in his life, that everything was too much. It created such a feeling of helplessness that struggling was futile. It was a fight with an invisible enemy, a spectre that would always have the upper hand, and each time it took more of him. He raked his hands through his hair as if he could push the thoughts away at the same time. He couldn't afford this now. He had to focus on the case.

After placing the cigarette on the side of a heavy glass ashtray, Sam pulled himself out of the sofa, stood, and stretched, another wide yawn making him shudder. He rolled his neck back and forth until the vertebrae clicked, and then moved towards the large windows that took up most of one wall. The dome of St Paul's Cathedral was almost dwarfed by the brutalist architecture of the Barbican towers. They were stark and commanding, piercing like needles into a pale sky tinged with red. Cranes like metal dinosaurs leaning over their developing young hovered beside futuristic office blocks of glass and steel. Nearby were council-owned high-rises, and Victorian warehouses converted into loft apartments much like his own. Ancient and modern pushing against each other, a symbiotic symphony of city life.

Ten floors below him, a police siren broke the seal of quiet on the streets. Living up high brought him a sense of solitude and security that made him feel untouched by the world below, able to view life from a safe distance – unlike his work that often demanded dangerous proximity – that was why Sam had bought the place. From this height, London looked beautiful, like a small world trapped inside a snow globe. Only at ground level did the truth of the city intrude, its reality sometimes too much to take. The streets were not paved with gold after all, but rather with dog shit and spit – and the bodies of dead women. Somewhere out there was the killer he was looking for.

He turned from the window. The faces on the dining table beckoned him. There was accusation in their expressions, but also a question in their eyes – the same one Sam had been asking himself for so long it formed the rhythm to his days: *What kind of mind is capable of killing like that?*

He whispered to the women the same words he did every morning. "Today we will find him."

Then his mobile phone rang.

"Stirling?" It was his boss, Detective Chief Inspector Albert Riley, his voice unusually loud, words crashing into each other. "Another woman's gone missing."

And just like that, Sam's hope for the day was snatched from him as swiftly as a plaster ripped from a wound, pulling the scab with it.

*

Sam hurried through Whitecross Street Market which was filling up with people on their way to work. It hummed with the banter of stallholders promoting their wares in powerful, Cockney voices, competing with the throb of food truck engines and spitting, smoking grills, the mouth-watering smells drifting down the street on a warm breeze. Farther into the market, a greasy-spoon cafe added its own intoxicating aroma of frying bacon, and Sam's stomach growled its approval, but he only had time to grab a coffee. As he headed towards the cafe, his half-asleep brain focused only on caffeine, a bicycle courier swerved to avoid him.

"Wake the fuck up!" the courier shouted. "Watch where you're going."

Words to live by, thought Sam; he doubled the size of his coffee.

Outside the cafe window, the lines by the food stalls increased. The market, once a little stale and half empty, now thrived as the gentrification of this section of the city took hold. Stalls that used to sell dodgy products off the backs of lorries had given way to gastronomy. But as new and shiny as this part of the East End now felt, it was merely the decoration on a poisonous cake. "All fur coat and no knickers," as the locals would say. The darker side of life flowed underneath the gilded topcoat like blood from a severed limb, pooling into the gutters and dripping into the drains before joining the Regent's Canal that ran through London like an artery.

Because of his job, Sam saw the city in a different way to most people. He couldn't un-see the terrifying ghouls that paved the path before him, the wickedness that was emblematic of another kind of world. He couldn't un-hear the words that lingered on the lips of the horrifying, the disturbed and the sick, who just wanted to see the world bleed because they liked the taste. His mind would never be clean, because he knew too much about those who made the world dirty.

Feeling more awake with another coffee inside him, Sam cut through the concrete confusion of the Barbican and hurried towards work. After weaving between the commuters around the entrance to the Barbican tube station, he jogged down Long Lane, passing the cavernous green-domed building in the heart of Smithfield meat market. A Grade II listed monument to meat occupied the space that had once been the place for public executions – now it was the place for the butchery of animals. The odour of raw flesh was so distinct among the traffic fumes, it seemed to have a texture. The coffee roiled in Sam's stomach, but he thought only of the woman who had been reported as missing. She might not be another victim of their killer at all, but Sam couldn't ignore the feeling of dread that the woman would never show up, at least not alive. She would instead be displayed with a hideous beauty, grotesquely vivid and sullied by the twisted imagination of the last person she ever saw.

He made his way to the offices of the police task force overseeing the investigation into the murdered women. The nearby police station was going through a lengthy refurbishment, so the task force had been relocated to vacant offices nearby and currently sat above a betting shop. Sam climbed two narrow flights of stairs and entered the security code into the keypad. As he pulled open the door, a wall of sound hit him that seemed far louder than the team of twenty assorted police officers and CID detectives warranted.

Inside, it was warm and uncomfortably stuffy, the desk fans successful only at distributing the odour of overworked bodies and overcooked fast food. Energy-saving lighting and yellowing paint gave the room a jaundiced feel that created a sense of malaise, and yet the mood was frantic, and it appeared as if every phone was ringing.

The man heading up the investigation was DCI Albert Riley, an experienced officer in his fifties, a company man since his early twenties. Standing in the middle of the room, he conducted his orchestra with calm authority. Eyes followed him round the room as he gave orders, frequently patting officers on the back to encourage them. His nickname, Smiley Riley, fitted him as neatly as his well-cut dark suits.

Despite his advancing years, DCI Riley was open-minded and willing to embrace new technologies and methods, and he was responsible for employing Sam as a profiler.

He pulled Sam aside. "You understood my garbled call, then?" he asked in his usual deep but gentle voice, his accent local. The stress of the job had made itself comfortable on his face years ago, but this case was etching the lines deeper. "It's already all over the news. Bloody irresponsible journalism. We don't even know if she's dead." He shook his head, looking as exhausted as Sam. "No regard for the girl's family."

"Do we think this is another one of our victims?" Sam's voice was husky with early morning smoking.

Riley moved across the room to the whiteboard where photographs of the murder victims were displayed, smiling faces immortalised in happier times.

"I'll be surprised if she isn't. The date seems like too much of a coincidence." Riley pointed to the first column drawn on the board in red marker with the header JANUARY. "Our killer murdered victims one and four on the same day in January, but a year apart."

He then pointed to the next column headed MAY where, for now, only one photograph was displayed. "The second victim was murdered this time last year. Hard to believe we won't find victim number five in the next three days." Riley touched the vacant space on the board. "If so, it will be the second time the killer has stuck to his routine. Obviously, you know what this means." He pointed to the third column on the board marked SEPTEMBER that contained the third victim's image. "If we don't find this bastard, we can expect victim number six to turn up dead in September, same time as number three last year."

Sadness and frustration dragged his features downwards, but his posture remained as ramrod-straight as ever.

"It has to be him, then, doesn't it?" Sam asked. "If the missing woman turns up dead soon, according to schedule, it's got to be our killer." He tried to keep the alarm out of his voice and wondered if his eyes were as bloodshot as Riley's.

"It's him. I can feel it. We won't find her alive." Riley sighed. "There's fuckery afoot." He scanned the photos. "Fuckery and trickery." He gave Sam a once-over. "You look exhausted. Everything alright?"

Sam remembered his tired face in the mirror earlier and looked down at the creases in his shirt. "I'm okay. Bit of a sleepless night, that's all."

"Well, I appreciate you being here so early, then. A Stirling effort, as usual." Riley patted him on the shoulder.

It was a frequent joke, but it made Sam smile all the same.

"I'm giving a briefing in a minute," Riley said. "I'd like you in on it, but then I want you to concentrate on the previous victims, look back over the case notes, personal histories, anything you have, anything at all that might help. I know you've done that dozens of times, but something may jump out at you. You know the story – it's what you always tell me – we have to go backwards to go forwards."

"Nice to know you've been listening," Sam said, as he moved off into a quiet corner.

"I'm always listening," Riley said. "It may not look like it, but I hear everything that goes on in this room. A lot of it is utter bollocks, but you'll be happy to know that most of what you say doesn't fall into that category. Now, head down, arse up, and get on with the files. If it's too noisy out here, take my office for a few hours." As he turned to leave, he said, "And by the way, that whistle needs a visit to the dry cleaners, it could stand up on its own at this stage."

Sam looked down at his suit and noticed the coffee stain on his lapel; he wasn't sure if it was from this morning. "Noted, thanks," Sam replied. He picked up his phone. "I just have to make a quick call before the briefing and the profiling and all the murdering and the dry cleaning."

He left a message cancelling his first session with Emma Malone, his new psychotherapist. Today wasn't the day to start therapy again, even though he hadn't worked with another therapist in a supervisory capacity for over a year. Maybe it was neglectful of him. Succeeding at his job meant attending therapy himself on a regular basis to be at his best as a psychological profiler. The nightmares and insomnia were diverting his focus at work and therefore needed to be addressed. He promised himself he would book another session during the coming days. For now, he had to direct what little remained of his energy towards work.

He moved across the room and looked at the crime scene photos of the murdered women. The scenes were intricately staged, shocking, and yet disturbingly beautiful. Sam knew the killer was communicating, and all he had to do was listen.

4

Annie waited in the corner of the room, almost motionless and facing the wall. Her spine was straight, her shoulders back and feet evenly spaced, just as she had been taught long ago. Perfectly balanced, holding herself taut, poised and ready to move when the moment came. Ready to glide like blades across a frozen pond – smooth and steady and almost silent, but for the whisper of shaved ice sliced cleanly through. She might have been frozen too, if it wasn't for her large hands clenching into fists every few seconds, prominent blue veins pushing up through her milky, thin skin like the roots of a tree through pavement. She blinked rapidly, holding her eyes closed for a second too long each time, as if trying to dispel the last image registered there. Her head dipped, keeping time with the blinking.

When she returned to the reality of the room, it was with a slight surprise, but recognition of the familiar soon intruded, and with it came disappointment. She lifted herself onto the tips of her toes and moved away from the corner. Her movements were somewhat exaggerated, but fluid and graceful, the vestiges of the ballerina she had wanted to be clinging to her like cobwebs. She floated towards the windows and turned her face up to the buttery light of late afternoon, the sun warming her face. A gentle breeze moved through the trees surrounding the extensive gardens, the dense foliage almost obscuring the high wall of red brick. Sunlight glinted off the rusty barbed wire that sat atop the wall like balls of spun sugar.

Wooden benches were placed at various points throughout the grounds, some under the shade of trees, others by flowerbeds in full sun. Some of the benches were occupied by women deep in conversation, heads close together and faces animated. On others, individuals sat alone with a book on their lap. *You are never alone when you have a good book*, Annie thought. *A good book is company enough.* She had read all the books in the library, some more than once, although a new batch had been promised for the coming week.

Her eyes fell upon a man outside dressed in dark green overalls. He was on his knees weeding one of the flowerbeds, his head obscured by the heavy blooms of yellow roses drooping in the heat of an unusually warm May afternoon. He was methodical in his work but drew back when he caught his finger on a thorn and withdrew his head from underneath the roses, dislodging a few petals as he sat upright. He examined his injured finger and then sucked on it, removing the spot of blood. Annie smiled and copied him, sucking her own finger all the way into her mouth, pulling it in and out until saliva ran down her chin.

The man pressed his fists into the base of his spine to massage the tightness in his muscles, and then ran a hand across his forehead, leaving a smear of bloody dirt above one eyebrow. He looked behind him to retrieve his gloves and caught sight of Annie staring out at him. He smiled at her, exposing straight, white teeth, and gave a small wave, but she didn't wave back.

He wouldn't smile if he knew what I've done, she thought. *He wouldn't wave at me if he knew what I am, or what I'm supposed to be.* She was a What rather than a Who now. Although he must have known she was here for a reason. They were all here for similar reasons, like Liquorice Allsorts crammed in a box, all looking different but tasting the same.

Her breath steamed up the grimy window, creating a fogginess to the outside world, but she could still see the gardener amongst the rose bushes. She breathed onto the glass again and drew an outline around the man, framing him in a square like a living portrait. Another breath onto the window and she drew a dog, its mouth wide open, teeth jagged and completely out of proportion, close to the gardener's head. *It's behind you*, she thought, *and what large teeth!*

She laughed, a throaty rasp that was more like a bark, the only sound to come out of her all day. A guard looked over, frowned. Annie rubbed a hand across the window, smearing the drawing into the remains of her breath. She didn't want anyone to see it – they might jump to conclusions. Every action had meaning here – and consequences.

"Something funny, Annie?" the guard asked as he approached her.

"What do you think, Einstein? Does this seem like a place that lends itself to amusement?" Annie turned towards the guard, arms extended like wings, but more fight than flight.

The guard removed his hands from his pockets. "Come on, be nice."

"Where's our ill-mannered therapist? She's late for group." Annie moved closer to the guard and stared up at him. "Is her time more valuable than mine?"

He looked into her eyes, took a step back. "I'll go and find out what the hold-up is." He took two more steps before he turned his back to her and walked away, a patch of sweat on the back of his shirt.

Annie sniggered, but then noticed her hands. The dusty

window had left dirt on her fingertips. When she rubbed them together, the rough particles worked their way into the wrinkles of her skin. She brought her fingers to her mouth and licked the tips, gently at first, but then sucking them all the way into her mouth, tasting bitterness and saltiness and something unidentifiable that reminded her of unwashed hair on a pillowcase. The taste repulsed her, but she sucked until her fingers were clean. The dirt was now stuck in her teeth. Her molars ground it down into a fine powder she could swallow. She imagined herself swallowing the gardener framed on glass, eating him all up until he wasn't there anymore.

Bored now by the gardens, she moved into the centre of the room and sat in the corner of one of the sofas, the grey material worn but comfortable. She curled her legs awkwardly beneath her and held one of the cushions across her body, feeling protected by the soft barrier. There were other women in the room, some reading in armchairs, two side by side on another sofa comparing the progress of the brightly coloured hats they were knitting. A group of women sat at a long table together, heads bent over a quilt they were putting together, patch by patch. Faces turned downward, absorbed by their task, their advanced ages revealed by varying shades of grey hair. Younger women formed a group at another table. One plaited the hair of another, loose strands drifting to the floor. A different pair took turns painting each other's fingernails, the smell of nail varnish like pear drops in the warm room. Performing different tasks but sharing the same conversation, the women peppered their subdued voices with the occasional burst of laughter.

Not all of the women who lived here were present. Some were in other rooms keeping themselves to themselves. Others were in class at this time of day. Still more spent their time alone because they didn't play well with others. They were easy to spot on the other side of the building as they wore pale blue.

All the other women wore pink. "Pink to make the boys wink," one of the women repeated over and over again like a song stuck on repeat.

Various shades of pastels rendered the building insipid, inoffensive – and apparently soothing. Pale lemon or lavender for the walls, curtains the colour of weak green tea, and the sofas and armchairs in matching shades of pale grey and lilac. Pastel paintings on the walls depicted vases of flowers or country scenes of cows chewing their cud in green meadows. Worst of all were the kittens – lots of paintings of kittens. Some with balls of wool, others curled up and asleep on soft blankets. In the painting nearest her, five kittens tumbled over each other, small balls of fluffy fur. Women adored kittens after all, and flowers, and pretty scenes of country life, and pink, pink, pink. Women who knitted and played with cosmetics in a pastel world, like cupcakes in a bakery window. Women who should be seen but not heard. *Is it any fucking wonder,* Annie thought, *that some of us just want to tear off the pink and paint the walls blood red? Just make the whole fucking world bleed red.*

There was a low murmur throughout the room, the sound of words filling up the space, flying towards the high eaves of the ceiling until they mingled with one another, no longer making any sense. It was like being trapped in a room full of bluebottles buzzing around her face, trying to get into her mouth, reducing her to carrion.

She rammed her fingers in her ears to block out the sound and inhaled and exhaled deeply until the humming was replaced by her own breath. It was the silence she missed – there were so few opportunities for silence now. Her day was dictated by sounds. A harsh knocking on the rusted metal of her door early in the morning signalled the start of another day. And then, bells. Bells kept them all in line, provided discipline to their supposedly undisciplined minds. A ringing bell informed her that breakfast was now being served, so she had better be up and dressed and standing in line. The same bell an hour later told her to clear away her plate and cup and get on with the rest of her day. The bell was her boss. Later it would summon her to lunch and then dinner, and her stomach would rumble with hunger before the ringing stopped – so well trained was she, like one of Pavlov's dogs, conditioned by environment.

Every day was indistinguishable from the day before and the day before that. Unless it was the first Saturday of the month, when she was allowed one visitor, but only if she'd behaved. It was the same visitor each time – he never missed – but the visits made her feel bad. They were a reminder of the world to which she was denied access, a world without bells.

Sometimes she missed the silence so much it made her want to scream, but that would be beneath her. There was screaming of course, all day long sometimes, but never her screams – she wouldn't humiliate herself in that way. But she often settled for a quiet cry.

The guard came back into the room. "Can I have your attention please, ladies?" Most of the women turned towards him, some eyes more focused than others. "Group therapy is running late today." He turned to leave.

"Why?" Annie asked. She attempted a polite smile to disguise her irritation, but it struggled to form.

He ignored her and left the room, his shoes squeaking across the linoleum. He slammed and locked the door behind him. When he looked back through the glass panel, he smirked at Annie, holding up a ring of keys and shaking them at her as though flaunting their power.

Annie turned away. Her smile snapped off as abruptly as a power cut. As she headed back towards the windows, she swiped the bottles of nail varnish off the table and onto the floor. Bluebottle words silenced.

5

Ben watched her intently from the dark doorway of the room. She didn't know she was being watched, didn't realise her panic was being closely monitored as she struggled to breathe. He was tingling and shivering although the room wasn't chilly, alight with a tense excitement, wringing and twisting his hands, bending his fingers until the knuckles clicked back into place. Tension stretched across his shoulder blades and along the back of his neck, but repeatedly turning his neck left and right, as if waiting to cross a busy road, he loosened the muscles. He smiled as he remembered what he'd been taught in school about crossing roads, how he must always check both ways before stepping off the pavement. School had been a place where he'd excelled and blended in. Sometimes. But that era seemed far too brief and too long ago. Perhaps it was the last time when life had been simple. He remembered it that way. But then love consumed him for the first time, and life was never simple again.

He still missed his first love – he missed her every day, but thinking of her now didn't feel appropriate. If she got in the way now, he would feel dirty, and he didn't want to be dirty on this special night – a night that was already tipping over into day. He'd been very patient and waited for so long he wouldn't allow her to spoil things now. He had to stay clean, clean, clean. He shook his head violently, trying to shake his first love away, but it was too late, he could hear her now.

"Go away," he whispered, "stop talking."

But she was still there in the corner of his mind, spreading like a damp stain across a wall. He smacked the side of his head. "I'm not listening, you had your chance," he smacked again, harder this time. "You're too loud." She wasn't listening to him. "You've spoiled it, I was all nice and clean." He was shouting now, but her stain was growing bigger, turning darker. "Leave me alone."

In the end banging the side of his head against the door frame was the only way to get rid of her. She was a stubborn bitch.

He hit his head against the door frame again and again, harder each time, until he felt a stickiness in his hair and warm blood pooling in his ear. When he was finally free of her, he stopped, his head throbbing with glorious clarity and silence. The deep red smear on the wood meant purity, despite the clump of his hair encased within the thickening crimson like an insect caught in amber. He was angry with himself. He wasn't clean anymore. He was the dirty little piggy again, and dirty little piggies should be locked in a pen. Now that she was out of his head, he had to clean himself up all over again, scrub and rinse, scrub and rinse, until he was squeaky clean and shiny like a star. He switched off the lights and left the room, slamming the door so hard it shook in the frame.

*

Ben's rage alerted the woman tied to the chair – her rasping

27

breath silenced as she sucked it in with a strangled gasp. She held herself rigid, straining to hear more, trying to sense what her blindfolded eyes couldn't show her. Her arms were pulled tightly behind her and tied around the back of the chair. It had a high back that dug into her spine, the top of it pushing into the base of her neck. She tried to lean forwards, but the chair dug into the crook of her elbows sending a sharp pain across her biceps, swapping one level of discomfort for another. Her head pulsed with an intense pain around the top of her skull and behind her eyes as if it had a heartbeat all its own.

A strong but stale odour filled her nose. It had an unpleasant sweetness to it, and yet she inhaled deeply, relieved that she could breathe at all through the mucus caked around her nose and across her top lip. She must have been crying at some stage but had no recollection of it, and it suddenly crossed her mind that she had no recollection at all of how she came to be here, tied to a chair, and this thought spread ripples of panic throughout her body.

The gag in her mouth tasted like the iron of blood. Had she bitten her tongue? The material was rough against the corners of her mouth and pulled tightly behind her teeth, pulling her mouth open into a frozen grin, her lips so dry they'd cracked and split open. She felt thirsty suddenly, but just as that thought came, it was gone again, swallowed by her mounting panic. Tears formed behind the blindfold, and a sob escaped from behind the gag as the realisation of her predicament became horribly clear. Her legs started to shake, sending tremors throughout her body, but as she tried to stop them, she realised her legs were tied just like her arms, each tightly bound at the ankle to a chair leg. She couldn't move at all.

Suddenly she was freezing cold. She started to shiver, her body now shaking and vibrating with such intensity the chair creaked and shuddered beneath her. Saliva flooded her mouth.

She was about to vomit, but from somewhere in her head a voice told her she couldn't be sick, she would choke on the gag. And so, she swallowed rapidly, gulping the saliva back again and again, but as her stomach churned, she didn't think she could keep up, and a burning sensation spread across her chest and up into her throat.

*

In the bathroom mirror, Ben's eyes appeared sunken and his cheeks hollow, but the bright white light hanging above his head wasn't the most flattering, he knew he was attractive, strikingly so. *Movie star good looks.* He recognised his father's nose and jawline now he'd reached thirty-five and grown into his face. The black hair and dark, coffee-coloured eyes were those of his father too – at least that was how it looked from the one creased and blurred photograph he'd seen, its colours bleached by time. He'd never known his father. He was just a hazy man in profile, squinting into the sun.

He turned on the shower, the ancient pipes complaining and groaning like an old man struggling out of an armchair. But the fixtures in the bathroom were modern, the taps sleek and unfussy, the white tiles clean and clinical, and the chrome head of the powerful shower as large as a dinner plate. He'd fitted the bathroom himself, the old one torn out like a rotten tooth and replaced with exacting attention to detail. The room was spotless, a tang of bleach ever-present. He liked to be clean. It was the mark of a gentleman.

As the water heated up, the bathroom filled with steam and chased the chill from the room. He took off his clothes, folding his trousers over the towel rail but tossing his blood-stained shirt on the floor. He would put on a fresh one so he looked well presented, so she could tell he'd made an effort. He could feel his pores opening. They would purge the filth from his body – purge the piggy and make him feel pure again. In the shower, he allowed the water to fall over him. He liked this moment of stillness before the scrubbing started. The water felt like a warm caress from a gentle hand and made his skin tingle. The blood from his head swirled down the plughole. The wound under his hair began to sting, but he had to be clean. He picked up the heavy wooden scrubbing brush, its nylon bristles more suited to scrubbing floors than flesh, and rubbed a bar of coal tar soap across the top, the dense bristles cutting grooves in the orange soap. Starting at the top and working down, he scrubbed every inch of his body until it turned bright pink. The scars on his inner thighs throbbed, some pearlescent with age, others like red cord, but he didn't stop until his skin was on fire. Only then did he feel clean.

After wrapping himself in a large towel, he went to his bedroom in search of fresh clothes. He chose a dark, well-made suit that created a striking contrast with his pale complexion and fit his frame like a second skin. It was one of his favourites and would suit the occasion well. Too many of his younger years had been spent in hand-me-down clothes: trousers too short and flapping around his ankles, jumpers too large with frayed cuffs folded over more than once. Worst of all were the faded shirts with a ring of greasy dirt around the collar, coming into contact with his skin. Frequent washing in the homes in which he'd spent his youth had never been enough to remove the musty odour of second-hand, even third-hand clothes. But those days were gone. Never again would he endure a make-do outfit, a charity shop bargain hanging sloppily off his body and stained with food he'd never eaten. His clothes caressed him now – a fine figure of a man in a classic black suit.

He combed his damp hair into place, taking care not to remove the plaster and reopen the wound on his head, and then he chose a tie. A deep red felt like the right choice – it would match her dress. He enjoyed the tidiness of this, and hoped she would appreciate his thoughtfulness, the attention he paid her in choosing a complementary tie. Next, he picked up a small bottle and twisted off the lid. It was a little stiff, as he only used it on special occasions, and it hadn't been opened for quite some time. He tipped the bottle upside down and deposited a small drop of oil onto the tip of his finger, and then dabbed a little behind each ear and onto the nape of his neck. Soon he could smell the faint sweetness wrapping itself around him, intensifying as it warmed and sank into his skin. Finally, he was ready. One more glance in the mirror produced a small smile. He buttoned his jacket and congratulated himself on the choice of suit – just right for entertaining a lady, well-cut. It always came down to the cut.

*

She was swallowing less frequently now, although some of her spittle had spilled from her mouth. It hung off her chin in thin spools like a spider's web. She realised she wouldn't be sick after all, but her panic had not subsided. She had never been more frightened in her life. Every part of her body shook intensely, almost convulsing with sheer terror. Sweat dripped down her back and between her breasts, and yet she still felt freezing cold, her teeth chafing at the gag. Sudden warmth moved down the back of her legs, and she realised with a powerful sense of shock that she had urinated. Shame washed over her, and then a lucid thought informed her that her shame was misplaced. Without warning, her mind cleared, and she began to struggle.

Her hands were numb, but she rotated them as much as she could, flexing and wiggling her fingers until some of the sensation returned. As she did so, the ties loosened, and the blood rushed back into her hands, filling them with strength. There was a gap now between her wrists, and she was able to pull them a few inches apart – not much, but enough to flex her arms, her biceps straining with the effort. She kept pulling, ignoring the pain in her arms, and slowly the knots loosened. Sweat poured down her face and behind the blindfold into her eyes, and she was vaguely aware they stung, but still she pulled. Finally, she managed to drag one hand free, although it felt as if she had removed some of her skin, but there was no time to think about that now. She had freed her arms completely and shook the rope loose as she brought her arms back around her body, only briefly acknowledging the release of the pain. In her haste to remove the blindfold, she tore out a clump of hair, but she hardly noticed. She removed the gag from her mouth. The room was dark, a sliver of light coming from underneath the door behind her. She was alone.

The ropes that fastened her legs to the chair were very tight. She strained her legs against them but felt no give. There didn't seem to be anything in the room that might help her, so she bent forward and worked at the knot. Frustration made her cry, but she wiped her tears away – there was no time for that. She pulled at the ropes until the knot gave way, freeing one leg. Now that she could manoeuvre her body, she worked on the next knot. To her relief this one felt looser, and a little laugh escaped her lips – a lucky break at last. Finally, she was free.

She stood up quickly, the blood rushing to her head and momentarily clouding the edge of her vision, but she didn't hesitate. Stumbling on shaky legs, she ran to the door, but just before she reached it, it was pulled open, silhouetting a man in the doorway. She screamed and shrank back into the room, the man following her inside.

"Leaving so soon, my darling?" he asked in a voice clipped with irritation. "But our affair is only just beginning."

6

Mobile phones pinged and buzzed across the room, persistent and seeking attention. The members of the task force yelled back and forth as though the office were a construction site, and Sam's headache felt as if it were drilling its way out of the top of his head. He swallowed two painkillers with coffee that may have been yesterday's and briefly closed his eyes shutting the room out allowing the women to beckon him inside the end of their world.

The case files were open and pulled him into tattered lives on tattered pages. Four case files for four lost lives. Although a *lost* life wasn't quite right. A *stolen* life was more accurate, as if it had been there for the snatching rather than the living. Inside each file, four murdered women were reduced to pages of cold hard facts: their day-to-day lives, their friends and family and the places they worked. The details of their last known movements on a day that was all about last moments. Detailed information, practical, black and white and cold, devoid of the warmth of living colours.

Anger stirred inside, a sense of hopelessness that felt almost as tangible as the files in front of him, but he knew such feelings had to be channelled rather than pushed aside. He carefully positioned each file on the table, the first victim nearest him. He would start all over again, from beginning to end. As Sam focused on the files, the tangled office soundtrack emulsified and then dissolved. The murdered women reached for him, and he stepped into their stories once more.

The killings started over a year ago, just before threadbare Christmas trees were dumped on street corners and the season of goodwill turned into the resentment of long, dark winter. Glittery decorations still adorned the windows of shops and homes; fairy lights threaded between lampposts formed canopies of glowing and flashing lights above cold, frost-covered streets. But as the news of the first murder broke on 3 January, London was wrenched from the festive season into a horrifying reality that suddenly rendered the decorations gaudy and inappropriate. With the murder came a new fear that had women looking over their shoulders more often than usual and increased the anxiety of staying out late and walking home alone down streets that felt darker, longer. Parks and public gardens were turned from peaceful places of solitude into isolated waste grounds where one could, quite literally, lose their head.

Back then, Victim Number One didn't have a number – she'd simply been the victim of a brutal murder. It was only later that she became the first victim of a serial killer keen to establish himself in his chosen career. Four months later, towards the end of May, another woman was found murdered. The two victims had died under similar circumstances, which aroused suspicion that they might be the victims of the same killer. When a third murdered woman was found in September, the suspicions were confirmed, and the women were then given the numbers they would be known by forever: victims one, two and three. The tragic trio was joined by a fourth in January, a year to the day since the first woman had been murdered. Four women dead and now, as the end of May approached, another woman was missing. It seemed as if the killer was a creature of habit, one who enjoyed marking an occasion.

The first victim, Rosie Jones, had just turned twenty-one. As the youngest victim, she had the thinnest file. She was a student who had almost completed her training to be a teacher, evidently something she'd been born to do. Sam sensed that Rosie was going to be the kind of teacher who nurtured the potential of a child, one who would make a lasting impression. But in the end, she had made a lasting impression on the wrong person.

During term-time, she'd lived in a flat on Thornhill Square, a beautiful ellipse of Victorian houses in Islington surrounding a large, well-maintained, rose-filled square of protected green space. It was here that her body was found. She had promised to call her parents on New Year's Day, just as she always did, but when the call didn't come, they became concerned and alerted police. Their concern gave way to devastation shortly thereafter. When Sam spoke to Rosie's mother, she seemed stuck in time, like a mannequin in a shop window with a painted-on smile. Her life was now divided into two: the time before and the time after Rosie's murder. Rosie's father kept the *after* at arm's length.

It was the park keeper who'd found Rosie's body. He'd been out for his usual early morning patrol around the large square, which had been obscured by a midwinter mist so thick he'd felt as if he was the only person alive in the whole city, the only one blanketed by the kind of heavy silence that comes with mist. Sam remembered the keeper saying he'd always loved misty mornings and the way they made him feel, as if he were balanced on the edge of the world, preparing to fly, and another step forward would tip him into the arms of thermals waiting to lift him. He'd told Sam how he'd gingerly taken a few steps, half believing he would take flight, and then he'd tripped over something and fallen heavily to the ground. The frosty grass cracked and splintered as he landed awkwardly, the breath knocked out of him. Rosie's body lay on the crisp, frozen grass. Her blood, lots of blood, was like a red blanket under her body, surrounding her and framing her within the world of white. Sam held the photograph in front of him and recalled the park keeper's shock and confusion, that it had taken his brain a few seconds to register he was lying next to a body without a head, that his hands were sticky with blood and the awful, piercing scream shattering the silent morning was coming from him. Mist no longer held the same fascination or the daydream of flying.

Rosie hadn't just been lying on the ground on a bed of her own blood – she'd been displayed. There was a precision to the way she'd been left, placed rather than thrown. Positioned with care, as if a film director had framed her for maximum impact in the shot. The contents of her bag were piled at her feet, which were bare and tinged blue with the icy stroke of death. Her socks had been balled and neatly placed within her shoes, which stood next to her legs. A red hat was left where her head should have been, glued to the grass by her own blood. She lay on her back with her arms outstretched, a pear resting on one of her palms. It was unripe, with one large bite taken out of it, the white flesh of the fruit turned brown. In her other hand she held her own heart, deep red, almost purple, and coated with the frost of the cold day, glistening like a precious jewel dusted with glitter. The gaping wound in her chest was more shocking to Sam than her missing head somehow. It made Rosie's death all the more real for what was no longer beating there. The killer had ripped out her heart, her centre, but had then given it back to her. To Sam it felt like a final insult. Because the killer had chosen to give back Rosie's heart rather than take it with him, it seemed like he was taunting Rosie. This notion resonated deeply with Sam, as if the killer had considered Rosie's heart, and therefore Rosie herself, as worthy of nothing but rejection.

While Rosie's missing head and ripped-out heart would haunt Sam for the rest of his life, it was the pear he thought about more than anything else. Try as he might, he couldn't understand what it was supposed to mean. The pear had been tested after it was taken from the scene of the crime, but the results had revealed nothing. On closer inspection, it turned out that no one had taken a bite from the pear, but rather they had scooped out the flesh – probably with a spoon rather than a knife, because the edges of the fruit were smooth rather than ragged. This meant there were no teeth marks or DNA from saliva to study. The pear itself was the clue, but Sam and the team working on the murder had no idea why it had been left at the scene.

Sam had researched pears extensively to try to decipher their meaning. It turned out the pear was an ancient fruit mentioned by Shakespeare and Dickens and even earlier in Homer's poem *The Odyssey*. In some parts of Asia, the pear was a symbol for the human heart, which seemed to fit more closely than anything else, but Sam still wasn't convinced. There was something ridiculous about making a piece of fruit so important – that something so simple, so benign, could be potentially so revealing – and so he'd continued to research it, but the significance of the pear remained a mystery.

The crime scene was thin on evidence. The police examined Rosie's clothes, but these gave nothing away. The killer had been extremely careful and had left nothing of himself behind. Everything left at the scene, apart from the pear, belonged to Rosie. Her underwear had been removed and was left folded with her shoes and socks, and this was clearly important, as Rosie was still dressed in all of her other clothes. At first this suggested a sexual motivation to the crime, but again no evidence had been left behind, so the underwear left more questions than answers. Sam knew it had to be significant; he just didn't know in what way. Initially, he'd doubted his effectiveness at bringing a level of understanding to the murder. He had been brought in to read the scene, but this was a language he couldn't decipher. The lack of evidence went some way towards reassuring him that this was a careful, clever killer, and there wasn't much to read. He told himself it was less the case that he was failing at his job and more that the killer was excelling at his.

Sam knew another body would turn up. They were dealing with a killer who'd gone to too much effort to just stop. This was someone who'd made long-term plans for a project that had probably been germinating inside his dark imagination for years. He hadn't dumped Rosie's body like rubbish; he had displayed it with care, had been deliberate in the way he'd left her possessions. The killer was telling a story. It was up to Sam to understand what that story was, although he didn't expect a happy ending. A gnawing desperation told him another body would have to be discovered before Rosie's death would make any sense. Another woman had to die in order to give life to the investigation, and when, just a few months later, Riley informed Sam that a second body had been found, the first thing he felt was relief.

Suzy Peters was found dead on 23 May, just as the weather was warming and the last of the pink blossoms from fruit trees were scattered across the streets like confetti. She was found under a pale blue sky, on succulent grass full of buttercups vibrant with golden life, ushering in brightness and hope. It had been dawn on a Monday morning in Postman's Park, a small, quiet space tucked away on St Martin's Le Grand, close to St Paul's Cathedral. To Sam it felt like a secret place, a tiny green refuge that housed the Watts Memorial built in the 1900s to commemorate acts of bravery and sacrifice performed by local people many years ago. Sam was particularly appalled that the killer would choose this place to show that human beings were equally capable of evil.

Suzy had been a marketing assistant in an advertising agency, twenty-four when her body was discovered among the blood-spattered buttercups. She was displayed just like Rosie, on a bed of her own blood, turning rusty brown and thick by the time she was found by the gardener unlocking the park early that morning. Her head was missing, and she too was found on her back with her arms outstretched, a pear in one hand and her heart in the other. Her bag had been emptied and placed in a tidy pile along with her underwear, shoes and socks.

Once again, the killer had left nothing incriminating behind, although he did leave something that was obviously forming his signature – along with the heart and pear. Lying where Suzy's head should have been was a red hat identical to the one found with Rosie. The police had assumed that the hat they'd found with Rosie's body had belonged to her – it fitted the winter scene. But after another conversation with Rosie's parents, it became clear that it hadn't been hers. Rosie disliked the colour red and would never have chosen to wear such a hat. After that, DCI Riley had emphasised – sternly and definitely without his smile – they must never make assumptions at the scene of a crime. The red hat didn't fit the spring weather in which Suzy was killed, and indeed her sister, Sasha, with whom she lived, confirmed that it was not Suzy's. It had been left by the killer, like a name painted on a picture by an artist claiming his work.

Sam remembered one of the last things Sasha had said to him about female fear: she felt it was in-built, hard-wired into the brain from a young age. That women were always ready, always scared, but tucked the fear away and carried on with their life. Unless it was ripped from them.

Summer came, bringing with it long, warm days that filled the streets with Londoners wearing seasonal smiles. Every park, garden square and grass verge was crowded with pink and peeling-skinned city dwellers greedy for sunshine. Pollution was swallowed down with lunch at outdoor cafes, and people carelessly left their windows and doors open as if crime had taken a break, but Sam knew that wasn't the case. The third body was found on the first day of September, when the balmy weather decided to turn itself into an Indian summer. Lizzie Saunders was twenty-three years old and worked in a clothing shop in Shoreditch, close to the flat she shared with two friends. She worked very hard, sometimes seven days a week, in order to save money to go travelling for a year. She had almost reached her target and had bought her plane ticket just days before her body was found. That she had been so close to an escape made her death seem even more unfair.

A jogger had discovered her body just after sunrise by the pond in Victoria Park, a large expanse of well-tended parkland close to Bethnal Green. While looking at the body, Sam noticed a swan with its feathers splashed red, the deep crimson startling and disturbing against the bone white. It left behind bloody footprints before it flew away.

Charlotte Reynolds, a twenty-six-year-old copywriter who lived in Islington, was found dead on 3 January. The killer appeared to be celebrating the anniversary of his first kill, and perhaps in honour of this, he'd decided to leave a new addition at the scene: a comb. The comb itself was nothing special, just a cheap example that could be bought from any high street chemist, and it seemed never to have been used. It was carefully positioned above the torn skin of the neck, another clue, along with the heart, red hat and pear – another piece of the jigsaw Sam couldn't put into place.

Charlotte's body was found in Bunhill Fields, a cemetery dating from the 1860s that was close to the square mile of the City of London. For a copywriter like Charlotte, who was a devoted reader and made her living from words, there was something sadly ironic about her body lying at the foot of William Blake's headstone. Her mother was left to mourn her daughter and the plans that would remain unfulfilled, and the little things she left behind: the new dress hanging in the wardrobe that would never be worn, the pile of books beside Charlotte's bed, the corners of only one book folded to mark the last page read. There was still so much for her daughter to experience. That her life was too short to be properly considered a lifetime when Charlotte had so little time.

For Sam, time had become a waiting game determined by the killer. He lived by the killer's schedule rather than his own. He waited for him to kill, and after he did and things still didn't become any clearer, Sam knew he would have to wait some more. This wasn't a killer who would suddenly grow bored by his own game.

Sam spent his nights waiting, too. They were divided into snatches of disturbed, nightmare-filled sleep, hands clutching at him, pulling him under the surface of water until he was jerked awake struggling to breathe. The rest of the night would be long and lonely as he waited for daylight. Then, more waiting, ever waiting, holding his breath until the killer defined his day.

7

Annie stared at herself in the mirror. *Today is a good day*. Pleasure illuminated her face, as though she were lit from within. Her thick dark hair gleamed like polished ebony, her skin radiant with a slight pink blush that rose up from her chest and into her cheeks. Her cheekbones were high and sharp, reflecting the light that came from the small, barred window, defining her face, and adding contours and planes as if she'd been sculpted from flawless, creamy marble, not a blemish in sight. Her smile widened and the blush increased until the apples of her cheeks were flushed a deeper pink, and then she laughed at herself, a light giggle that would have sat better on a far younger woman. "Annie, are you blushing?" She gathered her hair and placed it over one shoulder stroking the length. "I suppose I am. I have an embarrassment of beauty." She covered her mouth in case her laughter was overheard. It was almost too much beauty for one woman, and yet she wore it like a made-to-measure dress woven from the finest silk.

"He always told me how beautiful I was," she reminded herself. "He couldn't stop touching me when I was his." She stroked her face with the tips of her fingers the way he used to, feeling the warmth from her flushing skin, but the skin didn't feel as soft as she'd expected. Her fingers weren't gliding across her face. They were dragging. Could that jawline be hers? The skin was too loose, and there was too much of it. The neck was ringed like the inside of an ancient tree. It was like touching crepe paper. She noticed her hands then, mottled with brown smudges, knuckles swollen with arthritis, the fingers twisted and gnarly like the branches of an apple tree that no longer bore fruit.

Her long hair didn't have the sheen of dark wood but was instead the grey of dirty snow with a few strands of nicotine-yellow hanging limply about her face. The reflection in the mirror didn't match the one in her head at all. It wasn't beauty, it was blotchy with dry red patches scattered with broken spider veins like cracks in glass. She did look lit from within though – like a pumpkin hollowed out on Halloween, the dying light from a candle flickering its last.

She smashed her forehead into the mirror once, twice, three times, enough to lose count, almost enough to lose consciousness, all the while screaming at it, and at the old, ugly thing that lived inside it. The glass shattered, the old woman inside now distorted like one of Picasso's women, but red rather than blue. Red with her own blood that now seeped from the gash on her forehead and dripped like thick paint down her face. "Now she is gone," Annie shouted, smiling once more. "Now that ugly old bitch is gone.

"Am I pretty now?" she screamed, as a drop of blood pooled into her tear duct.

Her cell door crashed open, the hinges complaining, rusty metal flakes floating to the ground like dead leaves.

Men entered her room without permission. They certainly weren't gentlemen – intruding and uninvited – they didn't know how to treat a lady. "Look at me!" she demanded. "Look at my beauty. The mirror is lying. Can't you see how lovely I am?" She gestured towards the wall, frowned at its emptiness and the smeared blood where a mirror should be.

The orderlies agreed that she was lovely as they each took an arm, their gloved hands squeezing her flesh as they dragged her from the room.

*

It had been another fruitful session with Simon, and Emma felt their work together was ending. As she left her office in the city, she came across a group of police officers huddled around the main entrance to her building. They wore serious, grim expressions that seemed at odds with the spring sunshine. One of the officers was holding an intense conversation with a group of women, some of whom Emma recognised as workers from the offices on the floor below hers. Two of them were crying, and the others looked frightened and pale. Apparently, a woman had gone missing – a co-worker and friend of the women talking to the officer. She had been missing for three days, "…as if she'd disappeared into thin air." Emma overheard. "As if we imagined her."

When Emma moved around them, an officer with dark circles beneath her eyes stopped her and seemed to examine her closely. It was unnerving, to say the least. She handed Emma a leaflet. Along the top in bold typeface was the word, MISSING. Beneath that was a picture of Polly Richards, the missing woman. Emma's breath caught. It was almost like looking at a picture of herself. Polly had long, dark hair, a little curlier than Emma's, but the same colour. Apart from a few freckles scattered across her nose and cheeks, she was pale-skinned, her eyes the same light green as Emma's. According to the information on the leaflet, she was twenty-five years old, ten years younger than Emma, but she could easily have been Emma's younger self, so alike were they. It certainly explained why the police officer had studied her face so closely.

Emma shivered in fear as her own mortality brushed up against her. Polly's disappearance underscored her own vulnerability in a city where it was becoming common for women to sink and vanish without a trace. Her legs suddenly felt weak, and a cold sweat broke out across her back like a rash. She took a seat on one of the newspaper-strewn benches near Moorgate tube station. The thought of going underground right away and getting onto a crowded tube was overwhelming. She sat very still and breathed deeply and slowly, the sweat beginning to dry, but she couldn't stop thinking about Polly. The discarded newspaper lying next to her speculated that she was more than just a random missing woman. It suggested she had been taken by the killer who'd been stalking London for over a year. A killer with an appetite for a definite physical type.

A little later, after exiting Highbury and Islington tube station and crossing the road, Emma still felt uneasy. She scanned her surroundings, senses on high alert as her skin prickled. She hurried across Highbury Fields, ignoring the little cafe where she usually stopped for coffee, and instead headed straight for the prison gates, wanting to get inside as quickly as possible. She suddenly felt exposed and far too small in a very big world. It crossed her mind that the people inside the prison were the ones she should be wary of, but today the prison signalled safety.

Emma knew her fear was unwarranted, but she couldn't get hold of her racing thoughts. The likeness between herself and Polly was too striking to be dismissed and their offices too close for comfort. She wondered if she could have been the victim instead of Polly. Had she come into contact with the killer? Had he been inside her building? Had she brushed up against him in the street? The questions came thick and fast, flashing across Emma's mind like the blurred advertisements speeding by the windows as her tube pulled into the station just moments ago. She couldn't enter the prison feeling this unsettled. She had to get control of herself before she started therapy.

She made her way to one of the empty benches in the prison grounds shaded by a weeping willow, its long, drooping fronds like a waterfall of green ribbons offering a private hideaway. She was too early for work anyway – cognisant of her previous tardiness – so she sat and waited for the return of reasonable thought to push through the emotional turmoil. Inside the prison she would work with women who existed in a world of little else but emotional turmoil. It was her job to be the voice of reason.

*

Annie sat up straight on the narrow bed in the medical bay. She tried to ignore the brown stain on the mattress, faded by time but visible all the same, and too close to her thigh. Surely she warranted better surroundings. The nurse had thrown a disposable sheet across the bed, but it looked like it should have been disposed of days ago, and it did little to hide the stain. Her hands rested in her lap, the handcuffs loose around her thin wrists, but cold and irritating, nonetheless. But she had to wear them while receiving treatment. Those were the rules, for everybody's safety – inmates and staff alike. For peace of mind. *Such a frail concept*, she thought, *like gossamer*. The idea of creating peace of mind in such a place seemed somewhat ironic. It would take more than handcuffs and an adherence to the rules to find something so elusive.

The nurse had her back turned to Annie while she leaned over a table preparing to tend to the head wound. This was bad manners, to say nothing of being dangerous. *How quickly could I reach her?* she wondered. *Could I pull the handcuffs across her throat and strangle her before the orderly pulls me off? Would there be enough time for me to choke her to death?* But Annie resisted. She didn't want to touch the nurse's rippling blubber. Her uniform was pulled tight across her shoulders as she bent over, the seams straining to contain her considerable bulk. The stale smell of her sweat twisted itself around the sharpness of bleach.

"How are you feeling now?" the nurse asked in the singsong medical staff voice Annie found unbearable.

"Thin," she stated, with a cruel smile.

A hurt expression pulled at the nurse's features, but then the smile returned. "That's nice. Now, let's see about that cut, shall we? It won't need stitches, don't worry. Just a plaster. But I'll give it a good clean first."

The nurse turned Annie's head roughly towards the overhead light and cleaned the wound with an antiseptic wipe, dabbing at the skin and wearing a slightly different smile now, as if she rather enjoyed the stinging pain this would cause. "Almost done, apart from some dried blood in those deep wrinkles of yours. Crow's feet. Age can be cruel, can't it?" It was a voice that approached sympathy but didn't quite reach it, the melodic tone absent now.

She put a butterfly plaster across the cut, pressing it firmly into place. "There, all done. That should heal nicely but keep the plaster on for a day or two and keep it dry. I'll check it in a few days." She reached into the large bowl on the table behind her and handed Annie the apple with the most bruises, its green peel resembling waterlogged skin. "Here, this is for you. It's a bit wrinkled and well past its sell-by date, but an apple a day keeps the doctor away." The nurse beckoned the orderly who was standing by the door to take Annie back to her room.

"I'm allergic to apples, as you well know," Annie said. "Or

is your brain shrinking while your hips are spreading?" But the nurse ignored her and placed the rejected apple back in the bowl.

"Lump," Annie spat over her shoulder as the nurse slammed the door in her face.

"Despicable how some women let themselves go," Annie said to the orderly as he led her by the handcuffs along the lavender-walled corridor. "That nurse is obviously a spinster left on the shelf like a sack of flour while she continues to feed her loneliness with a diet of junk." She pretended to gag. "It's like throwing rubbish into an overflowing dustbin. She's too fat to be loved and thus lonely, so she feeds the loneliness, and on it goes – a vicious circle. But not an ever-decreasing one." Annie's laughter spluttered like the engine of an old car.

She would never allow herself to fall so far. She wasn't that weak, and she certainly hadn't been lonely, at least not back then, before she'd been forced to enter this place of pastels and plastic forks and rounded-off corners, this place where the only sharp angles were the inmates themselves. Back then she had known true love, an innocent love of purity and a lightness of touch, clean and fresh. It had been like breaking the glass surface of still water. Such love didn't happen to everyone, and certainly not often, but she had known it three times in her life. She had been so lucky.

Her first love had been her greatest. She'd learned quickly how to please him. He'd told her she had to, if she wanted to keep him. But it came to an end, and the pain of rejection had been as great as the love itself. The void he'd left in her life had been a black hole into which she'd fallen and lived for a long time, unsure of how to climb out.

Eventually she'd filled the space he'd left with meaningless flings, a way to pass the time until another great love came along – which, after a long time, it did. It had been a brief encounter, but all the more intense because it was made up of stolen moments, secret whispers, lingering touches when no one was watching. But it was snatched away from her as if she were a naughty child playing with an unsuitable toy.

After that, she was alone for a while, licking her wounds and waiting, waiting for the time to be right again. And eventually, it was. The third love was still fresh in her mind, even now, after all this time. He had been her last love. Perhaps that was why the memory of it burned all the brighter. That one had ended when she'd wanted it to. She had been in charge at last, determining her own fate, escaping the pain of rejection even as she caused it in another. His love for her had been too desperate, grasping, and almost pitiful. He'd become too intense in the end, which she couldn't abide. Now her memories were all she had left, and they only kept her warm at night in short spells.

$$*$$

Emma managed to get hold of herself with the aid of some self-administered cognitive behaviour therapy. Ellis's theory, based in part on rationality, proved useful whenever irrational thought processes obscured her thinking, as they did today. While Emma had a great deal of sympathy for Polly, she also understood that her reaction had been a little extreme, and before she could go on, she had to restructure it into something more manageable. She reminded herself of Ellis's premise: if she was responsible for creating her own emotional discomfort, then she likewise had the power to change it and render it comfortable once again.

She sat under the shaded arch of the weeping willow, eyes closed, running through a list of questions she knew would calm her and help her restructure her thought patterns around the event. On a scale of one to ten, how frightened did she feel by what had happened? She answered her own question with the number eight. Then she asked herself: how likely was she to be the victim of a killer? Statistically, the possibility was remote, so she answered with a two. Given her response to the previous question, on a scale of one to ten, how over-the-top had her reaction been to Polly's disappearance? She smiled as she answered with the number nine. She wasn't really sticking to the traditional pattern of CBT, but Ellis would have approved of her pursuit of a rational viewpoint; she was grounding herself by employing logic over emotion.

Another question: how unhelpful had this reaction been to her day so far? The number ten came to mind. After running through these questions several times, her anxiety had decreased significantly, so she asked herself again how frightened she was feeling, and she was satisfied when the number three was the first that popped into mind. Polly was still in her thoughts, but in a more considered way. Emma was calmer now, her head clear and ready for group therapy.

8

Working in the cathedral-like back rooms at the Museum of Toys and Playtime in Bloomsbury suited Ben's temperament. Most of his time was taken up with repairing and painting toys from a bygone age. He made rusty clockwork cars run once again on wheels that no longer squeaked. He tinkered with trains and robots, cleaning them with care until the original paintwork appeared and the mechanics moved without stuttering. The worktops in the cavernous room were crowded, rolls of paper and bolts of fabric leaning precariously against any remaining wall space, hundreds of small boxes filled with nuts and bolts and different tools in varying sizes. The people who worked there were patient and meticulous, their heads bent over well-lit tables as they brought the old and neglected to life once more, preserving childhood history for adult visitors enraptured by the nostalgia of their youth, and children sometimes confounded but mostly intrigued by the brilliance of simplicity.

Gary, one of the longest-serving employees, gently placed the Bulgarian rod marionette on his workbench – two of the strings still unattached and the papier mâché head remaining decapitated from its nether rod – and groaned as he stood up, unfurled his back and rotated his neck. "My puppet has a haunted face and I need a break, so anyone fancy a cup of tea?" The room came to life, most seeming grateful for the opportunity to unfold themselves and stretch, cracking joints and the downing of tools rotating about the room.

Ben glanced at Gary, attempted the approachable smile he'd practised in the mirror. Gary seemed to notice it and then ignored it as he headed towards the kitchen.

It's never enough. I am never enough, thought Ben as his smile froze and then abruptly shattered on his face.

Henry, his boss, must have noticed his dying expression, because he wandered over – again – hovered at his desk, and placed a hand on his shoulder, making Ben's skin clammy beneath his shirt.

"How'd you like to go out for a beer after work?" Henry asked, his wiry eyebrows climbing up his forehead.

A pity beer. "No, Henry," he snapped, like an elastic band at breaking point. "I can't. I have other plans." After work, he was going straight home. *She* was waiting for him.

He couldn't breathe with Henry standing at his elbow, looking over his shoulder, his breath warm against the back of his neck.

Henry frowned – as if somehow Ben owed him something – and moved off, hands thrust in pockets and his back rounded from decades of leaning over and staring into large magnifying glasses to repaint the smiles on expressionless dolls.

Ben liked Henry. He was a good man, a kind man who'd hired him when he was only seventeen and taken him under his wing. He was more than a patient mentor; he was a friend – had even lent him money for the deposit on his home, tolerating the odd late payment – but he wasn't his father. Ben had gone all his life without one. He'd made the mistake once of confiding in Henry that he'd been taken into care when he was only eight years old and that his younger years had been a blur of government-subsidised children's homes and brief stays with various foster families who had failed to foster love for him. Since then, Henry wouldn't leave him alone. He needed Henry, wanted to be close to him, but he didn't need a fucking father, and mothers were too much fucking trouble, too.

As soon as Ben finished work, he avoided Henry's gaze and left as quickly as he could, almost tripping over the electrical cord of a floor buffer in his haste. His footsteps echoed in the emptying museum, the synthetic citrus smell of glass cleaner signalling departing visitors and the smeared fingerprints they'd left behind.

Concentrating on minute machinery at his desk for hours made the world feel vast when he stepped outside. After feeling too big in a toy-town world, it jarred to adjust to a normal size again. The sky seemed endless, the smell of cut grass intensely fresh after silver polish and glue, and the colours of nature soothing after the vivid rainbow shades of make-believe. Compared to the air-conditioned workshop, the heat outside felt dense enough to push through – more like swimming than walking. But he didn't mind. He loved the heat – he was more a summer than a winter man, and it felt as if summer had pushed spring aside to arrive early in May.

As he neared home, he felt his speed increasing, his strides lengthening, as if muscle memory had kicked in, driven by excitement, and was setting the pace, willing him to move faster and faster. His shirt was sticking to the sweat on his back and a smile – one that came as naturally as breathing – formed in anticipation of the welcome he knew he'd find there. He could feel her pulling him home. He had been away from her all day, willing the hours to move swiftly, but he was nearly home at last.

"I'm coming, my love, I'm almost there." He resisted the urge to run. "I've picked up your scent, I can smell you now."

He wondered if she had missed him as much as he'd missed her. Had she pined for him like a dog waiting for its owner? Was the sensation a physical one, a dull ache that throbbed more intensely with each passing hour? His own body pulsed now, a vibration in his chest, reaching a crescendo like a building storm about to burst open. But the waiting was almost over; in the near distance he could see his front door.

"I'm close now, so close," he whispered, although there was nobody to hear him. "I can feel you under my skin."

The street was deserted. It nearly always was. Badly lit at night, it was the street that time forgot. He glanced at the low-rise, abandoned office blocks, empty for years, with smashed windows and graffitied doors hanging off their hinges. He marched by boarded-up houses overgrown with weeds, tendrils of determined ivy weaving their way through rotted wood and broken glass. Shafts of daylight pierced the remains of a roof, the eaves torn and blackened as if they had once caught fire, a rusted fridge without a door in what had once been a front garden.

He hurried by a small run of shops, abandoned, and embedded in the not-too-distant past, rendered obsolete by innovation and technology: a shop that used to hire out videos, the dusty windows still adorned with faded movie posters advertising films long since viewed; the empty shell of a record shop, a few smashed LPs lying scattered across the dirty floor inside, shards of a different era gathering dust. At the end of the row stood one last place, a butcher's shop with the torn remains of a striped awning hanging over the permanently shuttered doors and large window. The name, Churchill and Son, was still visible above the rusted shutters. The shop was apparently established in 1932, successfully defending itself against bombs and wartime rationing but crumpling at the rise of supermarket chains.

Derelict and decayed, but it suited Ben perfectly. He was a solitary man who wanted to pass unseen, uninterrupted, who depended on not being overheard. He had bought the flat above the butcher, and the shop itself, for a very reasonable price a few years ago. Nobody wanted a business that was no longer viable and in the middle of nowhere – nobody but him. Nowhere was his ideal somewhere. An invisible street meant no neighbours, no nosy parkers to disturb him while he worked. He required peace and quiet and space, all of which his flat provided – the empty shop below accommodating the messiest jobs. He needed to be absolutely certain that nobody could hear them scream. They didn't scream for long, he was careful about that, but his women did scream. It couldn't be avoided, really. It would have been disappointing if they didn't.

Keys in hand, he stopped outside the front door and let himself into the narrow, dark hallway. He wiped his feet on one of the only doormats in London free from the litter of pizza takeaway menus and, after switching on the light, made his way up the long staircase. The floorboards creaked, the aged wood protesting but shiny and free from dust. He had taken his time sanding the wood and applying the dark varnish, the natural grain highlighted by the rich, deep polish. He let himself into the main door of his flat, closing it quietly behind him, sighing with pleasure into the silence. Shrugging off the neutral expression he wore outside, as if it were a coat, he allowed his features to relax. He was safe from the world outside.

The shambolic exterior of his home gave no hint of the precise minimalism and fine taste that existed behind the closed door. More hideaway than shelter, it was a home made for secrets and particular pleasures. It was the home of a single man living a very singular life. "I'll be with you soon," he told her. "Just be patient for a little while longer."

He opened the shutters on the windows, flooding the living room with late afternoon light, taking a moment to watch the dust motes drift in the sunlight before he walked through to the kitchen. He was biding his time, allowing the minutes to pass before he went to see her, wanting to prolong the moment until they were back together for as long as he could. Anticipation was building like a constant beat, and he noticed the slight shake in his hands as he reached up and opened the cupboard next to the fridge, taking care to avoid smearing the brushed stainless-steel door. He removed a glass, held it up to the window to ensure it was clean, and carried it back to the living room taking a bottle of red wine from the rack as he went.

He took off his suit jacket and placed it across the black leather armchair, loosened his tie and sat down on the sofa, the leather cool against the thin damp cotton of his shirt. He poured himself a glass of wine, but before he could take a sip, he noticed with irritation that one of his framed pictures, an old book jacket, was slightly crooked on the wall, and he knew he wouldn't be able to relax until he straightened it. He rose, feeling his shirt unpeeling from the back of the sofa, adjusted the frame, and felt the satisfaction that came from precision. The wine would taste smoother now.

Across the room on another wall – perfectly aligned – was the collection of framed photographs he'd taken. "I'm home at last," he told the women he'd captured in saturated colours. The red was particularly striking. "We can spend the night together now, just us."

They read his smile and he saw understanding in their expressions, felt their acceptance. He moved towards them and ran his fingers across their faces, and he was sure he felt them writhe with pleasure at his touch. Then, with glass cleaner, he removed the smeared fingerprints he'd left across their mouths. He lingered a few more seconds, allowing the women to inspire him, fill him up with that sound they made – a deep sigh moving warmly across his face – and then he opened the box of new frames and placed them in a neat pile.

The silence and order of the room pleased him. It was such a contrast to the noisy busyness of work. It had to be. He needed his home to be tidy and clean if he wanted to think straight – if he wanted an uncluttered mind. He liked the extreme differences between the two places. They were two very separate environments, one never coming into contact with the other. Two versions of himself that he needed to move through life: the *outside* him working in the museum financing the *inside* him who was more suited to the shadow.

The moment for his shadow side had come. He couldn't wait any longer. He went to the kitchen, unhooked the key from the back of the door, and made his way downstairs. The kitchen stairs led directly down to the storage rooms behind the shop. There were two sizable rooms down there, always chilly, the air stale. One room held a large, wide, glass-fronted freezer he'd ordered specially from a company that usually supplied caterers. The freezer dominated the space, standing tall beneath high ceilings in the windowless room, its machinery endlessly whining and throbbing. It was dark in there and smelt a little damp, the stone floors cold and clammy. Opposite the freezer there were marble work surfaces where the meat had once been cleaned, butchered and prepared for display. Metal hooks dropped from the ceiling, still in place although animal carcasses were no longer hung and aged there. The other room was off to one side and slightly smaller with a wall of wooden shelves that used to house the eggs, milk, cheeses and other produce the butchers had once provided for their customers.

Some old jars of mint jelly and apple sauce still sat on the shelves alongside the wide reels of blue string and the large assortment of knives, cheese wires and metal hooks – the tools of the butcher's trade.

He'd restored the collection of knives with tools he'd borrowed from the museum's workshop. Once rusted and pitted with age the blades gleamed in the overhead light, as good as new. On the lowest shelf sat a large cardboard box full of overalls made of heavy white cotton, as if the former owner had anticipated his needs. He removed a pair and put them on. They were stiff and chafed his skin, but they covered him completely and were perfect for his needs. The name of the butcher was sewn in red above the top pocket. He reached behind the door and removed the dark leather apron that hung there, another relic left by the previous owners. It was long and heavy and covered him from collarbone to ankles, the brown leather scratched and stained in places, the blood from dead animals having deepened the colour.

He wanted to sharpen his knives again before he began – it was part of the ritual – but he wanted to see her first, wanted to check that his guest was comfortable in her special space. He crossed the room and unlocked the heavy black door that led downstairs to the basement, his favourite room in the house. Time passed quickly down there.

She appeared to be sleeping – they had certainly made quite a night of it last night – but he knew she was closer to an unconscious state. He had ground up four sleeping pills that morning, not enough to kill her; sleeping pills were safer these days, liver damage more likely than death, but that hardly mattered. He'd put the crushed powder into her orange juice and watched her drink it before he left for work, knowing she wouldn't be able to taste it and she was so thirsty by then, she'd just gulped the juice down without registering the flavour.

She had been fast asleep by the time he'd left, her head resting on her shoulder. She would have looked peaceful if her arms hadn't been pulled tight behind her and each ankle tethered to the chair. But she'd slept long enough, lazing about all day while he'd been hard at work. Now he needed her to wake up. It was time to play again.

9

Sam managed to grab a table outside the pub despite the throng of people basking in the last of the evening's sun. He dropped down onto the hard wooden seat which felt oddly comfortable as it took the weight of his exhausted body, the wood warmed by a day in the sunshine. The headache that had squeezed his skull all day was lifting at last. Each time he left the incident room, he felt like he was disembarking from a plane after a long flight. His ears popped with the shock of the comparative silence of the outside world, his eyes squinting in bright natural daylight.

He rolled a cigarette while he waited for Riley to return from the bar with drinks. It was only his fourth cigarette of the day. This case was forcing him to cut down. The sense of urgency circulating throughout the office was an unrelenting dark presence leaving little time for smoking breaks outside. He turned his face towards the sun and closed his eyes as the reassuring normality of everyday life flowed around him.

Riley finally appeared, two pints of dry cider catching the light and turning as golden as the day. "Doing a bit of sunbathing, Sam?" His tone was surprisingly light-hearted despite the day they'd left behind.

"Anything to cover the bags under my eyes. I'm starting to look like my father." Sam took his first sip of the crisp, cold cider. "God, that's good. I needed that." He took another gulp, savouring the chill that moved through his body.

"What are you now, Sam, forty? Hardly an old man," Riley said. He took his first sip and let out a deep breath, his shoulders relaxing.

"Forty-one, soon to be forty-two," said Sam. "But I feel older. It's like I've been ageing in dog years since this case started."

Riley laughed, the creases by his blue eyes reaching towards his greying temples. They sat in companionable silence for some time, sipping their drinks. Sam allowed the warmth of the evening to ease the tension in his tired muscles, but he knew the stress of the case was never far away, attentive as a stalker.

"You've been doing this job for a long time, Albert." Sam massaged the back of his stiff neck. "How do you keep going? How do you switch off?"

"Someone has to stop the bad guys. Whenever I catch one, that's when I can switch off – well, for a while anyway. Until the next monster from the reject pile comes along." Riley smiled back at Sam. "Are you coping alright? Struggling to switch off?"

"Not struggling exactly, but it's hard to quiet my mind at night. I spend more time awake at night than sleeping," Sam said. "Wandering about the flat, trying to find something I missed in the files, wondering if I'll ever get eight hours again."

Riley peered at him over the top of his glass. "Is it coming back again? The depression?"

When Sam had first started working with the police department, he had taken Riley into his confidence and told him that he suffered from depression, but that he knew how to recognise the warning signs and take care of himself, keeping himself functioning on the outside despite what was going on inside.

He sighed. "Yeah, it's coming back, but I'm coping. I'm still taking the antidepressants, and I've increased the dose slightly; that should help. I'm going to see a new supervisor too, as soon as I can find the time." He ran a hand through his hair, aware that Riley was watching him. "Don't worry, Albert. It's not like I'm new to this. I just wish I could sleep more, but I can't stop thinking about him. I feel like I'm always waiting for the next body to show up."

"We're all waiting for that," said Riley. "Unfortunately, from what we've seen before, it won't be too long a wait, but you must take care of yourself. You're no good to me if you're burned out. Easier said than done, I know, but keep an eye on yourself, will you?" His tone was reassuring. "Can't have the team shrink getting into a two and eight, can we?"

Sam frowned. "What?"

"State," replied Riley. "Two and eight means state, thought you would've picked up more Cockney slang by now."

"Right," Sam laughed. "I will try to avoid that." He dragged his thumb across his lighter flicking the flame on and off.

Riley hesitated. "Have you seen Maria lately?"

Maria, Sam's ex-girlfriend, had moved out almost two years ago, tired of competing for attention with his job and wanting the children he had no desire for. The last he'd heard, she was engaged to a man who obviously better fitted the bill, and he was happy for her. She deserved to be with someone who wanted a family as much as she did, and although he was upset and missed her desperately at first, he came to appreciate her honesty. Even so, it would have been comforting to return home to someone again, someone to hold him after harrowing work and wrap him in affection warm enough to push aside the cold, brutal light of day.

"I haven't seen her in a long time," Sam said. "She must be married by now. Just as well she moved on, I think. This case is taking the best of me." He swallowed the last of his cider.

"Just don't let it take all of you. Save something for when the right person comes along." Riley smiled across at Sam and pointed to the empty glasses. "Now, off you pop to the bar, there's a good lad. We've inhaled these with indecent haste, and I think we could both do with another. Smooth the edges off."

Sam laughed, wondering what it felt like to have a life with smooth edges.

*

Riley watched Sam head inside. He looked shattered, had done for weeks now, and the depression couldn't be helping, but Riley trusted Sam's judgement when it came to his mental health. He thought back to their first meeting years ago, a meeting his superintendent had arranged for him after he'd investigated a shocking case of arson in which two young children had died. He'd resisted his boss at first, told her he didn't need counselling, but fortunately she'd ignored him, and he'd attended his first session with Sam on a rainy afternoon in a nondescript beige office. It was Riley's first experience with counselling, and he'd been surprised and impressed by Sam's ability to read between the lines. He certainly no longer believed that a therapist's job was "money for old rope", as an ill-informed colleague described it, one whom Riley believed would benefit enormously from some self-awareness.

During the session, Sam suggested Riley was holding onto his sense of horror – as if it were a life vest that would prevent him from drowning in the strong currents of any future horror if he held on tightly enough. But Sam explained it would have the opposite effect. It would pull him under, would turn into a powerful sense of guilt and eventually suffocate him, that he would have to face the horror and let it go if he wanted to move on. Horror wasn't the life vest. It was the rocks in the pockets.

After Riley left that room for the first time, he had admitted, somewhat begrudgingly, that he felt better, lighter, and as a result was far more productive at work – and this feeling increased as the sessions went on, and soon after Riley made a few of his officers attend counselling too. His scepticism and reluctance towards therapy dissolved completely when he saw the changes in them. He had a new appreciation for the power that could come from understanding the driving forces of the human psyche. When the time came to take on a consultant to understand criminal motivations and behaviour patterns, Sam was the obvious choice.

Riley found Sam's assistance at crime scenes invaluable. His training as a psychologist and his research into criminal profiling meant he could provide a pretty accurate picture of the offender by studying the scene – whether the offender had been relatively calm and organised, or frenzied. He could ascertain whether the offender was risk averse or a thrill-seeker. He could tell how well-planned the crime was, how much emotion the offender had invested in it and, therefore, to what degree it had personal meaning. Such insights provided clues to the psychological and social factors that wired an offender's brain and ultimately drove their behaviour. All the understanding Sam provided helped Riley and his team narrow down their list of suspects and eventually convict the perpetrator. It meant one more piece of scum would be off the streets.

After Sam returned with the drinks and rolled a fresh cigarette, Riley asked him for Polly's file. He knew Sam would have the file with him – he took them all home every night. It was against policy, but under the circumstances Riley chose to overlook it.

He moved closer to Sam and lowered his voice, even though the crowd had thinned now that the evening was darkening and cooling off. "Let's go over what we know about her."

"Twenty-five-year-old secretary, originally from Liverpool," Sam said. "Came to London five years ago for a new job." He fiddled with his lighter, the flame coming and going.

"Right." Riley sipped his drink. "Boss reports her missing when she doesn't turn up for work."

"No chance she went back to Liverpool to see her parents?" Sam asked.

Riley shook his head. "I spoke to them. No one's seen her since she left work Monday evening." He frowned at Sam. "Bloody hell, Sam, light the fag or put that lighter down."

Sam lit up and placed the lighter behind his glass. "Sorry, Albert." He leaned back and exhaled slowly.

It was Thursday. Even though Polly's face had been all over the news, no one had spotted her. Her file was still pretty thin. As they studied the photograph of the dark-haired, smiling young woman, Sam and Riley silently finished their drinks.

Eventually Riley closed the file and rested his hands on the cover. "Where are you, Polly?" He suddenly felt very tired. "What's he doing to you?"

The basement below the butcher's was cold, brightly lit and had the musty smell of mildew crawling inside the walls, layered over something more pungent. To Ben, it felt like an underground cave secreted away from the world above, a space ideally configured for the sacred task at hand.

The room held nothing but two chairs, a long wooden table heavily stained and scarred, and an old sink in one corner. The air was stale and thick and floated about the room undisturbed and slightly sweet. It was the smell each of them left behind no matter how thoroughly he cleaned the floors afterwards. He had learned to live with it. More than that: he had come to enjoy the way it rose up to meet him each time he opened the basement door, like one friend greeting another. The bittersweet smell leeched from the blood that decorated the walls in shades from red to rust. Fine strokes of elegantly written words inspired by childhood, rendered in a steady hand. He didn't approve of waste. It was disrespectful to discard the blood – luminous with oily iridescence, it was too exquisite to throw away; instead it flowed around the room like liquid silk.

He always entered the room clean but didn't leave it that way. He would discard the clothes he wore for the killing. The overalls, rubber gloves and shower cap ensured he wouldn't leave any hair or fingerprints. The only one who would be present in the final location was the woman, he would leave none of himself behind. But they always left something of themselves for him before they departed, a memento. There was the blood of course, but there was also the head. Women always lost their heads over him.

The heads of his dark-haired, pale-skinned sweethearts, lips a little bruised from love's last kiss, sleeping forever inside the glass display domes he'd stolen from the museum. They were his very own playthings, eyes almost closed, hair brushed until it was soft and glossy and twisted around the large wounds across their throats. He tried to be careful when cutting off the head, tried to do it with one clean movement of the blade, but it wasn't easy – a bone saw was needed halfway through – and the wounds were jagged and messy, although he was getting better with practice. He made sure the glass of the dome was clean after he'd placed the head inside, wiping away any smears or drops of blood, before taking them on one last journey upstairs where they were finally home, their last resting place the frosty domain of the freezer, crystals of ice like diamonds glittering on their eyelashes and hair. Glass coffins in a cold embrace, warm memories in chilled confinement.

Polly's glass dome waited for her, and a bucket by the sink was ready to catch her blood. Some of it would accompany her outside to form the canvas on which she'd be displayed; he knew pale skin contrasted beautifully against blood that darkened as it dried.

He laid out the bone saw and knives on one end of the wooden table, clean and sharp. This time he intended to experiment with a cheese wire to see if that would solve the untidy edges problem after the severing was complete. The plastic and tape he wrapped the body in afterwards were spread across the rest of the table. The red hat, plastic comb and a hard, under-ripe pear waited for him by the basement door. Preparation was key, and he was a man who liked to be prepared. He crossed the room and looked down at Polly, asleep in her chair, and wondered if she'd miss him now their affair was ending. But it was time to put her out of her misery before her disenchantment with him set in.

He loosened her bindings, lifted her gently from the chair, and carried her to the sink across the room. She was very light, just a small thing really, and she fell across his arms with loose limbs and a placid expression that erased years from her features. She remained asleep as he placed her on the second chair in front of the old butler sink, the taps tight with rust, the enamel cracked, but serviceable despite its age. He placed the large square plastic bucket in the bottom of the sink and then laid out the deep brown towels. They were a cheap brand, a little too rough for delicate skin, but the dark colour would disguise the stains when the time came to dispose of them. He put on the shower cap. Next, he placed the heavy leather butcher's apron on top of his overalls and knotted it tightly around his back. He set the black rubber gloves to one side for now. He was ready – he was finally ready for her. He trembled with excitement, his groin throbbing and pushing eagerly against the rough fabric of the overalls. He'd waited a long time for this moment, and now it was time to be rewarded.

He removed her blindfold, taking care not to tug at the hair entwined in the knot at the back of her head. A low moan escaped her cracked lips, the gag still in place and wet now but pulled tightly behind her teeth. He knelt in front of her, waiting for her to open her eyes, impatient for their last night together to begin. He moved closer to her face and extended his tongue, just the tip, and licked her lips, gently at first, then more forcefully flicked his tongue across her pale mouth.

"Wake up, sleepyhead," he murmured; his tongue moved across her eyelids, the moisture from his mouth glistening in her eyelashes. "I'm home and I've come to wake you with a true love's kiss."

Polly opened her eyes slowly, but she was confused. Her vision was blurred, her head foggy, but then it all came back, and a terrible, icy fear shook her entire body. She saw him clearly now, smiling at her, close to her face, tenderly brushing hair out of her eyes. She tried to scream, but her mouth was dry against the gag and it felt as if her throat was closing up, that she was about to suffocate. It crossed her mind that she wouldn't be that lucky. He was staring at her intently now, a look of concentration replacing the smile, and then he slowly and deliberately stuck out his tongue, curled the tip and moved it up and down like a snake about to strike as he drew closer to her mouth. He licked her lips, leaving a trail of saliva as he moved from her top lip to the bottom one, and then more insistently, much more roughly, he pushed his tongue up and under her top lip, probing, tasting, then across her teeth until she turned her head, repulsed by the smell of his drying spittle just under her nose. He forced her head back to face him and slapped her across the cheek, the sound like the crack of a whip in the silent room. He gripped the sides of her face and licked her again, tried to push his tongue farther into her mouth behind the gag, but there wasn't enough room.

"I want to kiss you, I want to taste you, but I know I can't trust you," he said. "I know you'll scream – won't you, Polly?"

She shook her head, tried to make a sound, anything that would persuade him to remove the gag so she could scream for help. She pleaded with her eyes but saw no softening in his – only dead eyes, flat and dark, as if his pupils had bled into the iris.

"I'm going to remove it now, but only for a while," he said. "Just long enough for me to kiss you. Nobody will hear you if you scream anyway. We're in the middle of nowhere. Nobody will come and rescue you. They don't know you're here. Nobody cares about you except me. Now, let me kiss you one more time. Let me kiss you goodbye."

At that moment, Polly understood he was going to kill her. Perhaps she had always known it, but her mind had buried it beneath hope to protect her. Too late now. She began to tremble, and tears spilled down her cheeks as the faces of her parents filled her mind. Images flickered like old home movies inside her head: family holidays, a group of her friends with her at graduation, the book by her bed only half finished, the cat at home who would be starving by now, and then the old, kind face of her grandmother whom she had dearly loved and lost the year before. This thought comforted her, the warmth of the memory filling her up, calming her, telling her not to be afraid.

When he removed the gag and she didn't scream, it seemed

to surprise him as much as it did her. Even after he forced his tongue deep into her mouth and a look of regret passed across his face. Even after he tipped her backwards over the sink, her dark hair filling the bucket – even then, she didn't scream. It didn't register when he pushed his hands into long gloves, the black rubber squeaking as he pulled them up to his elbows. She made no sound as he lifted a large knife with a long blade and rested it momentarily against her throat. When he stroked her hair and kissed her goodbye once more, it wasn't his face she saw. It was the face of her grandmother smiling down at her, a reassuring look of love that made her smile.

*

Sam stretched out on the sofa, his head a little fuzzy from the cider, and closed his eyes. Exhaustion lay down with him, its weight shrouding him completely, like a heavy blanket. He fell asleep where he lay, fully clothed and not entirely comfortable, but his weary body surrendered willingly to sleep, embraced it with relief. But the sleep was fitful and held images of red hats and pears, and blood, so much blood, drying crisply beneath the bodies without heads. He tossed and turned on the sofa, his clothes twisting against his restless body, the collar of his shirt rasping against his throat.

His dream wasn't the usual one that tortured him, but it was just as unsettling. Maria's head was next to a body on the grass. She was smiling up at him as she took a large bite from a pear, the juice dripping down her chin and mixing into the blood on the ground. She was saying something to him, something he couldn't hear. Her voice grew louder and louder until he woke up suddenly, pulling himself upright on the sofa, the dream still vivid in his mind. The shouting was coming from people outside making their way home, their drunken laughter stealing away his much-needed sleep. Sam sighed, unbuttoned his shirt and kicked off his shoes. His head felt so heavy. As he left the living room and switched off the light, the voices outside drifted away. He took off the rest of his clothes and climbed into bed, hoping that before long, he could drift away as well.

10

The prison in which Emma worked was a large building divided into two separate parts. One half was a traditional women's prison housing the inmates who made up much of the population. The other half was a secure hospital housing those women who'd been judged mentally unstable and in need of psychiatric care. The building was a stunning example of Gothic architecture, imposing but elegant, and always made Emma think of *Jane Eyre*. Large doors, deep red brick with turrets at either end, and windows that seemed oddly resistant to welcoming light, as if the rooms behind swallowed it. Emma felt the building retained a harsh beauty despite neglect and environmental damage, a quality shared by some of its inmates.

A residence for women of various ages and from diverse backgrounds, but all guilty of terrible crimes, all deemed a danger to themselves or others and therefore locked away. Working with these women was challenging, often disturbing, but always fascinating, and Emma gained satisfaction from helping women she'd once seen described as "beneath contempt" by a newspaper with a history of supporting fascism. They certainly were not above recrimination. Some had done truly horrific things, but some of them were imprisoned because they had reacted violently, but perhaps not entirely unreasonably, to the horrific things done to them. There were no levels of guilt, but Emma often thought there should be a little more compassion for the grey areas where human frailty resided, an understanding of why the women in the attic were *mad* at all.

"Hello, Emma. Come to pander to the *popolaccio* again?"

She ignored the sniggering security guard and his usual offensive greeting and made her way down the over-heated corridor; it felt as clammy as the guard looked. The psych wing was colder.

Emma watched Annie inside the large therapy room as she danced on the tips of her toes with a partner invisible to all except her. A waltz perhaps, although Emma knew nothing about dancing. Annie held out her arms as if in the embrace of a tall man whisking her about the room under a mirror ball, rather than the flickering strip lighting prone to whining at a high pitch. Head tipped back, she smiled widely, revealing slightly discoloured teeth. She moved well despite her advanced age, a little stiffly here and there but with control and precision during the turns, reminding Emma of Fred and Ginger in black-and-white musicals, lost in each other. Annie was also lost somewhere inside her own head, dancing to music only she could hear.

There was something ethereal about her, flimsy and light as she danced gracefully around the pale lemon room. If it wasn't for her eyes, she could have been dancing with a real partner in the real world – but the eyes gave her away. They were black and wet like bitumen, and so completely devoid of warmth that a partner couldn't fail to read the warning flashing in them. They were the kind of eyes that saw everything but gave nothing away, and they chilled Emma whenever she searched them trying to get a read on the woman in front of her, while always suspecting she was being read just as closely.

Emma tapped on the door before she entered the room, and Annie came to a stop mid-twirl, dropping her arms to her sides with her fingers splayed, as if she'd been accused of stealing and was keen to show her empty hands. She made no attempt to hide her annoyance at the interruption. This shifted to an appraisal of Emma from head to toe, a look of disapproval accentuating the deep grooves between her wiry eyebrows. Emma wore a light grey summer suit that was appropriate for sombre work in a sombre place, but Annie dismissed both the suit and Emma with one exaggerated toss of her head. Emma was used to this welcome, or lack of one.

Usually, Emma worked with Annie in a group therapy setting, but lately Annie had refused to take part, emotionally and sometimes physically removing herself from the other inmates, so Emma had decided to work with her individually hoping for more success.

Apparently, she was becoming aggressive towards others and had started to self-harm more regularly, cutting herself and smashing her head against walls until she was bleeding and screaming with anger. The cut on her head from her latest outburst was still an angry purple.

Even though there were two orderlies positioned just outside the door, it was with apprehension that Emma moved farther into the room to begin the session. She placed two chairs opposite each other, but at a comfortable distance apart – Emma knew better than to be within striking distance – and sat down.

"Good afternoon, Annie. Please come and take a seat." Emma hoped her smile was open and warm, but she made her voice firm so Annie knew she wouldn't be so easily dismissed.

"Are you going to dig around inside my mind like it's

a vegetable garden?" Annie asked. "Are you going to talk to me about penis envy and tell me I'm just another hysterical woman?" She sneered at Emma as she approached the chair.

Emma shook her head. "I think we both know there's very little about the penis we need to envy, don't we? I'm far more interested in where you learned to dance so beautifully."

Annie laughed, cocked her head and searched Emma's face. If she was looking for signs of sincerity, she must have found them. She sat on the chair, crossed her legs at the ankles and clasped her hands in her lap. She was demure in an old-fashioned way, with the type of posture once described as 'ladylike', although Emma suspected 'ladies' were not responsible for defining that quality.

Annie cleared her throat. "My first love taught me to dance when I was much younger, just a girl really. I wanted to be a ballerina, once upon a time," Annie said, perfectly lucid now, but with a degree of hesitation in her voice.

Emma nodded and smiled encouragement. She could see that Annie wanted to open up, but there was resistance there. The compliment about her dancing had resonated with Annie, though, and Emma sensed an opening, but she had to tread gently. *Careful*, Emma reminded herself. *Don't tell. Ask.*

"Am I right in thinking you're willing to talk to me, but you're unsure about something?" Emma sat forwards in her chair, hoping to create intimacy.

"Why do you want to know about my dancing? What has that got to do with anything?" Annie folded her arms across her body.

Emma leaned backwards again. "Something tells me you're a very interesting woman, and I'd like to get to know you better, if you're willing to share your story with me."

Annie had been institutionalised for a long time, and keeping yourself to yourself came with the territory, particularly when you were guilty of the kind of crime she'd been convicted of. But Emma suspected it went further than that. Annie seemed like a woman who was used to hiding, who was perhaps well trained in the art of keeping secrets. Maybe that's why she was so closed off in group therapy, reluctant to disclose anything significant despite numerous sessions.

The silence extended and became awkward, and the lights flickered and dimmed as if cowed by the tension. The room became gloomy, and the walls closed in and blanched from yellow to beige.

Emma sat in the silence, knowing most patients eventually felt compelled to fill it in individual sessions and Annie no longer had a group to hide behind. She watched Annie wrestle with herself, deciding what to say or even if she wanted to say anything at all. But apparently the silence had an unbearable weight and she seemed to decide. Her features softened, but only a little.

"I'm not the type to air my dirty laundry in public. It's demeaning. Those strangers in group with their blank eyes staring at me, gormless expressions, drooling for entertainment, all waiting for me to make my move like a pawn on a chessboard. I'm not a pawn, Emma. I'm the queen." Annie sat up straight. "So, do you still want to play?"

Amused, Emma replied, "Challenge accepted, your majesty."

Annie studied Emma's face, and appeared to embrace the spotlight of undivided attention. "They say you never forget your first love," she began, "and I have never forgotten mine. His face is there inside my head, even after all this time." As she spoke, a peaceful expression formed on Annie's face, and the beginnings of a smile stretched the sides of her mouth awkwardly. As the story emerged and gathered pace, Annie became lost in her own world again.

"My prince was so handsome, strong and sometimes angry – but never with me, I made sure of that. He used to stare at me when he thought I wasn't looking, but I could feel his eyes on me because my skin tingled and the back of my neck felt hot, as if he were standing just behind me breathing into my hair. Sometimes I couldn't catch my breath. There wasn't enough oxygen to take in because he sucked it all out of the room. He took my breath away, I suppose you could say." Annie giggled shyly, looking across at Emma with those dark eyes that had a shine to them now.

"Then one day he touched me, and when he did, I knew I had waited for that moment, wanted it, that I'd been holding my breath until it happened. It was as if my skin had been slowly heating, and when he touched me, it burst into flames. I felt myself tremble when he brushed my hair away from my face and pushed it behind my ear. There was a look on his face I'd never seen before, it pierced me, and I felt a warmth between my legs, such an intense warmth that I thought there was something wrong with me. I think I was scared. It was as if my body wasn't my own anymore, like I was standing outside myself, watching this man touch me where I had never been touched before. I was unsure about what I was feeling. It was all so new, and I was confused. I didn't understand why this grown-up man would be interested in me. He was so handsome, and I was so skinny and awkward, all angles and elbows, just a girl really, but he told me I was beautiful, and I believed him. I had never thought of myself in that way before. I'd always believed I was nothing special, and now suddenly I was."

Annie stroked her face, her fingers moving down to caress her throat. Her eyes were unfocused now. Emma remained still and silent, not wanting to disrupt the flow of her story, but she'd noticed the change in Annie's voice; it sounded softer, younger.

"The first time he undressed me, I felt so embarrassed about my body. I felt like a half-formed thing, like a baby bird naked without its feathers, but he didn't seem to mind. I think I tried to hide myself that first time, tried to fold my arms around myself as if I could disappear behind them. I put one arm across my breasts, although there wasn't much to cover, and I put my other hand between my legs. He told me I shouldn't hide myself, that I was a lovely girl and he wanted to see me, wanted to see all of me, and I wanted to show him. I felt very exposed, but also free, and my skin was alight. It felt too sensitive, and so good at the same time. But it took a while before I felt at ease when he undressed me."

Annie's breathing accelerated with a slight wheeze.

"It hurt the first time, and I cried out, but he covered my mouth so we wouldn't be overheard. I think I might have cried too, but he kissed me to make the pain go away. It didn't, not for a long time."

There was a slight quiver across Annie's lips, she swallowed loudly, and then her smile reappeared as quickly as it had fallen away.

"Sometimes it was a struggle to breathe when he was on top of me – he was so big and heavy – but it was special to be under him. I was small, and he covered me, and I felt safe beneath him, like I was hidden away. Sometimes I can still feel that burning pain that I felt when he was inside me, pushing too hard, breathing too fast, but I grew to like the pain. It made me feel nice. Although I'm not sure if it made him feel nice. He didn't smile at me afterwards. Generally, he looked angry and pushed me away, told me to cover myself up and I didn't know why. He smiled at me when he undressed me – he looked happy then, but not afterwards. Perhaps it hurt him too."

Emma began to feel claustrophobic inside the story. Words

like glue, sticking to her skin, getting caught up in her hair, clogging her lungs.

"He always gave me such thoughtful gifts," Annie continued. "Little things he knew I would cherish, because he knew I took great care with my toys. He said they were the prizes I'd won for being the best at keeping secrets, and he was right – I never told a soul. Why would I? The time I spent with him was so romantic. I was his secret, and he was mine. I didn't want anyone to know. I craved him, craved his attention, and used to wait impatiently for him to come home from work. That time, our special secret time together, was magical, intoxicating. It was like a forever summer, it went on for years, and I never wanted it to end, but then one day it just did."

Annie was crying now but seemed unaware of the tears falling down her cheeks and settling into the crevices at the side of her mouth. She looked so small as she sat in the chair, still heartbroken after such a long time. Emma wanted to take her in her arms and make all the pain disappear, and yet she couldn't move. She knew who this woman was, what she had done, and that knowledge held her motionless. She couldn't reach Annie anyway. She was far away now.

"I was bleeding when he came into my room one night, quite heavily, and with a deep pain in my back and stomach different from anything I'd ever known. I knew what it was. Mother had told me the year before, just after I had turned eleven. It meant I was a proper woman now. When he came to my room that night, I showed him the blood. I was so proud to be a grown woman at last, and I thought he would be proud too, thought he would love me even more because I wasn't a little girl anymore. He was disgusted. I tried to kiss him, but he pushed me away and slapped me across the face so hard it made my ears ring. He told me I was too old to play games anymore, that games were for children and I was no longer a child, and then he left my room and he never came back." Annie paused for a moment to gather herself, which took considerable effort. A tear shuddered on her chin before falling.

"I was so lonely for a long time, but nothing I did brought him back. I waited for him by the door when he got home from work just like I used to, but he pushed by me like I wasn't even there. He barely spoke to me. He didn't look at me. I was a stranger to him. I felt like I would die. Eventually I couldn't get out of bed – there didn't seem to be any point. Soon though, Mother got tired of my behaviour. She stormed into my bedroom one morning, threw back the covers on my bed, and shouted at me to get up. She told me to stop sulking, told me those days were over now and I had to leave Daddy alone. Daddy was hers again, and he didn't love me anymore."

Emma didn't know how to fill the silence that followed. Her training and experience deserted her just when she needed it most. She'd heard similar stories before from the other inmates, yet she felt at a loss in the face of childhood abuse confused with true love and entwined with heartbreak, and still so present. What was it that Shakespeare had written? "…*what's past is prologue.*"

Emma finally uncrossed her legs and unclasped her fingers – numb and white with tension – and the movement seemed to rouse Annie. She blinked rapidly, as if surprised to find herself back in the therapy room with company present. She wiped at her face. Some of her tears had dried, leaving shiny, salty patches on her cheeks.

Before the words were fully formed in Emma's mind – and she became conscious of the misplaced judgement they held – they fell from her mouth. "Didn't you know what your father did to you was wrong?"

Incredulity pulled Annie's eyebrows towards her hairline.

"But how could a love that consuming, that pure, be wrong?" she asked.

In that moment, Emma felt as lost as Annie.

11

Superintendent Nina Hepburn wanted to sit in on that morning's daily briefing before her meeting across town. She was in DCI Riley's stuffy office drinking a poor imitation of a latte while getting an update on the case. She removed an elastic band from the pocket of her navy suit jacket and pulled her dark blonde hair – still damp from the shower after her morning run – into a tight, no-nonsense bun.

She leaned forwards in the chair opposite Riley's desk and grimaced. "Why is it so difficult to get a decent cup of coffee in this bloody town? It's a cosmopolitan city full of what we're supposed to call baristas and artisan blends, and yet more often than not the coffee tastes like crap. This is apparently a latte." She held up her cup for both inspection and ridicule. Her name was misspelled, with an *e* and *r* on the end. "But it tastes more like dirty puddle water with hot milk thrown at it. How a chain can be established around this swill I'll never know. I've found one decent place in Shoreditch, but then I have to watch some bearded twat wearing glasses he doesn't need make a production out of one coffee."

Riley smiled. "I'm more of a tea man myself, but I

sympathise." He pushed a pile of paperwork to one side and dragged another in front of him. "We've worked together for ten years and I've yet to see you happy about your coffee. Do you think it's time to call off the search?"

She sighed, depositing the cup into the full bin, some of the coffee splashing out and adding more stains to the worn carpet tiles. "How are you coping with the press attention around this case?"

Riley put his elbows on the desk and rested his head in his hands. "The press is the press – I can't blame them for chasing the story. The public is worried: another woman is missing, and we're no closer to catching the killer. They need reassurance. I just wish I had more to tell them." He rubbed at his bloodshot eyes, making them water.

Nina nodded. Riley looked worn out, but he still had a controlled air about him; a calmness, something she had long admired in him. He would take the press attention in his stride and then focus on the matter at hand, just as he always had. She had absolute confidence he was the right person to lead the task force investigating London's serial killer.

"Do you think the missing woman is the latest victim?" she asked, although she was fairly certain of the answer.

"If the killer's previous form is anything to go by, I think we'll find her any day now." There was a note of resignation in his voice, but anger too. "We'll get the bastard, boss. They always slip up, give something away. This type of killer can't resist showing off. He wants to show us how smart he is, give us the run-around, but they're never as smart as they think they are."

Nina smiled at him. "He's underestimated the people who are out to catch him." She moved to one side to avoid the shaft of sunlight shining directly into her eyes.

"The bad guys often do. Even the smart ones can be

criminally stupid." Riley's smile opened out into a wide yawn that he attempted to suppress as his phone rang.

Nina left the office while he took the call and walked into the large outer office that was humming with activity. It was warm, the air sticky and as stale as some of the food abandoned on desktops. She made her way across to Sam who was organising the victims' case files into a neat pile ahead of his part of the briefing.

"Look at Stirling doing his housework over there," said a young detective named Pattinson to the officer sitting next to him. "He's doing that OCD thing again, Little Miss Tidy Up. He's like a fucking girl. He needs to man up."

Superintendent Hepburn approached him from behind. "I cannot wait for the day when 'like a girl' isn't used as an insult anymore by insecure little men like you, Pattinson." She leaned over the detective's desk. "Doing the job you do and working on this type of case should have educated you a bit, don't you think? Let me set you straight. Women represent only five per cent of the prison population in this country, and a significant number are there because of men. Men who have coerced them into prostitution, drug offences or theft, and that coercion is usually in the form of violence and emotional blackmail either towards the women themselves or their kids."

Pattinson leaned back into his chair with his mouth hanging open and started to blink rapidly.

She put her face closer to Pattinson. "Forty-six per cent of those women have been the victims of domestic abuse, fifty-three per cent have been physically or sexually abused in childhood, and yet, somewhat remarkably given what they've been through, eighty-one per cent of women prisoners are serving sentences for non-violent crimes." Nina's angry voice now carried across a much quieter room. "Might be worth considering before you talk of 'manning up'."

Most of the people in the room had likely overheard the exchange. "Something you all would do well to keep in mind while you try to stop another monster who is preying on women," Nina said. "Pattinson and his attitude are an example of the problem women deal with day in, day out, so ask yourselves if you want to be part of the problem or someone who helps solve it." Nina continued across the room to Sam, furious that this challenge was still called for, and far too often.

"Pattinson," barked Riley from the doorway of his office, "in here, now. The rest of you get back to work."

Pattinson blushed a furious red as he made his way across the room. A deafening silence followed the confrontation, everyone else in the room suddenly occupied by anything other than him. Clearly Pattinson wasn't a popular member of the team – Nina saw no support in their lowered faces. She took a brief pause to enjoy the moment.

Riley's office door slammed closed as Nina reached Sam's desk. "How are you, Sam?" She still felt a little flushed in the face after the exchange with Pattinson.

"I'm okay. Trying to get a read on this bastard." He closed his notebook. "Are you sticking around for the briefing?"

"Wouldn't miss it." The pens on Sam's desk were all aligned, his briefing notes ready to go. She resisted the urge to straighten his tie, deciding instead that his priorities didn't require adjustment.

She went to the kitchen in search of some water – anything to wash the bitter taste of coffee and the argument with Pattinson from her mouth. Soggy teabags were scattered in the bottom of the sink, staining the white enamel with tannin rust. She ignored them and filled the last clean glass with lukewarm tap water.

After Riley finished reprimanding Pattinson – Nina knew

he had no time for officers who were as lazy in their work as their thinking – he called everyone together and began the briefing. She sat at the back of the room and listened. They had gathered a great deal of information over the preceding months, and yet obviously not enough. The vital piece of the puzzle seemed just beyond reach, making it a challenging case to work on. It felt as if the killer would always be one step ahead. He ruled the city by night, like a vampire leaving blood in his wake, seemingly able to disappear into the walls come daybreak. London was his camouflage.

They had begun the investigation by following the same procedure they always did, pulling in the usual suspects – the perverts, rapists, those with previous convictions who were now out of prison and free to roam the streets again. But they had all been discounted. Some had been back in prison at the time of the murders. Others had alibis or had been out of the city.

Once those suspects had been vetted and ruled out, the detectives had taken the next step. They'd studied the women's lives and backgrounds – working life, home life and social life – trying to find connections between them, a person or place they may have had in common. They were looking for any kind of commonality, no matter how tenuous, that would have placed the women within a killer's eyeline. Perhaps a specific area where they had crossed paths with their murderer, something to help the detectives narrow down the place where he slaughtered them – but no such place had materialised. The monster's lair remained a dark secret behind an invisible doorway.

The background searches were a laborious, ongoing task, but necessary in order to discover where the killer had met his victims. But there was nothing to find. It was as if the victims had disappeared into thin air, like whispered words lost on the wind, before their bodies were discovered. The women hadn't known each other in life, and they had nothing in common. They didn't go to the same gym, or doctors, or frequent the same bars. They hadn't dated the same men or women and had no friends in common. There was nothing to link these women except being in the wrong place at the wrong time. They led normal lives. They didn't exist on the periphery of the city, the dark and seedy places that would have made them vulnerable or in any way an easy target. So far as the detectives could tell, the women hadn't risked placing themselves in danger. The normal rules of investigation, although closely followed, didn't seem to be helping. The women had nothing that united them in any way, nothing except for the last person they'd met.

Nina watched Riley closely as he talked to his team. The early days of the investigation, so long ago it now seemed, had been filled with the energy and adrenaline rush that fuelled a fresh hunt, but it was difficult to sustain that level of enthusiasm when efforts went unrewarded. Riley's frustration was echoed around the room, displayed in the faces of all those present. The detectives had dedicated long days to the search for the killer, and yet they were getting nowhere. Riley, however, was a driving force, adept at reading the mood of those who worked with him. He kept the negatives, the things they didn't know, as brief as possible, and moved on to the positives – the information they did know.

"Right, revision time. The only common ground in our investigation is the locations where the bodies were found," Riley said. "So far, these have been within a small area of the city, mainly east London or close by. This suggests that the killer is familiar with this part of the city. It's his chosen dumping ground, the area where he feels confident."

The killer seemed to know the places he left the bodies would be either locked or empty at night, his chosen hours of work. He could therefore count on being undisturbed when he displayed the women. The autopsies had shown that the heads were cut off and the hearts cut out prior to dumping, so the killer hadn't spent too long at the place where the bodies were discovered – thus minimising the time when he was most vulnerable to being caught.

"The killer is also meticulous in his research," Riley continued. "He's obviously paid close attention to the CCTVs installed at each of the scenes." Although some of the locations were close to cameras, the bodies were left out of their range of coverage. The killer was able to discard his victims and then disappear like smoke into the night sky.

Riley straightened and looked over at Sam. "We know from Sam's previous briefings that the killer is a creature of habit. He has a specific plan in his head when he creates his death scenes. They are his works of art." Some of the detectives in the room grimaced. "He pours blood on the ground like a backdrop, the women in the foreground like incomplete sculptures."

Nina studied the array of crime scene photos displayed around the room. She understood what Riley meant about works of art. The shoes, socks and the contents of the women's bags were displayed at the edges of the tableau, the red hat and pear along with the victim's heart, the artistic flourishes he included in his masterpiece.

He was methodical in his work – the personal belongings of the women were neatly placed and lined up in the same positions each time. She recalled that Sam had previously suggested that the killer was taunting them, attempting to demonstrate just how completely he had invaded his victims' lives, that nothing was off limits, not even their underwear, the most intimate of clothing.

The timer of a microwave oven announced its job was complete, but nobody moved.

"But I want to remind you all," Riley said, "that although

the killer has always stuck to his plan and meticulously recreated each death scene, he's evolving."

He started to pace back and forth and almost tripped over an empty box of photocopier paper; he absentmindedly pushed it under the nearest desk. He gestured towards one of the latest photos.

The plastic comb was the latest addition to his work, but as yet it was an unfathomable clue, just like the hat and pear, but it suggested there might be more to come – although Riley said he hoped there wouldn't be many more scenes to witness.

"This is a careful, well-prepared killer who leaves no evidence of himself at the scene," Riley said. "Everything he's done has been carried out with precision and attention to detail."

Nina wondered if that might be a clue in itself but was distracted by the aroma of something spicy as it escaped from the microwave and circulated about the room. Her mouth watered, but she focused again on Riley.

"He also seems to be sticking to a schedule," said Riley. "There are four months give or take between each murder, four months in which the killer remains seemingly dormant." Riley asked his team to consider this quiet period: was it reserved for finding new victims? For stalking them? Or was this a time for self-control and reflection? "This last question is more Sam's area of expertise. Any questions before I hand things over to him?"

"You said there was no forensic evidence from the hats, Albert," Nina said, "but what about the hat itself? Any idea where the killer got it?" She removed her jacket and put it down beside her, her thin, gold bangles rattling as they moved along her arm.

"No, there's no label," Riley said. "It isn't shop bought. We showed the hat to a textiles expert and also a lecturer from a fashion college, and they told us the wool is an unusual shade of red, but not so unusual that it's rare. It has been finished with a distinctive stitch, though, and that might help us eventually. We think it might be homemade." Riley loosened his tie.

"A serial killer who knits? That would be a first." Nina noticed that Pattinson had turned towards her. "He is dedicated, I'll give him that."

Pattinson laughed loudly. Nina – unconvinced – glared at him until he turned away.

"Yes, it's a bit weird, isn't it?" Riley smiled at Nina with a thoughtful expression on his face. Somehow, they needed to find out more about the hat, but where did you find out about something that was homemade when you knew nothing about the home?

Riley looked across the room. "Alright, Sam. You are in charge of the *why* he is, which will help us find out *who* he is. And make no mistake, we will find out who he is." He nodded at Sam to continue, as he moved behind Nina at the back of the room.

Sam walked to the front of the room, exhausted eyes looking back at him. Every day that Polly remained missing brought a new level of dread almost strong enough to paralyse the team, and yet somehow, they remained focused. They were clinging to the hope they might find her; they hadn't given up looking, but Sam suspected they were all waiting for her body to turn up, a uniquely disturbing situation that gave the detectives a haunted quality.

"As DCI Riley mentioned, our killer is going to a lot of trouble to create a story around the bodies," Sam said. "He's trying to share a particular vision with us, but it's one that we don't yet understand. The fact that we don't know what he's trying to tell us will likely leave him frustrated. He will become increasingly angry that we're missing the point. As his anger escalates, he'll feel he has to make things clearer for us, and that means he'll have to leave more obvious clues – and the more clues he leaves, the more of himself he gives away. The fact that he's added a plastic comb to the latest scene suggests he feels the pressure to spell things out more clearly, which is good news for us." Sam spoke with hope in his voice – a hope he wanted to share with the room.

"I think it's safe to assume the killer is a younger man who is physically strong – strong enough to handle the weight of the bodies. Lugging a dead body around isn't an easy task, so a young, able man would pose a significant threat to our victims, because he can overpower them with relative ease."

Riley nodded to him from across the room and leaned back against the wall, an EXIT sign flickering above his head.

"We know the physical make-up of our killer in the broadest sense, so let's think about the emotional. Although I have discussed psychopaths in previous briefings, I think it's worth reminding ourselves who we're dealing with here. We know from years of scientific study that a psychopath has a profound lack of empathy towards his victims. In layman's terms, he is lacking a conscience. He has no remorse. A serial killer, however, is a complicated beast. He is not an impulsive creature; he has self-control."

Sam noticed more than a few puzzled faces. "Let me explain. The amygdala is the emotional centre of the brain and is a key area when it comes to violent impulses. In an impulsive murderer, this part of the brain has become overactive and drives him. However, a serial killer is better able to control those impulses by engaging another part of the brain, the prefrontal cortex, which is, simply put, like the brakes on a car. It controls impulsive behaviour. It is this deadly combination, a profound lack of empathy coupled with self-control, that makes a serial killer a force to be reckoned with, and difficult to catch. It is also this discipline that allows him to be patient, to take four months off during which time he will most likely find another victim and plan ahead for the next kill. The routine is important to him – it's all about control. If he maintains a four-month schedule, he maintains control of himself." He took a deep breath. "If he changes this routine, it will signify to us that he has lost control, that his brakes aren't strong enough to hold back the violence anymore." Dread brushed up against him, but he tried to ignore it.

Sam looked down at his notes. "I think we can also say our killer has a deep loathing for women. He has never murdered a man – that we know of anyway – but he is unlikely to do so. Most serials stick with one sex. There are exceptions to this rule, of course. Dennis Rader, also known as BTK, killed men and women, but that is fairly unusual. From what we know from previous studies on the behaviour patterns of murderers, most psychopathic tendencies take root in childhood, the time when the brain is young enough to be malleable and neural pathways are conditioning what a person will become later in life. Therefore, his mother, grandmother or female guardian would be the most likely candidate for the original woman to set him on this path, someone who was able to shape him from the time he was a young boy."

Sam removed his lighter from his pocket and ran his thumb over the jagged wheel as he ordered his thoughts. He felt a little uncomfortable addressing a room full of people, but he moved on. "I would like to suggest there is also a psychosexual dynamic at work here, which may seem a bit of a leap in logic from what we know so far, but I know of very few studies of serial killers where there isn't an element of sexual deviance at play, so I think I'm on safe ground. Although there has been no sign of rape or masturbation at the scene, the fact that he removes the victims' underwear is significant, I think, particularly when the rest of the body remains fully clothed. I wouldn't be at all surprised if we later find evidence of masturbation at the place he actually murders the victims. Sexual gratification for him is most likely achieved by chopping off the victim's head. To me, this suggests that a female figure in his early life may have sexually abused him. Psychologists like me believe abnormal sexual behaviour is formed in early childhood, that the erotic world of that child is formed from learned behaviour from a primary adult within their lives. They have, in essence, been moulded, and this mould, in extreme cases like that of our killer, persists throughout their lives and drives their sexual desires as an adult. What we may think of as sexual perversion is not perversion for the killer. To him it is completely normal."

Nina waved her hand to attract Sam's attention. "You're suggesting that our killer was abused as a child by a female? How common are female paedophiles? I have never come across one myself."

Sam nodded. "They are rare, far rarer than male paedophiles, but they do exist. However, the kind of abuse they carry out is generally different from their male counterparts. Maternal behaviour becomes exaggerated, I think is the best way I can put it. Caregiving extends beyond normal boundaries, becoming too intimate – more like seduction. It can start simply with the mother or female guardian undressing or bathing in front of the child, in some cases bathing with the child. This can be normal bonding behaviour for some mothers when the child is young, but if these behaviours continue as the child grows older, when he is developing a natural sexual curiosity, then the normal attachment he develops with his mother will be warped. Children by their very nature are needy and will do anything to avoid abandonment, even if that means attaching themselves to a caregiver who is sexually abusive. At that vulnerable age, sexual abuse and love become entwined in the mind of the child. In other words, to be sexually abused means to be loved. Now, if the parent fulfils their child's needs with normal nurturing, then all is generally well. If, however, that need is abused sexually in some way, then it harms the critical period of sexual development that begins in early childhood. There is a lot of research that tells us that if a child relates and attaches to a parent in an abnormally sexual way, then that way of relating becomes hard-wired into the brain and drives sexual desires and behaviours in adulthood. In other words, our killer is probably repeating the lessons he learned from his female abuser. Freud wrote a great deal about the early stages of sexual development. He said that if the crucial stage of development is somehow damaged, in this case, by sexual abuse, then it could influence a person's thoughts and feelings about sex as a fully grown adult. As I said, our killer is repeating only what he learned, what he perceives to be normal."

"But even if the killer learned this sexual behaviour at a young age," Nina continued, "he surely still knows it's wrong, that society thinks he's a psychopathic pervert."

There were a few laughs in the room. It was clear from the faces staring up at him that others had the same question. It was something Sam knew he had to explain as clearly as possible, particularly as there were so many conflicting theories out there. Some psychologists believed sexual deviancy was an acquired behaviour, something that had been learned and could therefore be unlearned, but others, himself included, didn't agree that something so deep-rooted could be unlearned; at best, it may not be acted upon. Others argued that sexual deviancy was innate, but this view was controversial. There was currently no academic consensus when it came to sex offenders, which made explaining it to the room full of people in front of him such a difficult task.

Sam put the lighter back in his pocket and ignored his

cigarette craving. "A significant number of abuse victims go on to lead normal lives, relatively speaking," he said. "By that, I mean many of them do not go on to abuse their own victims. However, some victims of childhood sexual abuse carry out sexual abuse as adults because they are repeating what they perceive to be love and affection. They are very aware that society on the whole is repulsed by this behaviour, but they do not know of any other way to demonstrate love. It becomes a never-ending cycle of abuse: a significant number of abusers have been the victim of abuse. As I said, the child's brain is a malleable thing, and if it has been hardwired to think that to be sexually abused is the same thing as being loved, it's almost impossible to break this cycle. Just consider for a moment how easily you perform tasks you learned when you were little: tying your shoes, telling the time. Now try and imagine how it would feel if somebody came along and tried to break you of those habits of a lifetime by telling you that you've been tying your shoes incorrectly, or that you can't really tell the time properly after all. Well, that's how it is for some sex offenders. Telling them that perpetrating sexual abuse is wrong is like telling them it's noon when they are absolutely certain it's midnight."

For a while, there was an uncomfortable silence in the room, the air crackling with a tension that crawled along Sam's skin. He went to reach for his lighter again, stopped himself.

"Let me be clear: I am in no way condoning or defending sex offenders. I'm merely trying to explain why they do what they do. Sex offenders in general, and our killer in particular, know that their behaviour is unacceptable in normal society, and that's where the anger that our killer feels comes from, the anger that drives him to kill. When our killer murders these women, he is in fact carrying out something called displacement, or more precisely in this case, aggressive transference. He is transferring his rage from his female abuser onto our victims."

"I'm not sure I follow," Nina said, frowning and sitting forwards.

"Let's say you've had a bad day at the office. You might go home and take it out on your partner, or the kids, or even the dog. You are displacing your rage, transferring your aggression. This is what our killer is doing. He's transferring the rage that he feels towards his abuser, onto our victims. He is killing his abuser over and over again."

Sam noticed a few officers taking notes. "He knows that what his abuser did to him is wrong. He absolutely understands that he is damaged goods. His abuser has destroyed him completely, has removed any possibility of a normal life, and he is furious. Love, sex, anger and ultimately murder are intertwined in his mind. He is broken. He's killing the one who broke him, in the shape of his victims, over and over again. I strongly believe he is killing the one who broke his heart. This is why he cuts out the heart of his victims, because his own heart has, metaphorically speaking, been broken. When he leaves the heart, which is the symbol of love, behind, I think it's because he's rejecting it, perhaps because he was also rejected. Paedophiles tend to be attracted to a specific age group. Maybe our killer was rejected when he got too old, and that would have been devastating for him. His heart would have been broken, so he breaks hers in return."

"And the head?" a detective enquired in a detached tone perfected over the months.

Sam pointed to one of the gruesome photographs on the whiteboard. "He removes the head because that is the essence of an individual. The face is what we present to the world. It's generally the first thing people notice when they look at us. By removing the head, he removes the person. This might explain why all of our victims have dark hair. I'm certain his abuser would also have had dark hair. But this is a conflicted person. I suspect he keeps the head because he cannot entirely let her go. He needs to keep a part of her close by as a reminder. Having her close to him comforts him. He hates his female abuser as much as he loves her. In fact, to our killer, love and hate are the same thing. He is reliving his childhood, but he's also trying to kill it."

"But why now?" the same detective asked, as he tapped a pen against his chin. "Why is he killing now?"

"That's a difficult question to answer." A note of exasperation crept into Sam's voice despite his best efforts to prevent it. "We have to consider the situational circumstances as well as the psychological. We have to ask ourselves what else is happening in the killer's life other than murder. It could be that other aspects of his life are breaking down and this makes him feel like he has no control over his own destiny, and so he kills. Killing makes him feel like control has been regained, he is back in charge. We have to remember that he was once a victim; he will strive to ensure that he never feels victimised again. Another possibility is that something triggered him, and he finally snapped."

"Something like what?" Nina asked, a pile of paperwork sliding across the desk as she adjusted her position.

Sam shrugged. "It varies. Job loss, the breakdown of a relationship, a stressful work environment, prolonged loneliness or serious illness – or being rejected by one too many women. A triggering event can cause years, sometimes decades, of anger, repression, fear and frustration to explode. It's like giving the final push to a person standing on the edge of a cliff."

Sam let the information he'd shared sink in a little before asking if anyone had any questions. Team members shifted in their chairs and shuffled their papers, but Riley stepped in with a question that was most likely on everyone's mind.

"Will he ever stop?"

The room became very still, as if everyone was holding their breath. The high-pitched whine of a desktop fan infiltrated the silence.

Sam couldn't lie. "No, he will never stop, because his pain and anger will never stop. He'll kill more victims, because he's trying to kill his female abuser, but ultimately it won't work. His life is ruined, and that will never change. He can't have it back. The damage can never be repaired. The more women he kills, the more he will realise that it won't solve his problem. His pain hasn't gone away. Life isn't all better because women are dead. His abuser will always be inside his head, no matter what he does or who he kills."

This was something they probably already knew but, wanting to end on a positive note, Sam told them something they might not know.

"His abuser is his driving force. She might be the voice forever inside his head, but she's also his weak spot. She's the one who makes him angry, and when he becomes angry, he will also become careless, and that's how we'll catch him in the end. His abuser may be his weak spot, but she is our lucky charm."

"Let's hope so, Sam," Nina said. "We could do with a little luck."

12

The empty room held her smell, even though it no longer held her. The air was heavy with a stale, powdery sweetness, like a vase of decaying flowers. As Ben moved into the room, her smell opened its arms to embrace him. He inhaled deeply, savouring what remained of her, and was comforted by this strange intimacy that had been denied him when she'd been warm flesh and blood. He had tried his best to reach her. He'd tried to reach all of them, to forge something meaningful out of an uncertain and hesitant beginning, but they refused to apply themselves.

It was the lack of dignity he couldn't stand, the way they pleaded for a way out, prostrated themselves at his feet and asked for a mercy he just didn't have. The way they cried until they made themselves swollen and ugly with tears, a slug's trail of mucus from nose to chin. They didn't appreciate they'd been chosen, not taken. *Where's the fucking gratitude?* At least they left something behind.

Polly's blood was still warm as he poured it from the flask into the bucket, although it no longer had the same vibrancy, that shocking blue-red that was so frustratingly temporary.

Nonetheless, it was a gift he received gratefully. There had been a time when the ephemeral nature of blood irritated him, the red diminishing in power to brown as the blood cells and plasma separated. But he grew to respect its properties: the remarkable way it coagulated when it came into contact with air and unfamiliar molecules, and that it clotted to prevent further blood loss in an inhospitable environment. He had to admit the basement walls were a poor host. But mostly he admired the way the lifespan of blood was as fleeting as its human home, a mayfly substance. It decomposed and decayed, just like flesh. All that remained from a life drawing to a close was a brown stain, a haemorrhage of words on a basement wall.

He took off his clothes and folded them in a neat pile in the far corner of the room. Naked, he studied the space on the wall, the sheen of sweat on his muscles glistening as he dipped the brush into the blood. He inhaled the heady, raw scent of iron, sucking it into his lungs. Tipping his head back, he opened his mouth to allow her blood to drip off the tip of the brush and onto his tongue, where he let it settle before swallowing it. It was a taste unlike any other – not the same as tasting his own blood after he'd cut a finger. It was less bitter, though it still had the sharp tang of iron, but coupled with a burnt sugar taste that reminded him of candy floss from a fairground. He absorbed her sweet taste hungrily, her blood the only fix he needed to feed his addiction, for now anyway. His stomach turned as the unnatural liquid tried to settle there. But he wouldn't vomit – it was getting easier each time. It just took a little self-control.

As his stomach settled, an image formed in his mind and became clear. He knew now where he wanted to leave her, and as he saw the place, he knew what to write on the wall, saw the words as if he had painted them already. He plunged the brush into the bucket of blood like a knife into flesh.

He had a steady hand, his writing as delicate and precise as if it had been done with a fountain pen. Each individual letter was a work of art, swirling and twisting around the next like the branches of wisteria, until the story blossomed across the wall. It was a story from his early years but still vivid in his mind despite the brevity of his childhood and the passing of time. Sometimes he forgot the finer points of the tale, in which case he retrieved his tattered copy of the book to ensure that his words were a faithful rendition. He liked to get things right.

The blood dripped down his arm and onto his torso as he worked, but he liked the way it felt on his skin. Polly was mixing in with his perspiration, the sweet and sour aroma growing stronger as it warmed. He liked the feeling of tightness on his skin as the blood and sweat dried to a salty crust, the way it flaked as he stretched to reach the top of the wall. He could feel it in his hair and on his face. There were times when it was thrilling to feel like a dirty piggy again, wallowing in the stink. Wallowing and swelling. His erection took him by surprise, and he orgasmed almost without warning. *Naughty, dirty piggy.* He was covered in his own fluid. It slid down his legs, slippery and gelatinous, turning the blood a milky pink. He would have to scrub, scrub, scrub when he was all done, scrub until he glowed, but not until the story was complete, until the words ran across the wall as unbroken as a daisy chain.

He always illustrated the stories he wrote. They didn't feel alive until he did. This time he filled the space with a tower pushing high into the sky, the sun bouncing off the many square windows, each one a mirror for passing clouds. He didn't want to replicate the tower from the book. He wanted to stay true to the place where he planned to leave Polly. It would be her headstone, so it was important to get it right.

As he completed the tower, he began to cry. He thought by now there would be a callous over his heart, but the sobs shook his body and made his chest ache. He dropped onto his knees, the concrete basement floor sending a shuddering, searing shock into his kneecaps that made him clench his teeth. Love was always painful. It lifted you up and swept you away, and then slammed you back down to the floor like an elevator with snapped cables. It showed no mercy. It had never been kind to him. It only teased him from a safe distance. He had called its name, but it just waved at him as it passed him by. Now here he was again, all alone with love to give, but it didn't even meet him halfway.

When the newspapers first wrote about him, they only told half the story, sticking to the familiar labels when they didn't even know him. He wasn't supposed to feel love – apparently it wasn't part of his emotional make-up. But wasn't that a bit too easy? Certainly, it was more palatable. They asked their hungry readers how somebody could be capable of such cruelty, then answered their own question: he must be a psychopath. A normal person could never do such things.

The newspapers vilified him so the public could feel better about themselves, could pat themselves on the back for suppressing their own violent desires. Could take comfort in thinking they were normal, moral, and lived on the right side of the street opposite the likes of him on the wrong side. The truth was, maybe he was more like everyone else than they were prepared to accept. In fact, braver, more honest. Living true to himself, finding his own interpretation of love. After all, wasn't love a different thing to different people?

Or maybe he was the one telling lies to comfort himself. Trying to convince himself that he felt love, for Polly and the others. They would never abandon him – not like his first love. They couldn't. This was the thought that niggled him. They didn't choose to stay for him. They stayed because he had chosen for them. He closed his eyes and curled into himself, his long limbs knotted around each other, head tucked into his chest, making himself small in the cavernous room. An adult foetus smeared in blood.

He might have fallen asleep. He realised with shame that he had allowed self-pity into the room. *Grow up and be a man,* came the voice of his first love. *You should be ashamed of yourself for being so weak.* She was right to reproach him. He was pathetic. He banged his head on the floor, his knees protesting as he kneeled, but he deserved to feel the pain; his skull vibrating, he deserved to be punished. He banged his head again and again until she was gone, taking the self-pity with her, and then he got up, feeling dizzy but stronger now. It was time to clean himself up and wash Polly away.

He scrubbed himself clean with the stiff brush, the last of Polly's blood disappearing down the plughole. When the water ran clear, he started again, covering himself in suds from head to toe until the acrid fragrance of coal tar soap filled the steamy bathroom and left his skin so clean it squeaked as he rinsed himself off. The towel felt harsh against his skin, but it felt satisfying to be clean again – inside and out – as the remnants of shame drained away.

He thought of Polly and what he'd created in the basement in her name: a soaring tower pushing up through the words and almost touching the ceiling, a testimony to their shared experience. A bloody epitaph, still tacky to the touch.

He was ready to visit her again, to ensure she was comfortable and had settled in nicely with the others. He smiled at his reflection in the mirror and brushed his hair forward so they wouldn't notice the lump that had risen above his left eyebrow. He didn't want to spoil the moment.

He went down to the storage room behind the shop. It was a cold room and he shivered, but it was more from excitement than the chill in the air. This was the first time he'd visited Polly since she'd moved into her new home. He'd placed her there just last night, but he wanted to touch her again, to stroke her skin with the tips of his fingers, even though she wouldn't feel as warm and soft as before. As he opened the freezer door, he hardly dared to breathe until he saw Polly up close, saw they were all there waiting for him. He needn't have worried. They would never abandon him now.

Five heads were lined up in rows: two on the top shelf, two on the middle, and Polly, all alone for now, on the next shelf down. They were equally spaced like tins of food in a supermarket, the aisles yet to be fully stocked. Their eyes were open. Their mouths were slightly open too, waiting for him. He brought his fingertips to his mouth and transferred a kiss from his lips close to theirs, his affection leaving marks on the glass barrier that separated them.

He lifted Polly's glass dome. Her beauty still took his breath away. The cold had transformed her pale skin into a dove grey pearl, her eyelashes crusted with tiny icicles, her lips, slightly parted, still full and welcoming. She was a masterpiece preserved while still in her prime. Perhaps he had put too much blusher on her cheeks – they were a little pinker than he would have liked – but it would fade with the cold, and the lips were just right. The red lipstick created a dramatic contrast to her skin, like fresh blood on snow. A sliver of pear rested on her tongue, the white of the flesh maintained by lemon juice and frozen while still vibrant and fresh, just like Polly herself. It wasn't caught in the throat as the story dictated, but he permitted himself a little poetic licence. He liked to see the pear, that hint of whiteness against the red of the lips. It was only visible if he looked closely, a secret just for him.

He wanted to pick her head up and cradle it in his arms, wanted to dance around the basement with her again like a love-struck couple clinging to each other, but she was at her most delicate now, almost frozen but not quite. Polly was settling in very well, the frozen droplets in her hair like raindrops on a spider's web, shimmering and catching the light. She was his favourite so far, although they each had something unique about them, a star quality that made him choose them over others.

He still had another hour or two to wait before he could move Polly's body from the basement. He had wrapped her torso, fully clothed, in plastic sheeting, and yet the smell of her flesh was leaking from somewhere. She was beginning to turn. But it wasn't fully dark yet, and he had to be patient before he could create the scene where he would lay Polly to rest. You could get away with murder if you waited until dark.

Finally, it was time. He tied a rope around Polly's waist so she would be easier to haul up the stairs and used a stainless-steel butcher's block with wheels to transport her to the boot of his car. On the backseat, he placed a large black bin liner that contained the red hat, the plastic comb, and Polly's shoes, underwear and leather bag. Underneath the front passenger seat, he set down two small plastic boxes: one held the pear, the other Polly's heart. The boxes were wrapped in the same plastic as the body. And, last but definitely not least, he placed a final object on the passenger seat, something very fitting just for her.

He felt a familiar ache as Polly's chapter drew to a close, but his ice maidens would soothe him when he returned home. Rosie, Suzy, Lizzie, Charlotte and now Polly: five pale-skinned, dark-haired beauties, decorated with frosty glitter, mouth-watering to behold. Frozen desserts.

13

Sam fidgeted in his chair, glanced around the room, and tossed his lighter from one hand to the other. He was aware his new therapist, Emma, was watching him and reading his body language; an open book, he suspected. Despite being well versed in the process of counselling, he wasn't keen on this reversal of roles, undoubtedly obvious at this moment.

He tried to hide his awkwardness, but Emma said, "Too late, Sam. Your discomfort is as obvious as a bad wig." She tilted her head. "You're not wearing a wig, are you? That would be awkward."

"What?" Sam was so taken aback, he spluttered with laughter. "That has to be the most unconventional opening to therapy I've ever heard. Is that your usual approach?" He noticed thin fingers of sunlight reaching into the room highlighting the red in Emma's dark hair.

"Only when a patient displays unusual levels of tension," Emma said. "It felt like we needed to break the ice rather than allow it to slowly thaw. I suspect your needs require immediacy."

Sam let out a deep breath. He placed his lighter on the table in front of him and slouched into the chair. Her voice had a soothing quality. The ache under his ears eased as his molars took a break from grinding; the absence made him feel lightheaded.

"You mentioned on the phone it's been some time since you attended supervision," Emma said.

"It's been a while. Almost a year, I think." Sam gazed at the patterned carpet, feeling embarrassment at the thought of such neglect, but glancing at Emma he saw no judgement in her expression.

Emma shook her head. "Let go of the self-criticism, Sam, you're here now. What brings you to me?"

Everything. Work, unhappy relationships, maybe loneliness. Maybe destiny. You. He caught himself, surprised by his thoughts. He needed to shut them down before Emma read them on his face. He felt hot suddenly. His eyes travelled the room again as he tried to focus on therapy rather than his therapist, but instead the case intruded. *Wasn't this the same building where Polly worked?* Her face appeared pushing other thoughts to one side. *Where was she? Would they find her in time? Was it possible she had just—*

"Sam, where are you right now?"

The question snatched him from his turmoil like he'd been rescued. The sensation was familiar, like waking abruptly from the nightmare just in time to catch that vital breath before drowning. Sam realised he'd been drifting and hadn't answered her original question. He tried to concentrate on Emma and the gentle encouragement she offered. "I'm sorry. The case I'm working on involves a missing woman who used to work here – I mean, works here. Maybe, I don't know. Now I'm here to see you. It's just odd, that's all, the chances of that happening."

Emma put a hand to her mouth. "Yes! I saw police officers by the entrance downstairs. They were interviewing her co-workers just after she went missing. That's the case you're working on?"

Sam hesitated. He couldn't go into the details of the case – it would be unethical – and yet the case was the thing that had brought him here. It was the source of his stress, and triggered his recurring nightmare. He had to discuss it to a certain degree if he was to get the help and support he needed.

Emma must have sensed he was conflicted, because she said, "Everything you say in this room is confidential. I know there will be some things you can't discuss, but please feel reassured that nothing leaves this room."

The space between them, although not more than a few feet, suddenly felt like a chasm. Her expression, expectant and sincere, invited him to be open, but he didn't know how to bridge the gap. They worked in the same field, and yet their worlds were so different. The nature of his work dragged him to dark places. He couldn't ask her to meet him there, and yet how could he pull himself out without a helping hand from someone who lived above it all? Finally, he made a decision: if he wanted to function effectively at work and in his life away from the job, then he had to open up, had to find a way to jump to the other side. He took a deep breath and leaned forwards.

He told her as much about the case as he could without breaching any ethical guidelines. He told about the last year of his life, the horror story of the murdered women ending with the disappearance of Polly, whom he suspected was the latest victim. He talked about his role on the task force and admitted out loud for the first time his sense of hopelessness. It felt like he was unpacking a heavy rucksack that had been strapped to his back, discarding useless items, even if only temporarily, long enough at least to catch his breath and stand up straight. When he was finally done, his throat felt dry, and he took a long drink of water from the glass on the table in front of him, emptying it quickly.

*

After Sam finished talking, Emma was emotionally drained. Hearing about the case felt like an onslaught. She could only guess at how exhausted he must be. To spend each day side by side with brutality must feel like being poisoned over time. She had glimpses of violence and its aftermath in her work at the prison, but not to the same degree.

Emma leaned towards Sam. She was tempted to advise him to get out of that world as quickly as possible, to run and not look back, but that wasn't an option. The killer had to be found before he destroyed more lives – before he destroyed Sam.

"Tell me about the anger I'm sensing." She could see it on his face but noticed it hadn't entirely eroded the kindness.

He sighed. "The anger is there all the time. I obviously experience it when I think of the killer and the fact we haven't been able to catch him yet, but I see anger all around me too, the world feels angry."

Emma couldn't disagree. There was anger in the faces of people crushed up against one another on the tube in rush hour. It was in the faces of pedestrians on the crowded city streets when they bumped into each other because one of them had their face buried in a mobile phone. When they stood in a line that never moved at the supermarket because there were just too many people in too small a space. It was in the way people behaved towards one another, no sign of courtesy or compassion. Sam carried that – a lot of Londoners did – but he carried a killer too. She wanted to help him with the weight.

Sam sighed. "The worst thing is, I can't let go of the anger because it fuels me. It drives me into work every day; it pushes me to keep going." His fists were clenched as tightly as his jaw. "It's what will get the job done."

It was encouraging that he was turning his anger outwards and using it like a tool. She would have been more concerned if he'd turned it inwards, where it would metastasise into a depression and consume him. This told her that Sam's depression, which he'd mentioned on the phone, was under control – at least for now.

She waited for his breathing to slow. There was something familiar about Sam. Something about the way he held himself reminded her of someone. The dark hair and eyes, the slight brooding quality – a sense of stillness, but on high alert – but she couldn't quite place him. She brushed the thought aside. There were only twenty minutes of the session left. It was time to start wrapping up.

"We've covered a lot of ground today," she said, "and we'll certainly revisit some of it in further sessions, but I want to pick up on the sense of hopelessness that you mentioned. You've described this feeling in your work but also in your life outside work. I'd like to know what it is about your life that makes you feel hopeless."

She wondered if he went home to someone, and if that someone made him laugh like she'd managed to earlier. She was drawn to his mouth and the subtle lines on either side that told her he smiled often, although maybe not lately. She glanced at his hands, imagined—

Sam sat forwards in his chair and reached for more water. Emma felt caught out. She suspected she was blushing.

"I've been having the same nightmare for years," he said. "When I wake up, what I mostly feel is a sense of hopelessness. Or maybe it's helplessness. I think the feeling comes from not being able to save myself in the dream, but it's more than that." A look of confusion creased his brow. "It's not understanding what the dream means."

Emma nodded and waited for Sam to say more, but he just shrugged and looked at her with a bemused expression. "Can you describe the dream?"

He hesitated.

"Talking about it might take away some of its power," she said gently.

He closed his eyes and took a deep breath. "The dream is about drowning. I'm either in a swimming pool or the sea, I'm not sure, but the water is warm. I know there's someone with me, but I can't see them. I don't know who it is, but I'm frightened of them." Sam gripped the armrests now and his words accelerated. "There's something tight around my ankles, but when I look at them under the water, I can't see anything. And yet it gets tighter and tighter, and then it starts to pull me under. I can see bubbles above my head. I struggle, but as I do, the bubbles grow bigger and I can't get through them. They stop me from breaking the surface. I wake up gasping for air and kicking my feet."

Sam snapped his eyes open and dragged his hands through his hair, leaving it sticking up in tufts. He actually looked to Emma like a man who had just awoken from a vivid nightmare. He was looking at her but not really seeing her, as if the dream had come into the room.

His eyes widened. "There's a smell. I've just remembered that." His words were slower now. "Or perhaps I've always known it, but it was in the back of my mind. It's strong. I don't know what it is, but I don't like it. It's sweet, I think." Sam curled his nose in disgust.

Emma glanced at the clock. They were a few minutes over time, but Sam needed a moment to gather himself. Maybe she didn't want him to go. She waited for his breathing to slow before she spoke.

"I think we should discuss this further next time. Meanwhile, I think it's important that you give some thought to the dream. Could it be a suppressed memory you're trying to work through as you sleep?"

Sam nodded thoughtfully, his eyes travelling her face as if committing it to memory.

"It may explain why there's a definite smell attached to it," Emma said. "As I'm sure you're aware, our sense of smell is more capable of triggering our memories than any of our other senses. If you feel a sense of hopelessness when you wake from your nightmare, it's probably because the smell you described is taking you back to a time when you felt hopeless – and also helpless, as you said those two states are intrinsically linked for you at the moment. If you can figure out the smell, you may also figure out the source of your nightmare. Once you understand it, you can disempower it. I'm sure if that happens, your sense of hopelessness will diminish."

Sam laughed. "Do I have to go to perfume counters now and sniff the bottles? Sneak up behind women and inhale their scent? Is that my homework?"

Emma straightened with excitement. "Don't you think it's interesting that a female fragrance was the first thing that came to your mind?"

"Blimey." He leaned towards Emma. "You might be right. That is the first thing I thought of." The look on his face was a combination of amazement and relief.

Emma smiled. His smile in return seemed to contain something warm, unspoken, and yet she heard it. The silence lingered and felt intimate, like a shared secret.

They rose at the same time, and as she held the door for him to leave, his scent – tinged with tobacco and spice – imprinted itself on her memory.

14

It was the first time it had rained in days, as if the sky had opened to mourn the loss. The sun was teasing the horizon, a hint of pink light mixing with the pollution to push a pale orange into the charcoal sky. The crisp dawn caressed the back of Sam's neck and ran its fingers through his wet hair. The rain that found its way behind his collar made him shiver beneath the third of the Barbican towers. The rain had also found its way to Polly, her blood pooling in the grouting between the paving stones. She lay beneath a large white awning now, the protection coming a little late – she had been open to the elements for at least three hours.

Sam waited outside the awning and watched Forensics photograph Polly from every angle, camera flashes illuminating the gloom of the morning. He couldn't hear their conversation; the raindrops drumming on the plastic awning drowned out their voices. He had to wait until the scene had been extensively recorded before moving closer. He wanted to see Polly's driver's licence for himself, but he really didn't need it or the DNA confirmation. He could feel it was her.

The Barbican centre was eerily quiet. Even the birds had

failed to announce the arrival of dawn. It was as if the city were offering a respectful silence. The entertainment complex wouldn't be open for hours, and it was still too early for staff to arrive. The rain had kept all but the most dedicated of joggers in their beds. Those who had braved the weather detoured around the crime scene that was cordoned off and guarded by uniformed officers. Lights were on in a few of the flats from the lower floors of the tower, the residents no doubt woken by the bright lights of a crime scene investigation in full flow, although those in attendance went about their work with the hushed tones usually reserved for church.

Sam moved away from the scene to a sheltered area and lit a cigarette, wishing there was somewhere open nearby where he could get a coffee. As he exhaled, he felt a tingling sensation on the back of his neck, like someone had crept up behind him. He turned, but there was nobody there, and yet Sam couldn't shake the feeling that somebody had been standing behind him just seconds before. The air surrounding him felt disturbed, almost as if a presence had moved through it and unsettled it, like a breath of wind kicking up dust.

He was just on edge. This was a crime scene, after all. But as he smoked, he wasn't convinced.

DCI Riley stood off to one side comforting the man who had discovered Polly's body. He was a young doctor returning home from a fourteen-hour shift, exhaustion ripped away from his body with the onset of shock. Tears glistened against his skin, his eyes swollen and bloodshot. He was experienced in accident trauma, but deliberate trauma was another thing entirely. Splashes of vomit were visible on his white trainers and on the front of his trousers.

Eventually Sam was alone with Polly, the pounding of his heart keeping time with the beat of rain on the awning above him. The space smelled of damp plastic. He squatted close to her. Most of her blood had been washed away, but enough of it still clung to her clothes to suggest that it had once been her bed, just as with the previous victims. The red woollen hat was placed just above her neck, which was ragged and torn like the end of a branch ripped from a tree by high winds. The hole in her chest was a large, deep gash full of congealing blood and shredded tissue. Her heart rested on the palm of her hand and resembled a large, crushed tamarillo, the blood staining her skin. A slice had been taken from the pear in her other hand, and the plastic comb was on the ground close by. Polly's underwear had been removed and lay next to her footwear. Under her red dress she would be naked and vulnerable, a quality that extended to her bare feet that looked small and delicate and as white as bone. The killer had stuck to his routine in every way except one. Lying neatly across Polly's waist like a belt was a thick braid of long blonde hair. It hadn't come from the dark-haired Polly. It felt synthetic, more like the hair from a doll.

Sam stood up, his knees cracking and his brain full of jumbled thoughts. The killer had added another clue. He was attempting to push them in a certain direction, trying to tell them a story, but Sam still couldn't read it. He rubbed his hands across his face in frustration and moved out into the rain once more. A part of him was relieved to see another piece of evidence at the scene. It meant the killer was growing frustrated with the inability of the police to understand him. At the beginning, he'd probably taken great pleasure in knowing he was confusing the police with the clues he left. He would believe he was outsmarting them, was incapable of making mistakes, and this would fuel both his ego and his desires. Sam considered how perfectly the killer exemplified the dark triad, the three personality traits common to serial killers. He was narcissistic. He had Machiavellian tendencies – both manipulative and amoral. And he was psychopathic, completely remorseless towards his victims. The dark triad was a formidable force. It made the man they sought into the great white shark of the serial killer world. A predator that would never stop swimming.

This time Sam welcomed the cold, cleansing splashes of rain. He looked upwards into the milky grey sky, praying for a hint of insight. He didn't know how long he could go on asking the same question. The Barbican tower stretched high above him. Until now, the killer had left the bodies in green spaces, but the Barbican was a concrete warren, utilitarian, urban; so, why the change? Everything the killer did was carefully managed, so the Barbican was a deliberate choice. It had meaning.

Abruptly, Sam straightened. The tower. His mind shifted like the barrels inside a locked safe, aligning and allowing access to the secrets inside. The tower and the lock of golden hair. *A tower with many windows when in fact there should only be one.*

DCI Riley chatted to one of his officers as the awning was being dismantled. The SOCOs were packing away their equipment and preparing for the removal of Polly's body. Riley made his way over to Sam, the dark circles under his eyes exaggerated against his grey skin. He walked slowly across the concourse, dejected and weary, but for the first time in a long time Sam felt like he had the power to defeat that state of mind.

"The scene of crime officers want to move out, Sam. Do you need to ask them anything before they go?" Riley's voice was croaky.

Sam shook his head and grabbed Riley by the biceps. "I've got it. I know what it all means now. At least I think I do. It's fairy tales. It's the Brothers Grimm."

"Slow down. What do you mean?" Riley asked with a hint of urgency in his voice.

"The killer is using fairy tales as inspiration for murder," Sam said. "The red hat, the comb, the heart, and now the braid of golden hair – it all fits. They're from fairy tales: *Red Riding Hood*, *Snow White* and *Rapunzel*. Look up. Look where we're standing. We're beneath Rapunzel's tower."

According to the Brothers Grimm version of the traditional tale, Rapunzel was a beautiful young woman imprisoned in a high tower by a vengeful witch. Rapunzel had very long hair, which she would lower from the only window in her tower to allow the witch to climb up it and gain access. Sam searched his memory for the details of the story, a tale he hadn't heard since he was a boy. After the witch discovered that Rapunzel had lowered her hair so that a handsome prince could climb into the tower, she had cut off Rapunzel's golden braids, thus denying the prince access to her. Sam seemed to remember that somehow the lovers were reunited and lived happily ever after.

Riley squinted up at the tower. "Are you suggesting the killer left Polly here because of the tower?"

"Yes. The tower is a clue – it goes with the hair. If the killer had just left the braid, it wouldn't have made sense. The tower gives the braid meaning."

Vivid childhood memories flooded Sam's brain, as if he were falling down a deep hole in time. His mother read the stories to him when he was young, one of the few memories he had of her before she'd died leaving Sam and his father alone. When he was a little older, his father had read the Grimms' tales to him to distract him from his nightmare, the same nightmare that had followed him into adulthood like an irritating tune on repeat. "There's a poisoned comb in *Snow White and the Seven Dwarfs*, isn't there?" He rubbed his hand across the top of his damp head sending a fine shower of droplets into the air.

"I think so." Riley stared at Sam and frowned. "You might be onto something – but what about the pear? It's been a long time since I read fairy tales to my kids, but I don't remember any pear." He chewed his bottom lip.

117

Sam nodded. "That's the only thing I'm unsure of. The pear doesn't fit as well as everything else. I need to do some reading. Might be time for a bedtime story."

The feeling of certainty warmed him despite the chilly wind whipping around the Barbican. After more than a year of doubt and confusion, suddenly there was a clear road ahead. Sam felt lighter, the weight of the case feeling manageable at last. The killer was closer now. Sam had brought him closer. Almost close enough to grasp around the throat. As his mood soared, the rain stopped and the sun came out.

Riley squeezed Sam's forearm and smiled. "Fucking fairy tales!" The dejection in his face was gone, replaced by something that looked like hope. "Keep this to yourself for now, Sam. We'll have a briefing when we get back to the station, but that's great work. A Stirling effort." Riley headed back across the concourse to dismiss the SOCOs.

Sam looked on as the forensics people zipped Polly's body into a black body bag and gently placed her on a gurney. Everyone at the scene wore grim expressions, including a few members of the public who had stopped to observe as they passed by on their way to work. Sam suspected they would share this bad news with their workmates, no doubt in that oddly enthusiastic way tragedy is passed on as gossip. Perhaps the slightly gleeful spreading of bad news was a way to express relief that the fate suffered wasn't theirs. Sam's relief came from a different place: they may be one step closer to finding their killer.

More lights were visible in the towers now as people woke up and went about their day. The Barbican centre grew a little busier, but not much; it never really did. The killer had known what he was doing when he'd picked it for his latest body dump. It wasn't just a clever representation of a fairy-tale tower. In the early hours of the morning, when he'd left Polly there, it would have provided silence and undisturbed dark corners.

Sam lit a cigarette and waited while Riley and the other officers prepared to leave the scene. He glanced behind him at the onlookers by the barriers as he exhaled, but didn't meet their eyes. He knew all too well the recrimination he would find there. People were fearful. They felt vulnerable and under threat, and they blamed the police – at least partially – for not moving fast enough. Sam hoped more than anything he could provide the peace of mind they so desperately needed.

15

Not all the eyes fixed on Sam in that moment held fear. Ben stood behind him like just another onlooker, close enough to smell the smoke from his cigarette. It was the first time he had allowed himself to linger at the scene directly after leaving the body. A policeman called Sam by name, summoning him over to Polly's body. *Sam.* It was always satisfying to put a name to a face, especially a face that wore such a look of sadness – but there was intrigue there, too. *He* had put that expression on Sam's face, had captured his attention and defined his mood. It gave him a sense of achievement. He longed to walk over and touch Sam, introduce himself. It was like a sense of vertigo pulling him over the edge of a tall building, giving him the overwhelming compulsion to jump. But he resisted. It was far too soon to claim the credit, tempting though it was. He wasn't finished yet. There were still three more to go.

Three more until he could have a well-earned rest. Eight was the magic number, the goal he'd set himself, and he wasn't the sort of man to leave a job unfinished. *When there are eight, the hunters will be too late.* He smiled as he repeated the phrase in his head. He liked the way the words became a rhythm, bouncing around up there like a trapped bird. *When there are eight, Sam will be too late.*

He enjoyed watching Sam move around Polly, liked the way he held himself. He was very still – poised – though he seemed tightly wound. There was an air of confidence about him, but it was a quiet, understated confidence that exuded rather than insisted. He noticed Sam puckered his lips when he concentrated, and small frown lines drew his eyebrows together above eyes that were as dark brown as his own but far more tired. He had the habit of running his fingers through his hair when he was thinking, which left it sticking up in scruffy tufts that he neglected to flatten down again. His movements were precise and considered, surprisingly graceful for a tall, strong-looking man.

There was something respectful about the way Sam moved around Polly's body, adjusting her position on the gurney, ensuring that she was securely zipped inside the body bag, brushing the rain drops away. He looked deeply moved by her, which Ben didn't understand. Polly was a stranger to him, nothing more than a bruised cadaver, and yet Sam seemed to mourn her passing as if there was a meaningful connection between them. The way he looked at her and then placed his fingers over his lips as if holding back his emotions almost seemed like an indulgence.

And then – Sam turned his back on him and walked away, as if he warranted no more attention than any of the other onlookers who had no business being there. *Look at me. Pay attention to me,* he wanted to shout. But no, that would be reckless. He would just have to be patient. There would be other occasions – their destinies were entwined like grapevines. He would invite Sam out to play again, sometime soon.

As Sam walked away from the scene, Ben felt exhilarated. *He can leave the scene of the crime, but it will never leave him.*

The feeling followed him home from the Barbican, making him shiver all over, his skin sensitive from its touch. The hairs on his arms and the back of his neck unfurled themselves like petals in springtime.

The exhilaration accompanied him down to the basement where the air hung thick and fetid with the last of Polly drying on the walls. Her blood, now terracotta in colour, was the tale of *Rapunzel*, the oxidised liquid a tower of strokes straining to reach the ceiling. He took off his clothes. Her scent was so strong in the enclosed space that it cloaked his naked flesh, sunk into every pore until he felt like he was drowning under the weight of too much Polly. She would never leave him now. She was a part of him whether she liked it or not. Polly had got under his skin, just like the song said, the one his first love had played over and over as she sashayed around the room. Sometimes he could still hear the swish of her dress.

Eventually, the women disappointed him, and sooner rather than later. It was always the same. He'd start out full of the enthusiasm that drove his best intentions – this time he would get it right, he would find the perfect fit. Each time he found the one he wanted, which took considerable effort, he learned as much as he could about her: where she lived and worked, where she liked to go in pursuit of hobbies or entertainment. How easily she could be taken. He ensured that her hair was dark enough, her skin pale enough. He asked himself if she was beautiful enough to meet his high standards. Was she the fairest of them all?

He was good at judging if they were tall enough, and if they were the right size, too – a perfect size ten. Size was important, he already had the dresses neatly hanging in a wardrobe, freshly laundered and ready to wear. Although he was partial to red, it was the style of dress that was most important. The lower half had to be quite long, about calf length, and it had to have enough material so that when he made them spin around, the skirt lifted high and billowed out around the top of their thighs. Just high enough for him to catch a glimpse of the nakedness beneath the dress, a little peep at what was no longer private. An intimate dance that was just for him, performed in the basement under the lights.

At first, each of them refused to wear the dress he had chosen for them, an ingratitude that angered him so much they always capitulated in the end. They only had to wear it for a short while. The dresses weren't theirs to keep, so he didn't understand what all the fuss was about. He let them put their own clothes back on in the end. It never failed to give them false hope they'd be going home. Each one was as misguided as the last. Every one of them had refused to remove their underwear, even when he'd explained they were disrespecting his memories with their reluctance. He had to remind them they were there for no other reason than to please him, which usually did the trick.

Polly had been no exception. She hadn't wanted to remove her underwear either, but she'd done it in the end, after he'd insisted that his vision was not to be tampered with. She had cried, which was tiresome, but she had regained her composure under his glare. Then she finally did as she was told and spun around the room for him with a clumsiness he had found endearing at first, but that soon wore off, and that was the trouble. They all wore off in the end. No matter how hard he tried to find the perfect match, none of them was quite right, none of them even close to the perfection of his true love. Although to be fair, they had a lot to live up to.

Was he wasting his time? Perhaps he would never know that type of love again, that complicated and consuming obsession that was as much about hate as it was about love.

Sometimes the hate choked the life out of the love, like a

weed entwining itself around a delicate flower until it withered and died. The hate was what he was left with, a suffocating feeling that hollowed him out, providing the space for overwhelming disappointment.

He couldn't deny how soothing it was to have some quiet time again after all the screaming and carrying on. That feeling of fulfilment wouldn't last long, though. Soon the hunger would take over again and form a chasm of loneliness. But for now, the mere presence of the putrid perfume was enough to quench his soul in the vacant space. It was a peaceful place once more, empty and still and waiting for more with a nice clean section of wall. But that very wall would soon tease him until he couldn't resist anymore. Until the teasing turned into accusation, felt more like recrimination, and then criticism that finally focused his intentions once more, propelling him into action. Eventually the need for company felt like starvation. His cravings would evolve into a particular type of excitement, enough to fuel a hunt, and man was a hunter at heart. A man had a primal urge to kill, a need to bring home the meat. Ben recognised this feeling when it came knocking, and he always let it in. He couldn't turn away so familiar a friend.

He brushed his fingers across the tower on the wall. The dried blood no longer flaked at his touch – the application of two thin layers of pale varnish acted as both protector and preserver. Why go to all the trouble of creating something beautiful, only for it to flake or fade into nothingness? He wanted it to linger, almost as permanent as a tattoo. He held himself flat against the cold wall, pressing his naked skin against the varnished words, the tower against his cheek. He rolled himself back and forth along the wall like a human rolling pin. Polly had been such sweet confectionary: as light as meringue, her skin as silky as custard. She had even smelled of vanilla in the end. On their last night together, he had bathed her in a scented warm bath, the vanilla oil leaving tiny beaded droplets on her skin as he washed her back for her, rinsed her hair and patted her dry. The memory of her soft, oily skin was with him now and made him feel alive.

Thinking about the scent of vanilla brought his first love back into the room. He couldn't resent her presence; it had been her scent first – before it was Polly's. Before it was his. Perhaps that was why he'd chosen to wear it. The fragrance had floated from her in waves whenever she danced for him. The way she would twirl until her skirt lifted and revealed that she wore no underwear. Each twirl was a scented tease, and she loved to tease him when they were alone. She stopped only when she was too breathless to continue, and then she would lie down next to him, her head on his lap, and smile up at him. Sometimes he liked the way she lay there, the vanilla oil strong on her warm skin. Sometimes he didn't.

He closed his eyes on the memory and waited for it to disappear, but she was too strong for him, easily resurrected in the basement, the only place where she was alive. He picked at the scabs on his inner thigh, the bloody skin sticky under his fingernails, but she refused to be purged. Her face lingered there, dark hair flowing as if she were standing in the wind, almost real enough to touch. In many ways, she had never left him. Daydreaming about her always brought her back to him, but only temporarily. Too often he had to remind himself she was nothing but a dream.

He couldn't go back to the wall now, back to Polly. The moment was gone. He got dressed and turned off the basement lights, closing the door behind him. As he climbed the stairs, he remembered it was almost the first Saturday of the month, and he had things to do.

16

Superintendent Nina Hepburn paused in the doorway, taken aback by the excitement in the room. She'd been expecting the strained silence of defeat that had followed the discovery of the previous victims. The task force had left the office in the crisp chill of the early hours to attend the crime scene at the Barbican, their moods darkened by disillusionment, but that was not how they'd returned. A restless chatter came from the team, anticipation winding around them, fuelling them. She caught sight of DCI Riley huddled in a corner with Sam, both men locked in animated conversation, almost feverish. She made her way over to them and tapped Riley on the shoulder.

"Morning, you two. What's going on?" She raised her voice over the multiple conversations swirling around the packed room.

Riley looked back at Nina with a flushed face. "Believe it or not, we might be closer to finding this evil piece of shit." He pushed through his team to the front of the room.

He looked energised, exhilarated, despite the way his morning had begun. It was contagious. Excitement built up in the pit of Nina's stomach, and the familiar tightness in her chest lifted, allowing her to take what felt like the first deep breath in months. She turned to Sam, searching his face. "Really?" She grabbed his shoulder a little too tightly. His usual frown was gone, and she suspected the odd expression moving across his face was relief.

"I think so." Sam rubbed his fingers through his hair. "We're just about to have a briefing." He followed Riley through the gap in the room, oblivious to the half-eaten sandwich he knocked off a desk as he walked by.

Members of the team occupied all the chairs. A young detective offered Nina his seat, but she declined, moving some folders aside and taking a seat on top of the nearest desk. The room fell silent as Riley cleared his throat, the mood turning serious, the team focused.

"Well, if the excitement in the room is anything to go by, I assume you've figured out we've made some serious headway in the case this morning. Despite finding poor Polly – and I know how that makes all of us feel – she may help us close this case. Sam thinks he knows what our whack-job is trying to tell us, and I think he's onto something. So, I'll let him explain."

Some of the team exchanged smiles. Others looked expectant but appeared wary of embracing hope too quickly. They shifted in their chairs, leaning forwards with impatience.

Riley stood to one side as Sam took his place at the front of the room. He had everyone's attention; the only noise was the sound of someone's hungry stomach. Nina thought he seemed a little anxious, but then he took a deep breath and planted his feet, and when he began to speak, every trace of anxiety was gone.

"Right, here we go. This might sound far-fetched but bear with me. I think our killer has an obsession with fairy tales, and I'm pretty sure he has a preference for the darker, more traditional Grimms' version of the stories." There was a murmur across the room. "There's nothing Disney about this killer. The clues he's been leaving at the scenes are lifted from the stories. Take this morning's new addition, for example. We have a long braid of golden hair that we know didn't come from Polly. This braid, and the fact he left Polly beneath a tower, suggests the story of *Rapunzel* to me."

Nina looked around at the surprised faces in the room. Sam seemed to be waiting for his words to settle. "Are you talking about the story of the girl who unwinds her hair so the prince can use it to climb into the tower?" she asked.

Sam nodded. "And it's not just *Rapunzel*. We have the red hat that comes from *Little Red Riding Hood* and the poisoned comb from *Snow White*. In the Grimms' version of the story, the evil stepmother gives it to Snow White and it almost kills her. She also tells a huntsman to take Snow White into the forest to kill her and cut out her lungs and liver as proof that he has finished the job."

"But the killer left a heart," one of the detectives said before taking a sip of coffee from a large take-away cup. "Why not leave the correct organs instead?"

"I think that's because it's more symbolic for him," Sam said, glancing at the coffee cup.

"He's playing about with the stories a little," Riley murmured, his voice almost drowned by the sirens from an ambulance departing St Bart's hospital.

"Yes," said Sam, "but that could prove useful to us." He waited for the sirens to drift away. "If you think about it, all our victims could be Snow White. If I'm remembering the story correctly, Snow White gets her name because her mother wished for a daughter with skin as white as snow and hair as black as ebony."

Which describes every one of the victims, Nina thought as she adjusted her bun, a blonde strand of hair landing on her shoulder.

She looked across the room at the whiteboard, at the victims' enlarged photographs, faces captured while smiling and full of life. She glanced at the other photographs further down, a different story captured up close.

"I'm pretty sure I remember something about her lips being as red as blood," Sam added, "but I need to check that. It's been some time since I read the stories. I think my old copy is gathering dust in my dad's attic, so I'll go and buy one, but I think blood is mentioned in a number of the other tales as well. It's a recurring theme. If I'm right, it could explain why the killer leaves the victim's blood at the scene."

Sam paused as he surveyed the quiet room. All eyes were on him.

Nina spoke into the silence. "What about the pear in the victim's hand though, Sam? If the killer is following this theme, shouldn't it be an apple?"

Sam frowned. "Snow White is given a poisoned apple, a piece of which becomes lodged in her throat and convinces the Seven Dwarfs that she's dead. So, this is another change the killer has made in the fairy-tale theme, but I don't know why. There are gaps in my knowledge, and I need to do further research."

"Maybe he just got it wrong," someone called out.

"I don't think so," Sam said. "He's far too detail-driven to make such an obvious mistake. He's left a pear for a reason. Again, it could be that it has personal meaning for him. As I said before, the killer wants us to figure this out so we can marvel at his brilliance. He started out intent on one-upmanship, but he has evolved and now desires admiration. He wants to be noticed. He wants to tell us his story. Maybe, like many insecure egomaniacs these days, he wants to be famous."

There were a few sniggers and an officer named Taylor shouted, "Couldn't he just have appeared on reality telly?"

The room filled with laughter, an unfamiliar sound in the incident room. Nina noticed the slightly hysterical nature of the laughter and understood how needed it was, the release it provided.

Sam offered them a tired smile. "Although reality television would have been a far easier way to gain notoriety, our killer is a different type of animal." Despite his obvious exhaustion, he stood straight and confident as he continued. "He wants us to pay attention to him because he was denied attention, or the appropriate type of attention anyway, during those crucial years of early childhood. We have previously discussed the likelihood that he was abused in childhood by a female caregiver, and now he is exacting that revenge on his victims who undoubtedly remind him of his abuser. When he kills them, he's taking back the power he didn't have as a child. He's also enjoying the sense of power he has over us. But most importantly for him, we are sitting up and taking notice of him. We're listening, and what he's telling us is the story of his own sad life. He wants us to understand him, to reinforce the idea that he matters."

"Are you saying the killer is asking for our sympathy?" Riley asked. "Because that ship has fucking sailed."

"It's fucking sunk," Taylor said.

There was a smattering of applause and the manic laughter returned once more, until Riley asked for quiet so Sam could continue.

Sam nodded. "In a way, yes, he is asking for our sympathy. He wants us to acknowledge the pain of his childhood. He wants us to recognise that what he does to his victims is a representation of what was done to him – and what he would like to have done to his abuser had he not been a vulnerable child at the time."

Sam paused and seemed to gather his thoughts. "What we're talking about here, I suspect, is a case of arrested psychological development, the roots of which come from trauma experienced during early childhood. Essentially arrested development means being stuck at an emotional level of development – childhood trauma determines adult behaviour. Because of our killer's fascination with fairy tales, I would suspect he was between the ages of four and ten when he experienced trauma. I said earlier that our killer is seeking attention and admiration, which are immature things for an adult to seek. He seeks them from others as an adult, because he hasn't outgrown his need for them."

Nina looked around the room. A few people were taking notes. DCI Riley looked up from his own notepad. "You've said before that paedophiles usually stick to an age group. I presume that means at some point the child grows too old to be attractive prey to the abuser and is rejected. Do you think this is what happened to our killer?"

Sam nodded. "Yes, I think that's exactly what happened. I think his abuser read fairy tales to him because it was a way to build a bond of closeness, an opportunity to groom him. During story time, she abused him, which is why the killer associates fairy tales with sex and also with love and closeness. The killer would have enjoyed this time with his abuser, his mother figure. For him, at that young age, abuse and love would have been the same thing, so it's no surprise that he's attempting to recreate this with his victims. He is trying to recapture the time when he felt most happy and loved. Then he grew too old for his abuser and she no longer abused him, which in the killer's mind meant she no longer loved him. This rejection would have been one of the most traumatic events of his childhood and no doubt made him into the killer we see today."

Nina raised her hand. "If the killer is trying to relive the happy part of his childhood when he takes these women, why doesn't he keep them alive so they can carry on playing Mummy for him?"

"Two reasons, I think." Sam paused. "The first is that they ultimately disappoint him. They are not a sufficient representation of the maternal figure that he idolises. She is an ideal that our victims can never hope to live up to. The other reason is that he rejects them before they can reject him. If he kills them, then they can't abandon him like Mummy did. He wants to recapture the happy part of his childhood, not the most painful part."

Nina nodded. "Thanks. That makes sense."

"Okay," Sam said, "let me summarise what I understand about our killer so far. Essentially, obsession rules his life – his obsession with his mother, or whoever the dominant female was in his young life – and that obsession is driven by love and hate. Love and hate are indivisible for him. He loves his mother, and he hates her too, and I'm sure that's how he feels about his victims – they are, after all, stand-ins for his mother figure. He is emotionally immature, locked in childhood and obsessed with fairy tales." Sam put his hands in his pockets. "So that's it, our nut in a nutshell." He smiled at the groans from the team.

Riley laughed and then asked them to concentrate as he posed a question. "How can we use this new information to find the killer?"

"We're looking for someone who spends the majority of his time in a world where he feels most at home." Sam's tone had become serious once more. "Perhaps he works in a children's bookshop, or somewhere that would attract the patronage of kids, because emotionally, although not intellectually, he is of the same age as the children who go there. It's terrifying to suggest this, but he could be a teacher of younger children. I suspect that because of his abusive childhood he wouldn't have done well in school, but the crime scenes and the fact he has avoided capture tell us he's clever. He may have educated himself as an adult, perhaps gaining a degree that would allow him to teach. He must live or work close to where the bodies are found, because he's familiar with the area. He leaves the bodies in places where they'll be discovered but he won't. His emotional immaturity results in his need for attention which he is getting from us and the press, an attention he thrives on."

Riley straightened. "If he's thriving on all this attention, shouldn't we be doing more to control the media?"

Nina shook her head. "That's unrealistic. The simple fact is killers sell papers because society is fascinated with them. How many of you have watched true crime documentaries or read a book about a serial killer?" She looked around the room and nodded at the raised hands. "Most of us it seems, including me." She raised her hand, bangles sliding down her wrist. "Perhaps it's wiser to work with the media instead of against it."

"We can use it to our advantage," Sam said. "I think what's needed is a carefully worded press conference in which you release the details of the crime scenes for the first time. It would be wise to keep something back in order to weed out the usual false confessors – perhaps the removal of the underwear could remain our secret – but let's tell the media about the fairy tale clues, about *Snow White* and everything else. Tell them about the kind of man we're looking for. We might get lucky, and someone might know a man who fits the description if we can be precise in the way we describe him. However, we also have to control the type of attention the killer gets."

"What do you mean?" Nina asked.

"We have to mock him, criticise the childishness of his behaviour, and accuse him of simplicity. We have to make him feel inferior. We have to essentially label him an idiot. He wants attention, but not that kind of attention. He wants to be thought of as special, so we need to make him feel as if he's nothing more than your average psycho. Doing this will draw him out. He'll be desperate to prove us wrong."

Pens scratched across paper. Someone coughed. Otherwise, the room was absolutely silent. "Let's think of him as a child for a moment," Sam said. "What does a child do when his accomplishments are dismissed? He has a tantrum, he defends himself, he demands attention, and he shouts until he gets it. If we mock the killer, we'll encourage him to show off. He'll become irrational, because he is desperate for recognition and praise, and this irrationality will cause him to make mistakes. As all of you parents in the room know, if you turn your back on a child when they're having a tantrum, they'll inevitably scream louder. Our killer will throw his version of a tantrum in order to gain attention."

"Are you saying we should in theory encourage him to kill again?" Nina asked.

Sam shook his head. "He doesn't need our encouragement, he will kill again unless we can stop him, and if we're realistic about this, we'll only catch him because he makes a mistake. We can't buy into the evil genius mythology that surrounds serial killers. They are not. They make mistakes: parking tickets and stolen cars, for example. Criticising him will to a certain degree cripple him with anxiety and a sense of failure. He views the creation of the fairy-tale murder scenes as works of art and they are deeply personal to him. If we tear the scenes down and ridicule them, we're also ridiculing him. He will refuse to accept this dismissal of his work. He will instead assume that we've failed to understand it and, by extension, him. He'll believe we're mistaken in our assumptions, that we are in fact the unsophisticated ones who have failed to pay him the proper respect."

"What do you think he'll do next?" Taylor asked.

"Two things, perhaps," Sam replied. "He may take a risk and contact us to explain himself and gloat, demand the respect that he thinks he's owed. By contacting us he hopes to elicit praise."

A few of the officers chuckled. "He wants a pat on the back?" someone said.

"Don't underestimate how essential praise is to him," Sam said. "Serial killers thrive on it. And he might go back to the places where he left Polly and the other victims to reassure himself that what he did there was valid. Being at the scene will allow him to relive those moments and justify them to himself. To praise himself when we refuse to do so."

Riley spoke up. "But wouldn't that be incredibly reckless?"

Sam nodded and rubbed his thumb across the cleft in his chin. "Yes. It would be an act of desperation, but for him it's a risk worth taking. It would also be a chance for him to revisit the time he spent with the bodies at the end, which will arouse him sexually. Bringing those memories back to life will give him an erotic charge, provide sexual gratification when his recall is intensified by location. We cannot overlook the sexual deviancy at play here. Murder, sexual arousal, love and hate are one and the same to him. Displaying the bodies as he does equate to sexual intimacy in his warped mind. While there is no evidence of rape, it's vital to remember that rape is about power and domination over the victims. This is our killer's version of rape. The way he displays the bodies is his expression of sexual domination. Also, returning to the scene will allow him to justify himself in the face of the mockery we throw at him."

Nina looked around the room at her colleagues and saw understanding and determination in their faces. They reminded her of a strong army, newly outfitted with effective weaponry. The briefing was over, and they were ready to fight.

Riley stood up and addressed the room. "Okay, everyone. We're done for now. Let's take a break, grab some coffee, and get something to eat or some fresh air, if you can find any in this town. We'll meet back here in half an hour to discuss our strategy going forward."

*

As the team disbanded, the room filled with the noise of scraping chairs and excited chatter. Sam was pleased with how the briefing went. The mood was one of optimism and energy. It wasn't just the surge of adrenaline that charged the room with electricity – it was also the hunger for a killer who felt closer than ever. The team that was squeezed into the temporary office above the betting shop finally believed their luck had changed.

Riley approached Sam and took him aside. "You mentioned needing to do further research, I might be able to help with that. My wife has a friend who works at the Museum of Toys and Playtime in Bloomsbury. I think she's the curator of children's literature and she's worked there for years. I'll get her details for you. It might be worth paying her a visit to help you out. She might at least be able to shed some light on the pear."

"Couldn't hurt," Sam said. "I've never been there, but it sounds like a good place to start." He agreed his theory needed confirmation from another source. The more he knew about the stories, the better he would know the killer. Chatting to an expert might also shed some light on the intricacies of the murder scenes.

Sam left the office feeling more hopeful than he had in months.

17

Emma caught the aroma of chlorine from her damp hair as she adjusted her bun. It was a smell she'd always loved, associating it with swimming away the stress of her work. Each lap, methodical and monotonous, took her further away from her patients and brought her closer to a place of internal stillness. Her arms felt loose and tired as she clinked her margarita against Clare's wineglass.

"Cheers. Here's to the end of another long day," she said, before taking a mouthful of her drink. The sharpness of the frozen lime made her wince.

"Cheers," said Clare. "There's something lovely about sitting in a bar above a swimming pool watching other people doing their laps, isn't there?" She twirled her red wine in the glass, its colour deep and rich in the subdued lighting of the bar.

"Only if you've done enough laps to justify the calories," said Emma, "which I have." She smiled. "Don't know about you, though. I thought you were a bit slow tonight."

"Piss off, Emma, or you can get the next round, too." Clare laughed and rubbed her eyes, pink from the chlorine. "I've had my boss on my back all day. I don't need you as well." She glanced down at the pool as the sound of a loud, ungainly dive filtered up to the balcony.

"Is he still a self-entitled letch?" Emma wiped the salt from her lips.

"If being entitled to sideswipe my breasts as he reaches across my desk counts, then yes, he is still a self-entitled letch. I've really had enough of him. Today he was telling me his wife doesn't listen to him anymore." Clare rolled her eyes and coughed after a large gulp of wine. "When I got up from my desk, I made sure my chair rammed him in the balls." She joined in with Emma's laughter. "I was deeply apologetic of course, but I don't think he'll be leaning over me again any time soon." She pushed her long red ponytail back over her shoulder. "He makes me envy you your prisoners. At least they're in cuffs."

"Oh, there's one I don't think you'd want to work with. She's so volatile – aggressive some of the time, defensive at others. I'm not even sure if I'm helping her." Emma massaged her eye sockets; she could still feel the indentation of her goggles.

"I'm sure you are, Em. You're brilliant at your job. Is this your self-doubt raising its head again?" Her gold hoop earrings flashed as they caught the light.

Emma's glass was dripping condensation. "Maybe. I keep reminding myself talking always helps, that being truly heard is a powerful thing, but she's so cold." She crunched down on a piece of ice. "All I can do is keep going back there, keep listening, providing the space for her to feel safe enough to open up."

"Exactly. What you're offering her, what you offer all your patients at the prison, is freedom from what they carry. Your work makes them less likely to reoffend if they are released – isn't that what you told me? You never know, you may save a life one day." Clare reached across the table and squeezed

Emma's hand. "How's your private practice going? You told me you were seeing a new patient the last time we met."

Emma smiled as Sam's face flashed across her mind. "It's going well. We've had a few sessions now. It started as supervision, but we both realised he needed traditional therapy." She felt herself growing warm.

"Are you blushing?" Clare leaned forwards and tried to meet Emma's eyes. "Is there something going on between you two?"

"No, of course not. But…" She searched for the right words but failed to find them.

"But what?" Clare asked as she placed her elbows on the table causing it to wobble.

"I'm attracted to him. He's intelligent, sensitive, seems kind. Very good looking. He has soulful eyes." Emma tried to ignore the surprise on Clare's face; instead, she studied the glimmering reflection of the swimming pool on the ceiling.

"He has soulful eyes?" Clare cracked up. "Are you Lydia Bennet now?" She moved their glasses to one side so she could lean further across the table.

Emma laughed. "I like him, that's all. But he's my patient, so there's nothing I can do about it." She felt a little sad now she'd said the words out loud.

"I haven't heard you say that about anyone for a long time," Clare said. "Is the feeling mutual?"

"I think so. We connected. There was something in the air." She smiled as she remembered the way he ruffled his hair leaving it messy, and his woody smell, warm and musky.

"Then why not refer him to another therapist? Wait a while, and then get in touch. That would be appropriate, wouldn't it? Isn't it time you did something for yourself?" She sipped her wine and then dabbed her lips, her lipstick staining the white napkin with a red kiss.

Emma shook her head. "I wouldn't feel right about that. He has a very stressful job. I can't abandon him. It's not the right time." She ran her finger around the rim of the glass, salt flakes falling to the table.

Clare finished her wine. "If he has a stressful job, there will never be a *right* time. A connection like that doesn't happen often. You should build on it, not walk away from it."

Emma tried to imagine a future with Sam. "But what if..."

Clare cut her off. "If you're about to say, 'What if it doesn't work out, or what if he turns out to be a weak, unfaithful prick like the last one?', then don't. Take a chance, Em. Don't listen to that doubting voice. Listen to the brave one that always shows up when I need great advice – the one that's trying to tell you to jump in, if only you'd hear it."

"Yeah, yeah, I hear what you're saying. You really are bossy, aren't you?" Emma laughed as she reached into her bag for her wallet.

"I'm not bossy. What I am is assertive and direct, and I wonder who taught me that?" Clare tapped the side of her head and frowned.

Emma laughed. "I don't know, but whoever it was, they must be smart."

"She is," said Clare. "Now get your arse over to the bar and be assertive. There are a few braying city boys hogging it."

Emma moved through the swelling crowd, waves of chlorine, soap and shampoo from just-showered bodies enveloping her. She declined the offer of a drink from a group of men who had imbibed one too many themselves. When she returned, Clare was leaning over the balcony and looking down into the pool below, as were a number of other people, their attention attracted by raised voices.

Emma placed the drinks on the table. "What's going on?"

"It appears to be a territorial dispute." Clare gestured

towards two men who were shouting at each other on the pool deck. "I think one of them was swimming the wrong way down the lane, and they collided."

The two men, dripping wet, stood close enough to shout into each other's faces, both clenching swimming goggles as if they were weapons. They gesticulated towards the pool and shouted over each other, their words echoing off the tiles. A lifeguard intervened, pushing between the men, his hands on their chests as he forced them apart. One of the men turned and walked away with a dismissive gesture and threw his goggles into the pool. The gesture lacked the drama he might have hoped for – he looked a little disappointed when they landed on the surface of the water with a small, almost soundless splash.

Clare turned away and reached for her new glass of wine. "Idiots," she said. "Time to put on their big boy swimming trunks, I think."

Emma watched as the man headed towards the changing rooms. With a shock, she realised it was Sam. He was talking to himself and gripping his towel in one fist as he stamped his way around the pool, heedless of the slippery wet deck. Sam's face was red, his usual friendly expression buried beneath a frown that pulled his eyebrows together and created a deep furrow between his eyes. The barely contained aggression in his hunched shoulders looked out of place on the man she'd thought she was getting to know. To feel affection for. She felt a mixture of disappointment and embarrassment but wasn't sure if it was in herself or Sam. The chorine wafting up from the pool suddenly burned the back of her throat.

Clare was watching her. "Are you okay? Do you know him?"

"No," Emma said. "I don't know him at all."

18

Emma stared at Sam, unable to reconcile his warm smile with the angry expression she'd seen on his face at the pool the night before. She usually appreciated her small office, the way it promoted intimacy, but today it felt claustrophobic. She noticed Sam's smile seemed to falter before it disappeared entirely, like the sun behind a black cloud.

Sam leaned forwards and squeezed the lighter in his hands. "Are you okay, Emma?" He flicked the lighter on and off, the small flame dancing in the air-conditioning before it was extinguished. "You don't seem yourself today."

"Could you please put that lighter down, it's very distracting," Emma said, swiping at a strand of hair before ramming it behind her ear.

Sam placed the lighter on the table in front of him. "And by that you mean irritating, I think." He smiled again and cocked his head to one side. "Do you want to tell me about the hostility I'm sensing?"

Emma assessed Sam and thought his smile looked strained. She suspected she was making him feel uncomfortable, that she'd allowed her feelings to dictate the tempo of therapy. She was annoyed with herself and took a moment to breathe deeply and retrieve her empathy, and a little humour.

"Very funny, Sam, but that's my line." She tried to return his smile, but it felt disingenuous. "Let's move on, how are you today?"

Sam seemed to shrink and fold in on himself, like a detonated building collapsing into its foundations. He stared at the floor and ran his foot back and forth across the carpet, until a small pile of dark red fluff began to form.

"We found Polly," he said, as he glanced briefly at Emma and then turned his attention back to the carpet once more.

The air-conditioning started wheezing, and Emma noticed tiny fibres rising from the carpet and drifting across the stripes of sunlight sneaking through the gaps between the slatted blinds. She heard sirens from fire engines as they rumbled past in the street below, a car alarm filling the space vacated by their departure.

"I know, I saw it on the news." She tried to catch Sam's eye, but his gaze was still fixated on the carpet. "I'm sorry."

Sam nodded, but didn't look up.

Emma waited; it seemed as if Sam was trying to contain his emotions. He ran his hands through his hair and then leaned forwards to retrieve his lighter. He stopped himself and placed his hands in his lap.

She studied him as he started to pick at a cuticle. He appeared to weigh his words, until the car alarm stopped and the abrupt silence – which sounded to her momentarily louder than the alarm itself – landed heavily in the room and seemed to halt his train of thought.

"What is it, Sam? I can't read your mind, so you'll have to tell me how you're feeling."

Emma leaned across the table and pushed the lighter closer to Sam. He finally met her eyes, and she noticed how tired he looked. He seemed hollowed out beneath the eyes, the dark circles very pronounced against his pale skin. She wondered if he had lost weight; his cheekbones were sharper lending him a gaunt appearance.

"Are you sure you can't read my mind?" he asked. "It always feels like you can." He waved the lighter at her, then shrugged and shook his head, paused for some time. "I was aiming for a light-hearted tone, did I succeed?" He offered a brief, apologetic laugh.

"No, you didn't." Emma tried to smile but found she still couldn't. "Do you feel light-hearted?"

She could hear impatience in her voice. It seemed Sam heard it too; there was anger in his response.

"No, of course not, but I'm so tired of feeling miserable, angry and completely useless that I just wanted to hear another note in my voice, a different fucking song from the one that goes around and around inside my head so often that I'm sick of hearing it." He put his head in his hands. "Even if the light-hearted note was bullshit, I just needed to hear it."

Emma waited for him to sit upright again, then asked, "What does the light-hearted tone signify?"

Sam didn't hesitate. "That this is all over, we've caught him, and that maybe I'm not bloody useless after all." He took a long breath that seemed to come from a place deep inside. "It means I don't have to come here and see you anymore."

Emma's stomach clenched and she felt very awkward in the lengthy pause that followed. There was a question on the tip of her tongue, but she didn't trust her motives in wanting to ask it. She tried another instead.

"Do you think of your colleagues as being useless because you haven't caught the killer yet?"

Sam studied her face. "No, they are working incredibly hard, they're doing everything they can." He winced as he picked at his cuticle.

"I know *you're* doing everything you can too, Sam, and yet you seem to be judging yourself far more harshly than you judge them. I wonder why that is. Are you questioning your commitment?" Emma asked.

"Of course not. Have I ever said anything in these sessions that would lead you to question my commitment?" Sam demanded.

Emma moved to the edge of her seat. "No, Sam, you never have." She tried to read his expression, but he seemed to have closed himself off. "I'm aware that you hold yourself to a high standard, and that's fine, essential for the type of work you do, but not always possible to maintain. There will be times when you doubt your commitment, and that's fine too. Normal."

"I haven't got time for normal," Sam snapped, his voice cracking. He squeezed the bridge of his nose and then banged the lighter back on the table. Some of the water from his glass splashed across the surface and journeyed towards the box of tissues. The table wobbled. "I'm sorry." He paused. "I didn't mean to sound so abrupt. I'm not quite myself." He reached for a tissue and mopped at the water. "I'm just so tired."

"I know, Sam, I'd be amazed if you weren't," said Emma as she topped up his glass. "In fact, that certainly wouldn't be normal." She glanced at him, the beginnings of a smile forming. He smiled back. "I'll repeat the question if I may. Are you doubting your commitment? I do sense doubt."

Sam shook his head, his smile gone. "It's not my commitment I'm questioning, it's my abilities. What if I'm wrong? What if my advice to the team about how to move forwards with this case is wrong?"

He let out a deep breath. "Did you see the press conference?"

"I did," replied Emma. She sensed concern in his question and took a deep breath herself.

"The tone of that conference was my suggestion," said

Sam, frowning. "Belittling the killer, dismissing his crimes, all of it. My boss did that on my advice." He rubbed at the stubble on his chin.

"So, what's the alternative, Sam? Do nothing and keep your advice to yourself? If I'm understanding you correctly, what you're really asking is a question, and I think that question is a *What if* question. *What if* your strategy leads to more deaths? We both know that *What if* questions are rarely helpful at times like this. So, let me ask you something. Do you honestly believe that you have the power to make this man kill again? That you can control him?"

Sam shook his head. "No, I can't control him." He absentmindedly chewed at his cuticle. "But I know where you're going with this. I can control my own feelings and behaviour. I can control the way I respond to this situation. Am I right, is that what you were going to say?"

Emma nodded enthusiastically. "Yes, who's the mind reader now? Great to see that you haven't lost your touch, Sam. Maybe you're not so useless after all." Emma found her smile easily this time and hoped that it would ease the awkwardness between them.

The room slowly darkened as a cloud moved lazily across the sun. The shards of sunlight retreated across the carpet leaving Sam's face in shadow while he sat in silence.

"So, what's the plan? Give up your job and go home?" asked Emma. She noticed that Sam's cuticle was bleeding. "Or accept that while you may not have the power to control the killer, you do have the power to catch him?" She noticed his frown. "Do you still believe that?"

Sam nodded and ran his hands across his face leaving a smear of blood just below his mouth. "Yes, we will catch him, I have to keep believing that." He rubbed his fists into his eyes.

Emma felt the tension in the room lift and the

claustrophobia she'd experienced earlier had vanished. She relaxed back into her chair.

Sam adjusted the cushion behind him, leaned back in the chair and looked up at the ceiling as the brakes of a bus screeched outside. He closed his eyes.

Emma was tempted to leave him there until he fell asleep; he looked completely exhausted, utterly defenceless. She regretted the tone she'd used at the beginning of the session, a tone that had been influenced by Sam's outburst at the pool. She felt a little ashamed that it had come from a place of judgement rather than a place of empathy for human fallibility in the face of intense stress.

Quietly, she said, "Sam, I'm sorry, we're out of time." She wished she didn't have another patient arriving soon. She wished time would pause, allowing them to remain still in the moment, silent in the peace, together. She didn't want to break the spell.

Sam rose from the depths of the chair, unravelling himself slowly as if it required too much effort. He finally stood upright, although his shoulders were rounded, picked up his lighter and headed towards the door, but turned to Emma before he opened it.

"I didn't mean what I said, Emma. I do want to keep coming here." He moved closer to her, slowly, step by step, as if unsure of himself.

Emma smiled at him, relieved and gratified she had the answer to the question she'd wanted to ask earlier. She felt the tightness in her chest dissipate as she moved towards Sam and reached for a tissue.

"May I?" she asked, as she gestured towards his face. "The blood from your hand…"

Sam looked confused, glanced down at his chewed cuticle and nodded at Emma. He stared at her closely as she approached, met her eyes as she gently touched him.

She wiped at the smear of blood, aware of the softness of Sam's lips as the tip of her thumb brushed across them. She lingered although the stain was easily removed and then reluctantly lowered her hand, threw the tissue away and moved towards the door, but just as she was about to open it, Sam reached for her hand.

"I want to keep seeing you, Emma." His voice shook as he entwined his fingers around hers. "Away from here, one day."

Emma stared at him. She saw vulnerability and hope on his slightly blushing face. She saw kindness. She smiled at him, feeling the spell hadn't been broken after all. But she also saw a patient in need.

"One day, maybe." She noticed that Sam was still holding her hand, his fingers through hers. It felt natural to her, comfortable, as if they had been holding hands for a very long time. "Perhaps when all this is over."

Sam pulled her closer, lifted her hand and held her palm against his cheek. He closed his eyes and Emma felt the heat of his skin as he leaned into her touch. She could feel it long after he left.

19

The press dubbed him the Grimm Creeper, though Sam felt conflicted by the new moniker. During the days after the discovery of Polly's body and the carefully controlled press conference that followed, they called him by other names, but the Grimm Creeper was the one that stuck. The new name elevated the killer's fame, gave him a brand – and thereby a stronger multimedia presence. They even provided him with a logo from which he was easily identifiable: a figure clothed in a hooded, black cloak, inside which only a skull was visible. The figure held a scythe in one bony hand, a full moon throwing light onto the skyline in the background. It was a brand now synonymous with London.

While Sam approved of the insulting and mocking nature of the articles that accompanied the Creeper imagery, he wasn't sure about the comic-book overtones. Although he believed the killer would feel diminished by the articles, Sam worried that the victims would also be diminished by association. However, as the story played out online and in the press, his fears proved unfounded. The victims were treated with the sympathy they deserved. Disparagement was reserved entirely for the killer.

He was rendered into an almost comical, stereotypical fairy-tale villain, which Sam felt would chip away at his fragile ego. At the first press briefing, Riley had referred to the killer as a man-child, which set the tone for all the stories that followed. The killer wasn't rewarded by a fearful public or an alarmist media. He was instead belittled, knocked down to size.

Because the killer remained on the front pages of newspapers and caused a great deal of speculation on social media, he stayed in the forefront of people's minds. They remained on high alert, and women in particular took fewer risks, but they were no longer governed by fear. Instead, the city was united by vigilance. It had come together against a common enemy. For the first time since the killings had started, the press wrote about the task force – or the Creeper Crew, as they had labelled them – with respect rather than recrimination. However, the high visibility of the case meant Riley and his team were subjected to greater scrutiny. The media and the public's goodwill would only last for so long, and only if they could provide the kind of ending such a story demanded: catching the bad guy.

It was this very pressure Sam had addressed with Emma in his session earlier that day. He was far more relaxed during his time with her now, slipping easily into the ebb and flow of therapy. He felt his transparency with Emma allowed for a deeper connection, that by revealing his feelings for her he'd removed a barrier between an intimacy that one day might extend beyond the therapy room and become something more. Their time together was a mere fifty minutes, but during this period he was able to release much of his stress and let his guard down so completely that he felt truly seen by Emma. He didn't want to leave her behind in her small city office when their time together was over. He missed her as soon as he left her.

He sat on the top deck of the bus to Bloomsbury and tried to ignore the beer can leaving a frothy stream as it rolled back and forth between the seats. Usually when he sat upstairs, Sam liked to peek into the cluttered and untidy stockrooms above shops that were proud of their ground-level minimalism. But today he thought mostly about Emma. He was surprised by his increasing feelings towards her. Earlier, his stomach had fluttered with nerves and excitement as he'd travelled in a lift keen to stop at every floor before hers; it was like riding a rollercoaster on a slow, steep climb – anticipation building and building and then the exhilarating free-fall when she opened the door. While he embraced these feelings, the psychologist in him also examined them closely. The pressure from his job and his nightmare-filled snatches of sleep left him tired and vulnerable. Maybe his feelings were less about a desire for Emma and more about the sanctuary from the darkness of his life she offered. After much contemplation, however, Sam believed his feelings to be only about her. He knew there was a connection between them, something deeper than a therapeutic relationship, something unspoken, but sometimes he sensed a reticence in her too. An unwillingness to entirely let go of professional boundaries, perhaps.

When the bus stopped outside the British Museum, he disembarked and made his way to the Museum of Toys and Playtime. He swerved around tourists and roadside stalls selling London-themed memorabilia and fast food. The aroma of frying onions competed with the diesel fumes belching from an ice-cream van, its engine panting like a dog on a hot day.

As Sam climbed the multi-coloured staircase, he smiled at the large statues of toy soldiers that stood like sentries on either side of the top step. There was a giant chess board off to one side, the outsized pieces abandoned mid-game as if a player had lost hope. The front of the building was painted with a snakes and ladders board, the bricks coloured red and green, a long black and yellow snake coiled around the entrance. Sam was enthralled and laughed out loud; he felt like a small boy again, dwarfed by the huge symbols of childhood.

The woman who greeted him in front of the bright orange double doors was a tall, thin, grey-haired lady called Mrs Lennox. She had huge brown eyes, pronounced cheekbones and a friendly face that immediately put Sam at ease. She was probably in her early seventies, but that didn't hamper the speed with which she walked past a row of dollhouses towards her office at the end of the first floor. She led Sam into a sizeable room that was windowless but glowed with the warm light from small lamps placed throughout. A framed poster on the wall promoting a Christmas annual from the 1950s was yellowed by age; the rest of the room was filled with dark wooden bookcases rammed with books and enclosed behind finger-printed glass. The room was essentially a well-stocked library with just enough space for a desk, three chairs and a small table with a kettle, teapot and an assortment of mugs – welcoming, cosy and musty with the smell of old books.

"I would love an office like this," Sam said. "It must be a pleasure to come to work here every day." His eyes travelled the room trying to read the book spines with a mixture of admiration and envy. "In fact, I could live here and be happy forever."

Mrs Lennox smiled, laugh lines like sunbeams at the edges of her eyes. "A room full of books is always a pleasure." She leaned back against the desk and brushed an errant lock of hair from her face with slender fingers. "From what Albert Riley told me on the phone, Mr Stirling, I suspect your office is quite a different place."

"Yes, I'm sorry to say it's rather soulless compared to this." He gestured at the bookcases, tempted to add his own fingerprints to the glass. "Please call me Sam, by the way."

Mrs Lennox smiled sympathetically. "How about a nice

cup of tea? Then you can tell me more about what brings you here today. Albert was a little vague when we spoke." She offered one of the chairs in front of the desk. "And call me Mabel," she said as she put the kettle on.

Mabel proved to be as knowledgeable as Sam had hoped. She told him a great deal about the Brothers Grimm and their travels in pursuit of folklore, and their admirable intentions to preserve the tales shared through generations of families. Apparently, Rapunzel was named after the rampion plant – Latin name *rapunculus* – that her mother had stolen from a witch's garden and consumed in large quantities while pregnant with her daughter. She drew Sam's attention to running themes: girls and women either portrayed as innocent and pure, often victims, or evil stepmothers. Fathers were often absent, off hunting or seeking fortunes in faraway lands.

When Sam asked Mabel about pears, she told him a story about a devoutly religious girl who ate pears from the trees in a royal garden. The tale was called *The Girl Without Hands*. After the king saw her eating the pears, he fell in love with her and married her. He had a pair of silver hands made to replace the ones her father had chopped off in order to pay his debt to the Devil. Those hands were eventually replaced with real hands by a thankful God. Apparently, the story had its origins in Italian folklore, and while the pear wasn't hugely significant in the story, the eating of it meant the girl's new life with the king had commenced. The pear symbolised love. It was enough to convince Sam this was the meaning behind the pear the killer left at the scene. The missing piece was perhaps a reference to the girl's consumption of the pear.

To finally possess an answer that had eluded him for so long flooded him with relief. At last, he could move on with the case, satisfied by his newfound knowledge.

Before he left, Mabel offered to show him an ancient

illustrated copy of the Grimms' tales that had been in the museum's collection for many years. It was currently undergoing careful restoration in the workshops situated behind the toy section of the museum on the ground floor. Sam jumped at the chance. He'd never seen an illustrated copy of the book and hoped it would throw more light onto the scenes the Creeper created when he left the bodies.

The workshop was filled with the strong, although not unpleasant, smells of paint, varnish and glue. It was quite a sizeable room, big enough to house five long rows of desks, most of which were occupied by workers immersed in their tasks. It was a cluttered space, but there was a feeling of organised chaos about the room. Every available surface was filled with the paraphernalia of toy repair. Mabel led him through the section of the workshop dedicated to the restoration of clockwork toys, the gentle drone of a pin vice drill from one workstation keeping time with the whispering hum of a small grinder from another. The sounds were rhythmic and oddly soothing, like cicadas at night-time on warmer shores. The workers were bent over their desks with faces of intense concentration, as if none of them needed to breathe or blink.

"One of our most skilled workers is repairing a rare toy train that dates back to 1882 and was made by a well-respected German company called Gebrüder Bing," Mabel said. "It's quite a find. We're lucky to have it in our collection; thrilled, actually." She looked excitedly at Sam. "Would you like to see it?"

"Absolutely." Sam found Mabel's enthusiasm endearing and contagious. He was relieved to discover he hadn't become so jaded that he could only feel excitement when a new clue had been added to a dead body.

She stopped at a desk where a dark-haired man was absorbed in his task. "Excuse me, Ben, I'm sorry to interrupt, but I wondered if my guest might have a look at the train you're working on." Her request was polite, barely audible.

The man called Ben jumped in his seat at the sound of Mabel's voice, as if she'd shouted in his ear. A look of irritation crossed his face as he turned towards her, but that expression disappeared as he caught sight of Sam. He flinched and his skin seemed to pale under Sam's gaze, his deep brown eyes widening like ink seeping into blotting paper.

"Is now a bad time?" Mabel clenched her hands, looking a little wary. "Are you in the middle of something difficult?" She glanced from Ben to Sam. Frowned.

A strained silence stretched for so long Sam thought there might be an audible crack when it was eventually broken. He looked into Ben's dark eyes and experienced a tingling sensation across the back of his neck. He smiled awkwardly and was rewarded with a surprisingly enthusiastic smile in return, one almost warm enough to smooth the edges of hostility. Ben unravelled himself, his chair screeching across the floor as he rose. He was taller than Sam expected, a couple of inches above Sam's six feet, and he was also rather thin; he reminded Sam of a snake uncoiling upon waking. He shook Sam's hand with both of his, lingering just a moment too long, which made Sam feel uncomfortable, but he seemed pleasant enough, although Sam wondered about his rapid transition from annoyance to friendliness. He sensed Ben was the kind of man who could change the atmosphere of a room just by entering it, that whatever mood he was in would leak onto other people like a red item of clothing in an all-white wash. The bottom of Ben's chin and the side of his nose was smeared with oil, the dark smudges stark on his grey, waxy skin.

"Of course your guest can have a look at the train, Mabel." He had a soft, gentle voice. "Sorry about that." He ran his fingers through his hair and laughed a little too loudly. "It's a fiddly task, and it's trying my patience." He glanced at Sam and blinked rapidly. "To quote Shakespeare, we are… '*mechanic slaves with greasy aprons*'." He blushed.

Perhaps it was shyness that hampered Ben's social skills. Sam smiled. "Is that from *Antony and Cleopatra*?" He used a light-hearted tone to encourage Ben to feel more at ease.

Ben nodded and looked pleased, although by now he wore his smile stiffly. He stood back from the desk so that Sam might approach and view the toy more closely. Sam admired the sleek train, a few parts yet to be slotted into place, but he could feel Ben hovering by his shoulder, staring down at him, which made him feel reluctant to linger for too long. Ben must have felt protective towards the train, perhaps worried Sam would attempt to pick it up. Sam stepped back to join Mabel, putting his hands firmly in his pockets as a way of reassuring Ben.

"Thanks for showing me," Sam said. "I'm sorry we disturbed you. We'll let you get back to work."

Ben was examining Sam's face closely, as if trying to commit it to memory. "It's no trouble, Sam, no trouble at all." He made another attempt to shake hands with Sam but paused halfway through the gesture when he saw Sam's hands were in his pockets. For an awkward moment Ben's hand was suspended in mid-air. Sam pretended not to notice to spare Ben any embarrassment.

He followed Mabel to a different part of the cavernous room, the area dedicated to books. Just before Sam rounded the corner, something made him turn. Ben was staring at him, the smiling expression still on his face, but rigidly now, as if it pained him to hold it in place. It was like the immovable smirk on a ventriloquist's dummy, painted on and insincere. Sam looked away and caught up with Mabel. Perhaps it was the climate-controlled restoration room that suddenly made him feel cold.

He spent another forty minutes with Mabel and a woman called Jenny who showed him the old copy of *Grimms' Fairy Tales*. The illustrations were indeed beautiful, incredibly detailed, but they revealed no further clues that would assist Sam in his work on the case. However, it confirmed his belief the Creeper was familiar with the works of the Brothers Grimm, and they'd been right to release the details of the crime scenes to the news outlets. The vindication felt good.

He'd enjoyed the time he'd shared with Mabel, especially the hour or so in her office soothed by her voice as if under her spell, time suspended. It reminded him of listening to Emma during therapy. He'd felt the same relaxation, the same sense of being able to let down his guard for just a while. He left the museum pleased at having invested the time there, although something about the visit had bothered him. When he tried to put his finger on it, however, it slipped away. He ran his hands through his hair as if trying to brush the uneasy feeling from his mind. *Probably just fatigue*, he thought as he boarded the bus back to the office, daydreaming about Emma once more.

20

After Ben recovered from the initial shock of seeing Sam at the museum, a tingling thrill throbbed throughout his body, making him feel almost giddy. That Sam should suddenly appear at his desk seemed miraculous, as if Ben had conjured him out of thin air like a magician pulling a bouquet of flowers out of his sleeve. It was intoxicating to stand so close to his hunter, Sam unaware of how near he was to his prey.

In the heat of the moment, Ben had taken a risk and used Sam's name, even though Mabel hadn't mentioned it. It felt reckless, but also deliciously naughty. They were on a first-name basis now. They were friends. For the rest of the visit, he kept his eye on Sam, trying to gauge if Sam had noticed, but if he had, he made no indication of it.

But now Ben was home, and the first flush of excitement had fallen away. Fear crawled along his skin like maggots across a rotten piece of meat. He'd acted like a child playing hide and seek with Sam. The papers were right, he was just a silly little boy. She had been right, too.

He took off his clothes and pressed his back against the basement wall, spreading his arms wide as if crucified against the completed tower. The cold wall raised goosebumps on his naked skin, but he forced himself to endure it. *Silly little boy*, she whispered in his head. *Silly little baby Benny, you can't do anything right. Useless little leech.* She was screaming now. *Baby Benny, little worm.*

"Shut up," he screamed back. "I'm a man now, all grown up. Leave me alone."

But she was still there, pulsating, pushing at him until he thought he could see her moving beneath his flesh, stretching it until it tore. *Is baby Benny trying to make a new friend? Why does a little worm need a friend?* She prodded him, on and on, her voice getting louder and louder.

"Because I'm so lonely," he screamed, the admission taking him by surprise, a shift somewhere deep inside, a new pain.

His words echoed in the emptiness, bouncing back to him unheard. He felt close to tears. She had won again. He was insignificant once more, but it was his own weakness that had permitted her victory. He'd behaved like a contemptible pauper when he needed to be a prince.

He gripped the handle of the boning tool, the hook protruding between his index and middle fingers, and sat cross-legged on the chilly floor. Pulling the skin taut on his left inner thigh, he dragged the hook from inside his knee up towards his groin, back and forth in long sweeping strokes. Warm beads of blood bubbled across his cold skin and dripped onto the floor, the droplets like rubies catching the light. He started gently this time. It was better to be patient and let the pain build and throb rather than explode. The scars healed neatly if he took his time.

With the pain came clarity and confidence, and a sweet release. No, he wouldn't allow Sam to get in his way. He wasn't finished with his task yet, and the thought of leaving it incomplete angered him as much as it scared him. If he didn't reach eight, she would still have the power to linger in his life. She was like a disease. He should have been immune to her by now, and it infuriated him that he wasn't.

She had developed her own immunity towards him, after all. As soon as he'd turned eight years old, she had turned her back on him. Eight was the magic number, she'd told him. Eight was too late. Too late for fairy stories at bedtime, too late for them to love each other and live happily ever after. Eight was too late for him to remain under her roof and under her wing. She had outgrown him and discarded him like old clothes that no longer fit. He should have outgrown her too, and while it was true she was losing her grip on him, she still hung on by her fingernails. He was growing stronger, though. Each time another one died, he felt more alive, more of a man. In control at last. Each time he killed one, freedom beckoned to him – it was just around the next corner. Eight wouldn't be too late for him anymore. When he reached eight, the tables would turn, and the world would make sense at last. When he reached eight, she would be too late. Too late to have a hold on him. Too late to matter anymore.

But Sam mattered. The newspapers said he was a profiler. They had dedicated one man entirely to him, to his personality profile and behavioural traits. One man whose sole purpose was to fathom him out and ultimately find him. Sam was his own personal disciple watching his every move, following along behind him with unwavering loyalty. Ben was flattered by the attention and wanted to feel closer to him. At first, he'd been sure Sam would feel the same way, would jump at the chance to shine his light of compassion onto a dark soul. After a lifetime of being misunderstood, he was convinced Sam could offer him understanding. He could trust Sam with his sensitive, interior self, a frailty that he protected from a cold world. It had never benefited him to reveal it. She had read it as an unbearable neediness that she'd found cloying and claustrophobic. Showing it to the princesses didn't count – they never stayed around long enough to be tested. But for a while he'd believed Sam would pass the test.

Sam had looked at Polly with such tenderness – even though it was wasted on the dead. What must it feel like to be held under such a gaze? Safe, like being tucked up in a soft bed while a storm raged outside. What would he have to do to make Sam look at him that way?

But in the end, Sam had let him down. He was the storm outside. He hadn't looked at Ben with compassion in the museum. He'd looked at him the same way as everybody else, the way people had been looking at him all his life: with confusion, wariness and ultimately dislike. It was such a disappointment. Sam was just another obstacle in his path, one he would either have to go around or run over if he refused to get out of the way.

But he wouldn't give in to the fear, it would metastasise into panic unless he held his nerve. His newfound fame was already getting in the way. He couldn't allow Sam's presence to add to his burdens.

He'd thought he would like the brand-new sensation of feeling like he counted. And he had, initially. Being the Grimm Creeper was a secret identity, like being Superman under his clothes. When Mrs Lennox gave him that look, like he was a bad smell, he wanted to tell her who he really was. He wished he could find a phone box and rip his suit off to emerge like Superman in his true colours; that would wipe the look off her face. But nothing ever worked out the way he wanted it to. Lennox wouldn't look at him with respect. She would look at him with the kind of pity only the most pathetic warranted.

The Grimm Creeper wasn't respected. He was being ridiculed. Despite the work Ben had put in, they still discounted him. He had opened himself up to them, shared his stories with them, even helped them out by making things clearer when it felt like they would forever miss the point, but they still wrote him off. It was Riley's fault, that bastard, courting the media like a desperate whore. Sitting there in his pressed uniform, freshly shaven and shiny, patronising Ben and belittling him while the hacks sucked it all up. The man was beneath him. They were all beneath him, like something he would scrape off his shoe. He needed a new distraction, something stronger than his sleeping beauties in their tidy rows. Something to take him away from the media and their daily insults.

He was already making plans, just pencil outlines on a fresh white wall for now, but the red would soon soak in. He hadn't found the final resting place yet, but he had found her – he had found them. He'd drawn them on the wall, arms entwined, the way they'd been standing in the rain at the bus stop, but the faces were blank. He hadn't been close enough to absorb their features. Not yet. But he already knew which dress each of them would wear. He could tell they would fit, snugly perhaps, but passable all the same. He would soon have them dancing for him, and when they did it would be double the fun.

"Twice as nice," he whispered as he ran his hands across the wall. "Twice as nice."

But he couldn't afford to indulge himself by sitting in the basement any longer. He had to revisit the sacred ground so he could bring the stories back to life. They were his stories, the ones he loved, and when he loved a story, he read it more than once. Standing on the spot where he had left each one aroused him, but he always waited until he got home before he welcomed the climax that signalled the story's end. A sticky, messy end, but deeply satisfying.

He didn't usually jump in again so quickly – a rebound was so undignified – but life was too short for procrastination. He could hear the whispers coming from inside the bloody walls, like a bubble of air trapped inside the plumbing. Rapunzel's tower summoned him too, and he wouldn't deny himself that pleasure. Going back to the last place would fill him with the strength he needed to go on to the next place. Now wasn't the time to hesitate, to fold over the page and leave the book to one side. It was time for the next chapter.

21

Emma waited for Annie in the therapy room. Apparently, she was refusing to leave her cell until provided with a clean set of clothes, and the staff had learned there was little point in refusing. Emma found the solitude eerie; slamming doors and muffled voices seemed far away, as if she'd been forgotten and abandoned. There was a smell of overcooked cabbage, sulphuric and determined to linger, a school-dinner-ish shepherd's pie, disinfectant no match for mass catering. Emma's thoughts drifted towards Sam while she waited; she'd also learned there was little point in impatience.

Having read the latest news on the Creeper case, she better understood the stress Sam was under. She wanted to see him. She felt herself missing him – missing the side of her that warmed when she was with him. She didn't want to lose that, or the potential of a future with him. Perhaps it was time to be as open with him as he'd been with her, to embrace the feelings she'd been keeping at arm's length. The thought of that made her feel less alone in the empty room, that somewhere Sam might be thinking about her too, and they were in possession of a secret shared only with each other. Sometimes, Emma thought, solitude allowed room for solace.

Approaching footsteps chased Sam away as Emma refocused. She'd been working one-on-one with Annie now for some time. The sessions occurred twice weekly, but after the startling revelation of the first session, Annie had remained tight-lipped. The fifty minutes now dragged with empty small talk and long, drawn-out silences filled with aggression and irritation. Annie made no attempt to disguise her profound dislike of being forced to talk. She'd returned to the stubborn, resistant mood she usually displayed in group therapy.

As an orderly finally led Annie into the room, Emma decided she would push her harder today, wouldn't let her get away with another ineffective session. Before she could begin, however, Annie presented her with an untidily wrapped package clutched in trembling hands. She'd used newspaper for wrapping paper, the edges ragged and torn. Emma noticed the ink had smudged onto Annie's hands turning them a dirty grey.

Emma raised her eyebrows, noticing Annie's shy smile. "Have you brought me a present? That's a lovely surprise." She hesitated before taking the proffered parcel, hoping her discomfort wasn't obvious. "It's not my birthday."

Annie's smile shuttered. "It doesn't have to be your birthday for me to give you a present, does it?" She sounded a little upset, her voice softer than usual, almost child-like. "It's not much, but I made it myself and I thought you'd like it." She placed her thumb in her mouth and chewed on the nail, the newspaper ink forming a bruise at the side of her mouth.

Kindness wasn't an emotion Annie displayed often or easily, which made Emma question it. She also doubted the sincerity behind Annie's hurt expression. Her exaggerated pouting was a performance Emma had seen before.

Emma smiled. "It's very thoughtful of you, Annie. Would you like me to open it now?"

Annie shrugged. "It's your present. You can open it

whenever you like. But it would be nice to know if you like it."
She clasped her hands together and held them under her chin.

Emma unwrapped the present. Inside was a knitted hat in an unusual shade of red. It was plain but beautifully made, with a complicated stitch running around the edges. Emma was amazed Annie's arthritic fingers could produce something of such fine quality. The wool was soft and the red vivid with hints of blue. It had a shape similar to a beret, although less structured.

"It's lovely. Thank you very much. Did you really make it yourself?" Emma scrunched the newspaper wrapping into a ball and placed it under her chair, the pages crackling as they unfurled. "The colour is very striking."

Annie looked satisfied as she sat down. "Yes, we are encouraged to knit. It keeps us quiet." A knowing smile replaced the pout. "I don't mind, though, it's nice to create something. I'm glad you like it. I thought the colour would look good against your dark hair."

Emma nodded. "I think it will suit me." She absentmindedly ran her thumb back and forth across the edge of the hat, her nail snagging a stich. "Can I ask what made you give me a present today?" She didn't want to appear ungrateful or suspicious, but she had to know the intention behind the unusual gesture.

The smile disappeared from Annie's face and was replaced by a thoughtful expression, the frown lines on her forehead burrowing deeper. She glanced at her hands entwined upon her lap, and awkwardly folded her legs beneath her, knees cracking as she adjusted them on the faded armchair, the seat sagging as the worn and aged tried to accommodate each other. She took a deep breath.

"The hat is a parting gift. I suppose I have to thank you for trying to help me. When I talked about my father with you, it felt strange." She noticed her dirty fingertips and rubbed them together, the ink blackening the edges of her nails.

"Why is that?" Emma asked, encouraged by Annie's apparent willingness to talk to her this time.

"He doesn't usually live in spoken words. He lives inside me, where he talks only to me. But I'm glad I shared some of him with you, because I wanted to show him off. I wanted you to understand that I am bigger and stronger because of him, because he chose me. But it made me feel lonely too, because now there is less of him for me. If I give you any more of him, this place will become too crisp. It's better if it stays out of focus. Talking about him made me feel like I was disappearing, so I'm not going to talk about him anymore. I know you think what he did to me was wrong, but I will never feel that way about him. I loved him, and I want to keep that for myself. It was my experience, and I don't want to dirty it by talking about it anymore."

Annie stared at the floor as she spoke, her face tense with concentration, her voice jittery with emotion. "I don't need your pity. I don't feel shame, because I don't feel like a victim. I wasn't abused or damaged. I was chosen. I was special. It's my choice what I live with, what I choose to believe, and I choose to believe in the love he gave me, and that's all I'm going to say about that."

Emma was stunned into silence. Internally she ran through years of training and experience, and only one answer felt like the correct response. Annie was right. Emma had made too many assumptions about Annie's experience. Should she dismantle the barricades of denial that Annie had erected around herself, or leave them in place? What would serve Annie better? She was an elderly woman who would never again taste freedom. Perhaps it was kinder to allow her to live out her remaining years with denial as comfort, but Emma wondered if this was the right choice therapeutically or morally. In her role as therapist, she wasn't supposed to judge. She was supposed to understand and facilitate understanding in her patients. She decided to move away from the topic of Annie's father until she'd given it more thought.

"I know what you want me to say, what you really want to hear," Annie said. "You want me to admit my guilt and take responsibility for what I did. You want me to say out loud that I'm a monster, a fiend, a pervert. That's fine. I'll tell you what you want to hear, and then we can both let this go and say goodbye."

Emma braced herself for the words she'd been waiting for and dreading: Annie's confession. It was as if Annie was preparing to disrobe and stand naked before her. Emma felt like she should avert her gaze, but she couldn't look away.

"I loved my son until he was eight years old. After that, he turned my stomach. I did everything a mother is supposed to do. I kept him clean, clothed, and safe. I made him his favourite food, read him stories until he fell asleep, and let him sleep in my bed whenever he felt lonely or afraid. Even when he was naughty, I never lost my temper, although sometimes I wanted to put my hands around his neck and squeeze so tightly that I never heard his screams again. Sometimes I would tease him, I admit, but only in a playful way, dancing for him, twirling until he blushed and giggled and wanted to run away, but I didn't let him. I pulled him close and held him. I can still smell his hair; sometimes I can still hear that music."

Annie smiled. She looked serene, almost beautiful. "I told him every day that I loved him. I would tell him my heart was so full of love for him it would burst right out of my chest and pop like a balloon, and that always made him laugh. Every time I said it, he would ask me if that meant I would die of a broken heart, and I would tell him I would grow another heart if I had to because I would never stop loving him – until I did, of course – but before my love dried up, I made sure he always knew he was my little prince."

Annie's eyes were closed, and she was smiling to herself. Emma remained very still. Then Annie shifted position and her smile fell away.

"Sometimes he'd go out into the garden and deliberately make himself mucky. He knew I couldn't abide an untidy house. He could be a very demanding child, and there were times when I didn't have the energy for the attention he needed. That's when he would roll around in the dirt or cover himself in paint from his artist set. On bad days, he would empty the dustbin all over the kitchen floor and sit in the pile of rubbish. He was a dirty little piggy sometimes, a filthy, smelly little piggy, and I would put him in the bath and scrub him clean. Coal tar soap was the only soap that drowned the smell of rubbish, that awful stink that matted his hair. Maybe I scrubbed him too hard, but I couldn't stand that mess, that odour. But once he was clean, I made the washing fun, like a game. I made it soft and gentle like my father did with me. I made it special. I'd wrap him up in a towel afterwards while he was still warm from the water, while I could still smell the soap on the back of his neck. Sometimes he asked if he could wear my vanilla oil perfume, because he knew it was my favourite. He said he wanted to smell nice for me after smelling like a dirty piggy. He told me he wanted to taste like vanilla ice cream, and he did."

Emma waited in the heavy silence until it became clear Annie needed prompting. "What changed after your son turned eight?" A part of her didn't want to ask the question, but she knew she had to.

Annie replied without hesitation. "Something inside me switched off. I still don't know why. Maybe it was because he became too needy. I never got a moment alone. There were times when I felt like I couldn't breathe. I couldn't enter a room without him following me inside. He was too desperate, and I couldn't stand that. I woke up one morning and it was as if

169

I was suddenly allergic to him. His skin looked shiny and felt slick to the touch, oily and damp like a fat slug. His pretty mouth was too wet. It was repulsive. He was repulsive. I didn't want him near me. I didn't want to hear his voice or see his face. When he reached for me, I slapped his hands away. It took a lot of slapping before he finally got the message. I did the best I could for as long as I could, and then I ran dry."

Annie looked straight at Emma, her dark eyes empty and devoid of emotion. Unburdened and yet seemingly unaffected.

"You know the rest. He opened his big wet mouth and gave our secret away to one of his teachers at school, just because I didn't pay him enough attention anymore."

She smiled at Emma as she ran her hands across her throat, the loose skin dragging like ripples in water.

"He wasn't as good at keeping secrets as I was." She sighed. "He was weak, a little tell-tale, so they took him away, and here we are. I went my way, and he went his. I'm sure he turned out fine, all things considered." She glanced at the hat on Emma's lap.

Annie stood up so abruptly her knees cracked, and she winced. She headed towards the door before Emma had a chance to react.

"Thank you, Emma, for everything, and now I'll say goodbye." She sounded like a polite guest thanking the host before leaving a party. "Enjoy the hat," she added, before nodding to the orderly who'd been waiting outside. He cuffed her, and then followed along behind her like a servant escorting a queen.

Emma took a moment in the suddenly empty room to process what had just happened. She was sure of two things: firstly, this wouldn't be their last session together – despite Annie's certainty; therapy was mandatory, and the next session would be far more intense, because Emma wasn't convinced by

Annie's story. Annie had only recounted some of her version of events, probably telling Emma what she wanted to hear. Playing at therapy rather than truly engaging with it. Secondly, considering how Annie had turned out, Emma highly doubted things had ended well for her son. There could never be a happily ever after for a story like that.

22

Sam and Riley were squeezed together on a small table outside a coffee shop. It was a bright sunny morning in late June, the sky the colour of forget-me-nots. The only break in the blue was the vapour drifting behind glinting aeroplanes like trailing kite strings. Some of the cafes and restaurants close to their office in Smithfield had set up outdoor seating in celebration of summer, and local workers drank in the warm day along with their morning coffee.

Sam was on his second latte and third cigarette when he noticed a black taxi dropping off a smartly dressed woman. She headed towards a sleek office building on the opposite side of the road. She was petite, with long dark hair falling down her back in waves and pulled from her face by a pair of large sunglasses on top of her head.

"I wonder if she's aware she's the killer's type?" Sam said, as he tapped his cigarette on the edge of the ashtray, some of the ash catching the light breeze and landing on his trousers. He brushed it away, frowning at the white smudges that remained on his thigh.

Riley poured himself more tea from the leaking pot. "I

was just thinking the same thing." A dark brown moat formed around the cup and he mopped up the spillage. The woman stepped into the building's lobby and disappeared. "It's an automatic reaction for me these days. I see black hair against pale skin and the words 'potential victim' run across my mind like news headlines across the bottom of a television screen." He blew across the surface of his tea before taking a sip, drips from the bottom of the cup splashing onto the table.

Sam waved his cigarette smoke away from Riley and nodded. A passing car with loud music blaring from open windows halted their conversation. He waited for it to drive away, a motorbike following the music down the street. "Every time I have therapy with Emma, I automatically think she's the Creeper's type." He flicked his lighter on and off until Riley snatched it from his hand. Sam apologised. He knew it irritated Riley, and it was becoming a nervous habit.

"How's the therapy going?" Riley asked as he undid the top button of his shirt and loosened his tie, a bead of sweat making its way down the side of his face.

Sam was due to see Emma again in a few days. As their therapy progressed, he was even more convinced of his feelings for her. While it was true that she gave him a way to alleviate his stress, she also gave him optimism for his future – one he hoped she would become a part of. Ever since his previous relationship had ended, he'd convinced himself he had little to offer, but when he was with Emma, he felt he might have something to give after all. She'd opened something in him, a softer side that had been closed off as protection against the brutality of the Creeper case. He felt both compassion and enormous sympathy for the victims, but he couldn't become emotionally involved with them or their families, it would obscure the cold logic he needed to employ to be effective. If he took their grief on board, he wouldn't be able to do his job.

Sam reached for his lighter, noticed Riley's frown, and put it in his pocket. "Therapy is going well, I think. I'm getting better at compartmentalising my emotions. Emma suggested I make a conscious effort to leave work behind for at least a few hours each week, and I'm trying to stick to that. I can never completely switch the case off – it's always in the back of my mind – but I've tried to take some time for myself each week. I'm still swimming, which I clearly need, as I'm not quite as fit as I thought I was."

"Who is, these days? It's not as if the bad guys are ever going to take a day off. After we catch this psycho, another one will crawl out of the sewers." Riley finished his tea and placed the cup and saucer to one side. "Maybe I'll take up golf when I retire, get fit on the fairway." Riley rolled his eyes. "Although I agree with Groucho Marx's opinion that golf gets in the way of a good walk."

Sam laughed. "I think my swimming gets in the way of a good sauna, it's the best part of going to the pool. I feel like I'm sweating the Creeper out, even if only for an hour at a time. I feel cleaner inside and out afterwards. It makes me feel sane again, like there's room in my mind for other things."

He immediately thought of Emma again and calmness descended.

Standing in the stuffy, urine-splashed phone box, Ben watched Sam turn his face up towards the sun. The increasing heat of the morning intensified the stench, but he couldn't risk moving. He held the phone up to his face, the lingering smell of stale breath in the mouthpiece deeply unpleasant, but he needed to look as if he was making a call. Posters advertising a local club were pasted to the windows alongside an assortment of takeaway menus and cards for sex workers who were – apparently – just a phone call away. The phone box offered him the perfect spot from which to view Riley forming sweat patches under his arms, and Sam as he enjoyed his coffee. He was the hunter now, stalking his prey. He was surprised to find he was aroused by the sense of power this gave him. The one Sam wanted to find was right here under his nose, just across the street. The temptation to touch himself was almost irresistible. It made him laugh into the phone, drowning out the shrill recorded voice that was telling him to please replace the handset.

Sitting in the sun, sipping his coffee, Sam looked complacent and smug. Much too happy and altogether too fucking pleased with himself – whiling away the morning as if he hadn't a care in the world. As if nothing mattered. As if *he* didn't matter. Ben's arousal dissipated. It had only been a few weeks since he'd broken things off with Polly, and already Sam and Riley had forgotten him. He was worth remembering. He was the Grimm Creeper after all. He occupied a place in London's history like Jack the Ripper or the Black Death. Others felt his presence. When women looked over their shoulders, it was him they searched for – and yet it looked as if Sam had forgotten he existed at all. He was obviously becoming lazy and needed something to keep him on his toes. Ben didn't want him turning soft. He needed a worthy opponent. Sam needed to sit up and take notice again.

Sweat beaded on his top lip, and his hair grew damp as the heat increased in the glass box. He envied his princesses, how cool they'd be in their glass boxes, kissed by frost as the frigid air moved around them in the freezer. His Snow Whites in their glass coffins, slices of frozen pear welded onto their tongues by crystals of ice. He wished he had a sliver of chilled pear to cool his own tongue, the sweet juices sliding down his throat to replace the urine he swore he could taste. The delicate, subtle taste of pear was so much more refined than apple. Of course, he knew he should be forcing slices of apple down the throats of his Snow Whites instead of placing pear slices onto their tongues, but they were his stories now and he could tell them any way he wanted to, just as she had done all those years ago.

"You lied to me, didn't you, my love?" he whispered into the phone, repulsed by the intimacy of his breath writhing around with the breath from strange mouths. "For years I thought Snow White almost died after eating a poisoned pear. You never liked to follow the rules, did you?" She'd told him that following the rules took the shine off life.

He laughed once, the sound like a bark in the confined space. It tasted acidic in his mouth, bitter as bile. He squeezed his house keys in his pocket, ran his thumb up and down the jagged blade until he could feel the familiar pain throbbing from his callus, until he was calm, and the story came back.

The dwarfs had laid Snow White to rest in a glass coffin, because she was too beautiful to remain under the closed lid of a wooden box. He liked that about the dwarfs. It demonstrated their love for Snow White, and he followed their example. He kept their delicate beauty alive. Unlike his own Snow Whites, the one in the book was only sleeping, the poisoned fruit stuck in her throat. She would magically wake after movement dislodged the apple and made her receptive to a kiss from her prince. No matter how many times he lifted his princesses' glass domes to place a kiss on their chilled lips, they'd never wake again. Sometimes he wished they would. They could dance for him again, read to him again. But mostly he was glad they were dead.

They all lacked the quiet dignity he remembered about her. They were incapable of employing the gentle, caressing tones she had used to soothe him when she read to him. When he made the princesses read to him, they spat out the words as if they tasted sour, resentment tainting every syllable. With her, the words had dripped like honey poured slowly from a jar and made the back of his neck tingle. Later, she did everything wrong, but back then, during story time, she'd done everything right.

"I didn't mind that you lied about the pear, my love, not really. It made the story ours, didn't it?" Ben felt her inside the phone box with him, her vanilla scent stronger than the urine, taking it over and making it hers, just like the story. Everything was always hers in the end. Her allergy to apples changing the narrative and making the pear synonymous with her. It was delicate and refined just like her, perfumed and sweet against the lips, just like her. Until she'd turned rotten.

After she'd turned her back on him, he ate only apples to spite her. It didn't matter that she would never know. It made him feel independent. It weakened her grip on him. But his resolve soon faded, the sublime taste of pear too strong a pull when it brought her with it. He yearned for its sweetness as he yearned for her, needed the memory of the sticky, sugary kisses to remain a part of him. Pears were often absent from the various homes in which he'd lived after she was gone, and this made them all the sweeter when he tasted one again. He still thought of them as forbidden fruit, a name she had occasionally called him – once upon a time.

*

After Riley paid the bill, Sam drained the last of his coffee and they crossed the road and headed back to the office. Sam's mind was so focused on the briefing he was about to give he tripped over the curb and fell against the phone box. He righted himself and waved an apology at the man inside, but the man was turned away and continued with his conversation.

"You okay?" Riley asked. "Do you need me to hold your hand the rest of the way, or can you manage?" He grinned and held out his hand.

"Thanks, but I think I can make it," Sam said with a laugh, and they turned the corner.

As they climbed the stairs to the office, the summer warmth ebbed away, leaving him with a strangely cold feeling on so warm a day. He thought he heard a footstep behind him, but a quick glance over his shoulder revealed only the dark stairs falling away below.

Sam made his way to the front of the incident room and took up his regular spot by the board where the victims' photographs were displayed, and stared at them as if they could tell him the things he needed to know. He knew their faces so well by now – the small scar above Rosie's eyebrow, the pale birthmark by Charlotte's ear – and yet this intimacy wasn't enough. Reading everything about the lives of the victims wasn't enough, but his colleagues had assembled and fallen quiet. He had to push on with the recap that Riley had requested.

"Thanks for your attention, everyone," said Sam. "So, we suspect the Creeper is now in his dormant phase, searching, perhaps stalking, but not striking – not yet. If he sticks to his schedule, then he isn't due to kill until the beginning of September. This gives us about three months to find him and prevent another death."

The team in front of him looked physically exhausted, mentally drained. He felt the same way, as worn down and burnt out as grass at the end of a long hot summer. They all needed it to rain, and soon.

He thought back to the psychological texts and old case files he'd been studying lately. Decades of horror had provided the theories Sam relied on for the psychopathy and behavioural traits common in serial killers. His job as a profiler was a paradox, only possible thanks to the deaths of previous victims. He constantly reminded Riley and the team they had to study the past to understand the present – and keep one step ahead of it by predicting the Creeper's next move. Sam had spent a great deal of time trying to put himself inside the Creeper's mind, to really understand the dangerous desires of his heart.

He gulped down some water, his throat feeling dry after too many cigarettes. "I just want to take a moment to remind ourselves of the basics. There is a considerable amount of documentation to suggest that serial killers usually kill within their own ethnic group, therefore, the Creeper is most likely white, but as ever, there are exceptions to the rule – the Hillside Strangler springs to mind – so this teaches us to keep our own minds open. They are also capable of great charm helping them to lure their victims. However, it can be turned off as abruptly as it's turned on. Their moods are like disguises – they can be worn or discarded at will, depending upon the killer's needs. Our killer is a terrifying chameleon who blends in with normal society, allowing him to go about the job of murder without attracting attention – at least until he wants it."

An officer waved his hand, hurriedly swallowed a mouthful of food. "Is the attention-seeking a consistent trait?" A blob of mustard landed on his tie. He attempted to wipe it away, but merely smeared it making it look worse.

A lorry pulled up in the street below, its warning signal sounding as it reversed. Petrol fumes crept around the room mingling with the smell of coffee.

"No," said Sam. "Serial killers often fall into two categories. There are those who like to go about their job as discreetly as possible, needing only to kill rather than to be seen killing. They never leave their signature – their calling card – because they have no interest in claiming credit. Such killers are rarely caught."

The atmosphere in the room shifted, as if some of the team had abruptly disengaged, the chance of a successful outcome snatched from their hands. "But I'm sure our killer falls into the second category," he said quickly. "Those who need to kill but also need an audience, which is why he signs his work, so to speak. His signature is the way he stages the bodies. The Creeper craves the recognition as much as he craves the murder, and this narcissism is one of his weak spots. Another is the women themselves. I believe the killer is in thrall of women. They have an unknowable quality that he finds intimidating. Perhaps this is why he removes the victims' underwear but not their clothes, thereby keeping their nakedness at arm's length. I suspect he's intimidated by the intimacy that the naked form represents. He will have no experience with true intimacy. Maybe this is why he chooses to remove the heads. The victims are rendered faceless – they could be anyone, and they could be no one – but either way, the possibility of intimacy is removed."

Sam went over a few more points discussed in previous sessions, ended the briefing and thanked the team for listening. And then it was back to the case files. He had to add his own stones to that well-trodden path for other profilers to learn from, just as his predecessors had done with the shared research he used. He would be passing on invaluable knowledge, but it was a knowledge that came with a heavy price.

*

Ben knew this was where Sam spent most of his days, long days that sometimes bled into the night. He rather enjoyed the fact that Sam worked above a betting shop, that the activities above and below were both driven by luck. He intended to be a winner, despite what the newspapers said. Each time he killed, he was that much closer to the finishing line. *When there are eight, Sam will be too late.* He mouthed the words as he stood under the shade of a tree opposite Sam's office. A woman quickly averted her gaze as she swerved around him.

Sam stood at one of the dirty windows staring out at the streets below, but Ben knew that look on his face. Sam wasn't observing the world below his window, he was thinking about the case. Ben waited for the now familiar moment when Sam would run his fingers through his hair, lost in thought. He could wait and watch all day, if it wasn't for the nagging voice of his boss, Henry, telling him he'd been absent from the museum too often of late. He longed to immerse himself more fully in Sam's life, but he comforted himself by the morning's efforts. He knew where Sam worked, where he liked to go swimming. He even knew where Sam lived, and he'd left a little something at his home, a gift to let Sam know his opponent wasn't a pushover. A reminder that it was the Creeper who had the upper hand.

Who was the profiler now?

Reluctantly he turned and headed towards the approaching bus that would take him to work. The sooner he got there, the sooner he could leave, and this made him feel quite cheerful, because after work tonight he had something to look forward to. Tonight, he had company to go home to, and it was always heart-warming to go home to companions who would be glad to see him. This thought made it easier to put on his public face, the one that smiled pleasantly at strangers. The one that reassured them he was safe. The one that said, *I look just like you.*

23

As soon as Ben arrived at work, his boss took him aside. "Can we have a quiet word?"

His co-workers stared at him. He felt their hostility burning into his skin, their mouths watering at the prospect of confrontation. Murmurs and stifled laughter took the place of the clangs and groans of machinery, work neglected in favour of taking pleasure at his expense. How was it possible to feel this invisible when he was the centre of attention?

Ben followed Henry to a corner of the workshop, bracing himself, attempting to figure out what face he should put on. He could feel their eyes boring into him.

Henry stood too close, as usual, and grasped his shoulder. "Ben, what's wrong with you these days?" His voice was soft, the words expelled on a wave of stale coffee.

Ben fixed a smile in place wondering if it was the right one. "I don't know what you mean." He tried to keep the tone light, but his clenched jaw clipped the ends off his words, making them harsh, snappy.

Henry's sad expression made his jowls droop even lower than usual, the weight pulling open his hair-filled nostrils. The 'quiet word' grew like fungus into one long poisonous sentence of admonishment and turned out to be not so quiet after all. "All the absences lately, you're barely ever here, and when you do show up, you're tardy. I hardly recognise you anymore. This is not the Ben I hired all those years ago, the man who dedicated himself to a job he loved. Where is that happy, reliable man? What's happened to him? That's the Ben I miss."

Henry stood so close that his coffee-flavoured spit landed in Ben's mouth. Rage flickered inside him. Henry was overstepping his role as usual, confusing 'boss' with 'father figure', scolding him like he was a child. Diminishing him in front of an audience straining to hear every word, hungry to devour his discomfort.

He wanted to tell Henry the Ben he used to know was long gone, now occupied by a higher calling. The new Ben didn't have the same enthusiasm for fixing toys anymore.

He only had time for writing the perfect ending now it was in sight. He kept the subservient employee mask in place, playing the role of dutiful surrogate son while this lonely man blathered on about how important it was to be a good employee. *A good boy.*

Good boys were supposed to look after their toys, treat them with care, and put them away when they were finished playing with them, but he wasn't a good boy anymore. He wanted to break his toys in half. He wanted to make a mess on the walls. He wanted to make such a mess of himself that he smelt like fresh death under all that stickiness. He wanted to make his toys bleed before they bored him to tears. Discipline and absolute dedication were required if he was going to breathe new life into old stories, if they were to escape the confines of musty, tattered pages and glisten on the walls.

"Yes, Henry," he said out loud. "I understand. I will certainly make more of an effort." His cheeks ached with the strain of the smile and a muscle twitched under his right eye. Meanwhile, he pushed the boiling rage deep down, as if his body were a bottle and the false smile the stopper keeping all the rage inside, stopping it from fizzing up and exploding all over Henry. The smile remained in place for the rest of the day, the disguise of happiness making his head throb. As he anticipated going home, the throbbing travelled down his body. It built with such an intensity he retreated to the men's bathroom when Henry wasn't around. He ejaculated into the toilet bowl, watching it swirl and flush away in viscous, milky strands.

He was saving his rage for later. He knew just how to use it so that something beautiful could emerge from something ugly and useless. That level of rage needed to be channelled into a confined space, like a bomb detonated under strictly controlled conditions. He could still taste Henry's spit, and Henry didn't taste nearly as sweet as the sugar and spice and all things nice that were waiting for him at home. One was brunette and fit the bill, but the other was a blonde – more Goldilocks than Snow White, but it was time for a change. They were mismatched delicacies, but they would taste the same going down. All Sleeping Beauties by the end.

On his way home, he made a brief detour – irritating but necessary. He had to make sure Sam was still at work, still pacing in front of the window where Ben had left him earlier that morning. Sam's complacent smile had been replaced with tension that was more appropriate, laying down its history in the lines across his forehead and the dark shadows under his eyes. Ben didn't want him to go home yet and discover the gift he'd left for him. It was too soon. Once he found it, the game would speed up, leaving Sam little time for lazy coffees in the sunshine. Ben still needed to put the final pieces in place, and he didn't want Sam jumping the gun. He was relieved when he saw Sam at the window deep in thought – relieved, but not surprised. Sam's schedule had become as familiar to him as his own face in the mirror. This was the day Sam swam after work – his feeble attempt to deal with stress perhaps. But it was helpful. It allowed Ben to plan ahead.

As he made his way home, his pace increased and his mind took off like a startled bird, thoughts banging against the sides of his head. His needs had returned with an urgency that took him by surprise. He'd never been this hungry before. Polly should have satisfied him for longer than this, but the memory of her was quickly turning weak and pale. She hadn't been hearty enough after all – just a sugar rush. He reached home, hot and out of breath, but as soon as he was inside his thoughts slowed and he felt calmer, soothed by the security behind his front door.

They must have heard him coming down the stairs. As he opened the basement door, the brunette began to sob, pulling against the ropes around her wrists with such ferocity he thought her arms might break. But the restraints didn't loosen. The room stank. The blonde was sitting in her excrement, her ankles bleeding from the struggle against ropes that would not give way. She shook her head from side to side as if refusing to accept her fate – but her opinion didn't count. Nothing either of them did would ever count again.

"I've got something for you," he said in a sing-song voice. "A present to thank you for dancing for me last night." He stood off to one side so they couldn't see what he held in his hands. He didn't want to spoil the surprise. They twisted in their chairs attempting to look at him, but they were restrained too tightly to manoeuvre their bodies.

"Poor little princesses, are you all tied up in knots?" He laughed as the brunette growled from behind her gag, her fear undisguised by the anger rasping from her throat. He assessed them – greed had lowered his standards. "I'm not sure if you two are worthy of such a generous gift. She wouldn't approve of either of you. You're nothing but cheap filler, second-rate women plucked from the gutters." When he'd taken them, they had been stumbling and vomiting after drinking so much he could hear the alcohol swilling around in their flabby bellies. No, they were not the fairest of them all, but their disgusting drunkenness had made them so easy to take.

The blonde was crying again, a strand of hair glued under her nose by mucus and dried blood. Her snivelling repulsed him. "Where is your dignity?" he screamed at them from across the room. "You looked like whores when I took you." Tight skirts had crept up dimpled thighs as they'd thrust their fat, floppy cleavages into the world with a pride they did not warrant. Glittery makeup pooled in acne scars, their skin the colour of nicotine on old men's fingers – a colour that came straight from a bottle.

One of the brunette's false fingernails was broken, revealing the natural nail underneath. Another was missing entirely – just a naked, bloody stub – but the rest of her nails, painted neon pink, remained glued in place.

"Floozies, she would call you," Ben shouted. "Filthy sluts. Nothing but fakery and trickery." The smell of the blonde's shit was intensifying. "But I have her approval for the next one. She personally selected her for me – the perfect ending. She'll wipe the taste of your inferiority from my mouth." He closed his eyes and allowed her to fill his mind. "Emma, Emma, Emma," he whispered, the sound of her name like a heartbeat. But he couldn't get ahead of himself. *Palate cleansers come before the main course*, he told himself, although he wasn't sure how clean they were.

He moved closer to them and lowered his voice. "You are nothing compared to her, but beauty is only skin-deep after all, and when your skin is peeled back and your hearts ripped out, you'll look exactly like the others. You will bleed like the others. And you will come to love me just like the others. You'll love me so much, your hearts will burst right out of your chests and pop like balloons."

The women stared into each other's eyes, but it was only a confirmation of horror, like they were staring into a mirror and terror was staring back. This was where life would end for them. This was all there was left.

The blonde screamed, the sound strangled by the gag, more animal than human. She rocked backwards and forwards frantically, until the chair tipped over and crashed onto the stone floor. Her face smashed onto the surface with a sickening thud and bounced once. It sounded wet, like an overripe watermelon dropped from a height. There wasn't a sound from either woman now, both instantly muted by the crack of a skull on stone.

Furious, he set down the present out of sight and struggled to pull her upright. "Have you broken my head, you selfish bitch?" he screamed into her face as her head lolled from side to side. He was relieved when he heard a low moan. "There you are." He searched her face for damage. Her nose was broken, pushed to one side and flattened. There was a deep cut under her eye, the socket soft and pulpy under his fingertips. Something dark slid down the blood on her cheek. When he touched it, he realised it was a strip of false eyelashes. It looked like a dead spider, its black legs curled in on itself. He flicked it from his fingers in disgust.

He slapped her face once, twice, until she opened her eyes. "Wake up! Don't you dare sleep through my surprise." He retrieved the present from the side of the room and held it out so they could see it, his biceps straining under the weight of the glass dome. "This is Polly," he said proudly. "She is my favourite princess."

Polly's eyes were half open, eyelashes so brittle with frost they could snap off. The flesh of the cheeks sagged and pulled the other features down into a mask of misery, pink iridescent blusher stark against grey skin. Her mouth hung open with the yellow-white slice of pear stuck to her tongue, red lipstick smeared. The torn, ragged flesh around the neck glistened, bruised in shades of green and black.

Ben searched their faces, but it took some time for the women to react, as if they were incapable of comprehending what they were looking at. He held his breath in the silence that swelled, anticipation building as if he were in a theatre and the play was about to begin. Then the curtain went up and muffled screams pushed against gags, exhausted limbs struggled against bindings. He indulged them for a while and then demanded a respectful silence for Polly.

"She is my greatest achievement so far, although I had so much to work with. She was a natural beauty, the perfect Snow White." He looked at the two women before him, disappointment increasing in the back of his mind. He'd have to work much harder with them.

Perhaps their reaction to Polly's entrance would have been more enthusiastic if he hadn't drawn their attention to the empty glass domes the night before. Their bodily functions cleaner if he hadn't shown them the cheese wires and knives, the leather butcher's apron that would cover him from head to toe – but he had shown them. Foreplay was so important.

"You were wondering about the empty domes, weren't you?" He looked from one to the other, but they didn't seem to be listening anymore, which was very discourteous considering the effort he'd made. "I wanted you to be excited. Have I been wasting my time, Snow White?" He grabbed the brunette by the jaw and yanked her head round to face him. There was defiance staring back through her tears. "Isn't it nice to have something to look forward to?" They were both sobbing so loudly it drowned out his words. "Enough!" He moved across the room to the table and picked up the knife.

Can you do it? Really? He was startled by the sound of that other voice, the doubtful one that made him feel weak, insipid, and not up to the task. *You're not strong enough to get rid of her. She'll never go away – not for long. She'll be back, like a stain, no matter how hard you scrub.*

The whisper worked its way in like woodworm, making him less stable on his feet, less sure of his endeavours.

That's it. Walk away. Hide, before it's too late. Stop. Stop!

But he wouldn't listen. What difference would another three deaths make when he was already so far in, so deep in blood it dragged around his ankles? He was the Grimm Creeper, capable of writing his own ending, and he was almost home. All he had to do was find a way to be close to Emma, close enough to see if she tasted as good as she looked.

Goldilocks sobbed and pleaded with her bruised, swollen eyes, but that emotion was far too small to have any impact on him. Snow White's eyes held a disgust, a fury far too big to look at for long. But bringing the blade down twice and feeling the spray of warm blood colour him with two happy endings – that felt just right.

24

Emma had never seen Annie so angry before. Her body vibrated as if she were outside shivering in the cold rather than inside the overheated therapy room. She twisted a strand of greasy hair around her index finger. It looked as if it hadn't been washed in days. Emma suspected that no part of Annie had been washed in days. The warmth of the room intensified her stale odour; musky and bitter, it came off her in waves.

Emma met her combative glare with quiet confidence while maintaining a neutral expression. If she allowed Annie to steep in the silence pulsing in the room, she would eventually calm down. Annie didn't like to lose control. Her surroundings had shaped her into the woman she was now – endlessly watched and equally watchful. She'd once told Emma a person couldn't afford to lose control in a place filled with violent and volatile offenders. Showing weakness was a form of surrender.

When she finally addressed Emma, her anger was simmering rather than boiling. "You're not wearing the hat I made. I watched you come through the gates outside, and you didn't have it on. Don't you like red? Or is it me you don't like?"

Emma took her time before replying. Annie wanted to play

one of her favourite games today: Queen Annie. She addressed Emma as though she were an inferior subject. It was what she usually did when she felt cornered.

"I like the hat you made for me very much," Emma said. "I have it with me, but it's too warm to wear it today. Tomorrow it's supposed to rain, so I'll wear it then and think of you. I'm intrigued by your question, though. Is it important whether I like you or not?"

Annie sat back in her chair with a smirk and folded her arms across her body. "Do you imagine for one minute that your opinion of me carries any weight?"

"So, why did you ask the question?"

"Because I want to know why you're here again if I'm not really your cup of tea. I told you I didn't want to talk to you anymore. We've said our goodbyes. But you seem to have missed the point, because here you are, prying and pushing. Talking makes me feel bad and it serves no purpose. Talking to you is beneath me. You are beneath me." She gestured towards Emma as if swatting a fly.

"Do you imagine for one minute that *your* opinion of *me* carries any weight?" countered Emma in a firm voice. It was a risky challenge, but one she thought worth making.

Annie looked momentarily stunned, but then burst into laughter. Her wide mouth revealed jagged, discoloured teeth. "Well, even if you don't like me, I like you. You're a strong one, aren't you? Refusing to take no for an answer. Refusing to hear an ending because you know there's still more of the story to come." Her dark eyes shone, but they appeared flat, devoid of the merriment contained in her laugh. She moved forwards in her chair and looked Emma straight in the eye. "You've read my files. You know why I'm here: too unpredictable for a normal prison, volatile and unstable, prone to violent mood swings and occasionally delusional, although I fail to see what's

191

wrong with deluding myself from time to time when this place is all the reality I'll ever know. Certifiably insane, to use an old-fashioned expression. I'm too dangerous for the world, unfit for human consumption, and yet here you are, wanting to eat me all up." She flicked her tongue across her lips, the movement reptilian. "Okay, Emma, we'll do it your way. It's feeding time."

Annie sat back in her chair and crossed her legs, tucking a limp, grey strand of hair behind her ear. She hesitated, as though tossing through her thoughts as she decided what to pick, but then she appeared to make a decision. Emma had already prepared herself for what she might hear today, knowing that if she pushed Annie further, she might have to endure a tale that would travel with her a long way down the road.

"I'm aware I have no control over being here today, that I have to attend therapy whether I want to or not," she said. "The only power I have is what I choose to reveal, and you can't make me talk about my father anymore. Surely you can't blame me for holding onto the one thing that keeps me warm at night." She ran her thumb back and forth across the prominent purple veins that protruded from the top of her hand like electrical cord.

Emma nodded. "What would you rather talk about? Therapy is only productive if you talk to me about the things you truly want to say, rather than the things you think I want to hear. I know you don't want to be here, but as you've said, you have no choice, so let's make the best of our time together. Perhaps getting some things off your chest will also help keep you warm at night."

Annie sighed, reluctant but resigned. "I'll tell you another secret – or more accurately, my biggest regret. Talking about that won't make me feel warm, but it will make me feel…" She moved her mouth from side to side as if savouring the taste of her words. "Clean."

"Alright." The air in the room stirred. Emma took a deep breath before it became too acrid and sat back in the hardwood chair.

"My biggest regret is that I became a mother, although not for the reasons you might expect. I should never have had a child. I should never have had children. I never once felt a maternal urge, like there was a hole in my life that needed to be filled. Motherhood just felt like a predictable route to go down – my only option, my natural role. But nothing about motherhood felt natural to me. It felt suffocating from the moment I became pregnant. A living thing inside me, moving and shifting about and making me sick. Controlling my body, my sleep, my appetite, my very existence, taking me over and living off me like a parasite. I didn't belong to myself anymore. I was an incubator, a source of blood for a leech. And then when it was born, I was just a source of milk. I tried breastfeeding it a few times, but I found it repugnant." Annie shuddered, her face filled with revulsion. "The sight of that little wet mouth sucking at me was one of the most disgusting things I have ever experienced." The tendons in her neck were taut and strained against her skin as if trying to tear through it. "To bear children, what an apt description that is: *to bear*. To tolerate, to endure." She squeezed her eyes closed. "Well, I couldn't *bear* it."

Emma waited for her to continue. The story had caught her off guard, but for all that it felt closer to the truth at last. She could see that Annie was troubled, lost in the past, and Emma was forcing her to revisit it. She started to question the validity of the exercise but decided to stick with it for now. She had to trust the process of therapy – a painful history was better expressed than repressed and allowed to fester.

Shifting in her chair, Annie went on. "Women just had kids back then, almost without allowing for the possibility of another way of life. I got married, and I gave birth. And then

I waited for the love to happen, that love that I was supposed to feel as a mother, the one that's supposed to come naturally, powerfully, the mother instinct – but it never came. The bigger the baby grew, the smaller I became, until it felt like I was disappearing under the weight of motherhood. The older it got, the more I resented it. The more needy it was, the more I pushed it away. I did what I had to: I looked after it and fed it and tried to play the role of a loving mother – my version of it anyway – but I hated every minute, every crying, vomiting, feeding, shitting minute. Each time I looked at its helpless little body, that large lolling head on a useless weak neck, I wanted to hurt it. I couldn't stand its weakness, its dependence on me, because it made me feel like I could lose control. It made me want to do something violent, something so spiteful that it would go away for good." Annie was crying now but seemed oblivious to the tears. Once again, she throbbed with anger.

Hot tears welled up in Emma's eyes and her throat tightened. This sudden and powerful surge of emotion surprised her. The woman opposite her was a convicted child abuser, a mother who had abused both the trust and the body of her own child. She had taken something sacred and smashed it into pieces until it was taken away from her dangerous and destructive hands. Annie had committed one of life's worst crimes, and yet Emma felt sympathy move inside her. As a therapist, she was supposed to withhold judgement and facilitate understanding. Her job was to focus on Annie and not her crime. She had to separate those two things if she was to perform her role responsibly.

Annie's life had been about a lack of choice from beginning to end. How could she have been expected to make the right choices for herself as an adult when she'd had no choices as a child growing up with an abusive father and a colluding mother?

As the tears slid into the wrinkles of Annie's pale skin, Emma wondered how many women felt the same way, doing what was expected of them rather than what felt right. How many mothers regretted having their children? How many mothers dared ask themselves that question, knowing it was an irreversible decision? Emma was lucky: she'd been able to choose that motherhood wasn't for her, and she felt certain and secure in her choice, never more so than when it was questioned by colleagues or friends. *Change is slow to come.* Too slow for women like Annie. Her choice had come too late, presented itself as a possibility to a different generation.

Emma knew how she would feel if she'd been pressured to become a mother. Trapped – an onlooker over her own life. Her empathy for Annie felt powerful, but she had to control those feelings and remain aware of their power. She couldn't allow them to manipulate the way she proceeded with Annie. She couldn't allow herself to become too soft in her questioning. It wouldn't help either of them.

"Where was your husband in all this?" Emma asked. "Didn't he help you, support you in any way?"

Annie snorted with laughter, a cruel look pulling her papery skin taut. "He was useless, one of those spineless, invisible fathers who goes off and leaves the children for the mother to deal with because it's women's work. He abandoned us. He didn't care."

Emma knew this wasn't true but resisted challenging Annie's version of the story. A patient's interpretation of events was often more revealing than the event itself. "You said you were afraid of what you might do to your child, that you might do something spiteful. How do you feel about what you did eventually do to him?"

Annie's head snapped around so quickly her neck cracked. Her lips turned white as she drew them tightly back across her yellow teeth, and her swollen, bloodshot eyes fixed on Emma coldly and without blinking, dark and wet. *Black ice.* Treacherous, dangerous, and unpredictable.

"I feel nothing. Absolutely nothing." Annie's voice was quiet and controlled but humming with fury. "What did you imagine? That I would be wracked by guilt, burdened by a heavy conscience that keeps me awake at night? The only thing I regret is the motherhood that brought me here, to this filthy place. I know you'd like me to think it was my own actions, but the truth is he did this to me. My son: that whining, snivelling, weak little worm who told tales the minute he didn't get his own way. A pathetic, needy parasite who sucked me dry before he was even born, and then took up all my space. He determined how I lived, where I went. He wrote all the rules, and now here he is running around free in the world. He took away my world in every possible way, continues to take it still." A white sticky crust had formed in the corners of her mouth.

Emma had been waiting for a confession of guilt from Annie, but realised she was unlikely to hear one. Annie wasn't looking for salvation because she didn't see herself as doing wrong, but rather being wronged. Emma knew the challenge was helping Annie to understand that being part of an abusive cycle across generations meant she was both. But for now, Annie only saw her version of the truth. She didn't care if it wasn't the right truth – the one that Emma thought should come out – she cared only that it was hers.

"Do you know what the most remarkable thing is? The most disgusting thing of all?" Annie's clipped voice was building in volume. "He still comes here to visit me. He still won't leave me alone. As soon as he turned eighteen and was legally able to make a choice, he chose me. After everything that happened. The first Saturday of each month, there he is. Sometimes I look forward to his visit to break up the routine, but as soon as I see that desperate, needy look on his face, I want my routine back. He still loves me. He still misses me after all this time, and there is nothing more pathetic than a son who still needs his mummy when he's all grown up. That's why I don't feel guilty. If he had the chance, he'd go back to warm baths and bedtime stories and our special little world that was supposed to be a secret." Annie was shouting now. "He would still cling to me and grab at me and suck me dry. He still loves me, and yet he makes my stomach turn."

She was almost out of her seat, so close to Emma that the angry words peppered her skin. The white substance congealing at the sides of Annie's mouth stretched in strands like the skin on boiled milk. Behind the door, the orderlies looked on with concern, prepared to intervene if necessary.

Annie's words were a torrent. "He's trapped me in this miserable fucking place while a monstrous, bloodsucking tick like him is free to roam the world and break rules I would never contemplate breaking. Isn't that ironic? He is free, and I'm the one behind bars. I'm the one who's supposed to be a danger to myself and others, and yet he's the unpredictable one. He tells me about what he does as if it counts in some way, as if I fucking care. He tells me with pride in his voice, as if his actions are his triumphs, his glorious achievements. Of course, what he wants me to feel is envy. He's replicating what we had together with other women as if that will hurt me. His mummy's attention is still important, but all I feel when he tells me about what he's done, who he is now, is relief. Relief that someone else has to endure him, *bear* him, that he's somebody else's problem now."

Annie stood above Emma, her words landing wet and hot on Emma's face. Her body odour was pungent, but it was more than just stale sweat; it smelt like sickness, as if the internal had become external. Emma leaned away, as if Annie's sickness were contagious.

The door crashed open and two orderlies rushed in to take Annie away. Emma stood up with relief and moved behind her chair, a safe distance from Annie's clenched fists.

"Do you know what the best thing is, Emma? You're his type. I've told him all about you. I've even pointed you out to him on one of his intolerable visits. My needy, pathetic little prince would love to meet you and turn you into one of his princesses. You would make the perfect couple, the two people who won't leave me alone rubbing up against each other until he sucks you dry, until I never have to endure either one of you again."

Emma was shaking as the orderlies cuffed Annie and dragged her from the room, but Annie had the last word – she always did.

"I hope you both fucking live happily ever after."

After the door slammed closed and Annie was gone, the silence was profound, but her words still echoed off the walls. Emma could feel them bouncing against the rafters and landing on the back of her neck. Annie's smell, indecent in its intimacy, coated the back of Emma's throat and became tangled in her hair. Her heart pounded in her chest and blood rushed in her head. Breathless with tension, her legs unstable, she collapsed back into the chair. She had come up against violent offenders often in her work at the prison hospital, but this was the first time she had experienced true fear.

Emma sat very still and breathed deeply and slowly until her fear subsided and the taste of Annie was gone from her mouth. She thought about Annie's parting words and wondered if she should be concerned for her safety. Was her son someone to fear or pity?

Emma packed her bag and prepared to leave, seriously

considering whether she should ever come back. She decided to stop by the senior psychologist's office on the way out and relay to her what had transpired in today's session. It crossed her mind that she could ask Sam to check out Annie's son, but she dismissed the idea. They would both be breaching ethical guidelines. Still, the idea lingered. Was she looking for an excuse to call him? She would have welcomed the comfort, just the sound of his voice, but she had to resist.

As Emma knocked at the doctor's door, she felt a wave of sympathy for Annie's son, a man who was so damaged, so broken, that he never failed to visit the one who had broken him. She hoped he was getting the support he so obviously needed and had found some way to live a happy, meaningful life.

Dr Florence Tice beckoned Emma to come in and sit down. "Are you okay?" She frowned. "You're looking a touch pale." She removed her glasses and pushed her unruly grey hair away from her face; it sprang back immediately.

"I've just had a run-in with Annie. She was incredibly angry at the end of her session. The orderlies had to remove her." Emma accepted an offer of water and drank quickly, a little of it dripping down her chin. "I also feel some concern for her son's wellbeing – and my own, to be honest."

Dr Tice passed her a tissue. "How so?"

"She told me I was her son's type. The way she said it, it felt like a threat."

Emma was aware she was talking too quickly, residual fear controlling the pace of her words. She inhaled deeply and finally noticed the scent of lilies in the room.

The doctor glanced at Emma's shaking hands. "Take a second to organise your thoughts and summarise the end of the session for me."

Emma did so and then reached for more water. "I don't

know how much I'm helping her. I feel very deflated – and a bit nauseous." She rubbed her stomach and noticed adrenaline was causing her hands to tremble.

Dr Tice gave her a reassuring smile as she removed an elastic band from her wrist and twisted her hair into an untidy top knot. "It sounds like Annie let go of a great deal of anger today because she discussed something deeply personal, something shameful. Even though she might not have fully processed that shame, it's there."

Emma nodded her agreement and clasped her hands in an attempt to control the shaking.

"Let me ask you: if she hadn't expressed that anger, what would it have turned into?"

She wiped lily pollen from the table, the tips of her fingers turning saffron yellow.

Emma didn't have to think about her answer. "Depression." Depression was often suppressed anger. With her mind in such turmoil, she had forgotten a basic principle of her work.

"Right, so let's reassess. If you hadn't pushed Annie today, all of that anger would still be inside her. Instead, it's been expelled, and now it has less power to fester." She tilted her head. "Still think you aren't helping her?"

Emma smiled. She felt calmer now. "Thanks, Florence. That's reassuring to hear." She finished her glass of water. "Did you know that her son is her only visitor?"

Dr Tice nodded and rested her chin in her hands as she studied Emma's face.

Emma wondered what drove a victim of abuse to visit the abuser he'd been rescued from. She could only assume Annie's son was so ensnared by the vicious cycle of abuse that his feelings for her were still wrapped in an unnatural form of love. That he was as incapable of turning his back on her as Annie had been with her father.

"Have you met him?" she asked.

"Once or twice, after the visits with his mother," Dr Tice replied. She sat back and twisted her wedding ring around her finger.

"And?" asked Emma, her attention caught by the light glinting from Dr Tice's ring.

"I seem to recall sweaty hands and a tendency to stand too close, but other than that, he seemed meek, almost child-like." She absentmindedly reached for her glasses and cleaned them on the front of her shirt. "I think he regresses during the visits with his mother. I'm going to get in touch with him and suggest a family therapy session with you. I think having Annie and her son sit down with you could be very useful."

It was the classic triangle of family therapy. Two opponents and the therapist as mediator.

"We need to assess him," Dr Tice added. "It would be negligent of us to allow visits with his mother to continue if they're damaging him any further. But ultimately, it's not our decision, it's his. Let's do the family session and go from there. Do you feel comfortable with that?"

Emma nodded and offered her thanks as she headed towards the door, but before she left Dr Tice called her back.

"Emma, you are a well-trained, highly effective therapist. Don't forget that. I'm sure Annie's son will benefit enormously from a meeting with you." She put her glasses back on as Emma left and closed the door softly behind her.

25

The night was closing in, the navy-blue sky giving way to deep purple. It was still pleasantly warm despite the late hour, and Sam didn't mind spending the evening in the jasmine-scented courtyard of the pub close to work rather than at the swimming pool. It was Riley's idea to have the meeting over dinner and a bottle of chilled rosé. He thought briefing Superintendent Hepburn on the latest developments in the Creeper case would go down more easily with pleasant wine in pleasant surroundings, but that wasn't the way the conversation was going. There had been no new developments to report, and Nina had taken the pressure that her superiors had placed on her shoulders and in turn placed it on Sam and Riley's, where it sat heavily.

Nina insisted that a press conference be held first thing the following morning. "The media are starting to turn. Their enthusiasm for the so-called Creeper Crew is waning, gentlemen. Their tone is starting to sound like thinly veiled criticism." She took a large gulp of her drink, sighing more with what seemed like irritation than pleasure at the chilled wine.

"I've seen the articles," Sam said. "The press is now writing about the case as if it's a melodrama, our victims the tragic heroines – and we are becoming the villains." He moved the bottle of wine to one side, condensation sliding down the label and onto his fingers. He wiped them on his napkin and rolled a cigarette. The smell of garlic coming from the pizza oven in the corner drifted across the courtyard and overpowered the jasmine. "Their frustration is all over the front pages."

"I can't say I enjoy seeing my photograph below a headline accusing us of apathy," said Riley, as he swiped at a mosquito. "We're working around the clock."

"Precisely." Nina pointed a finger at both Sam and Riley. "The public and the press need to know that even if the Grimm Creeper is still at large, our search for him is ongoing and thorough. So, before we top up our glasses, let's draft this statement and be ready to go in the morning." She pushed her glass to one side and scooted her chair around the table so she would be closer to Riley and Sam. It was best that no one overheard them, even though the nearest table had just paid the bill and left.

Together Riley and Sam drafted the statement with Nina, wording it as carefully as their previous press briefings.

"Teams are still in place at all the locations where the victims were found," Riley said. "We've been following up on tips from the public, but so far nothing has come from them."

Many of them were time-wasters intent on false confessions and fame. The team was doing everything in their power to find the Grimm Creeper, but he eluded them still, melting back into the shadows of the city.

By the time Nina left, her mood had improved. Sam and Riley decided to soften the impact of her words with another bottle of wine before the bar called time. Despite the tension-filled meeting, Sam was enjoying his evening. It had been a long time since he'd eaten a meal prepared by someone other than himself, and even longer since he'd savoured it. He would have to swim a couple of extra lengths at the pool to make up for tonight's missed session, but he pushed that to the back of his mind as he rolled a cigarette.

Sam's eyes felt heavy by the time he and Riley left the pub, and he was also feeling a little drunk, so he decided to sober up by walking the long way home via St John Street rather than cutting through the Golden Lane Estate. Although the street was busy and he had to swerve frequently into the road to avoid the boisterous, drunk gatherings outside various pubs and bars, walking this way meant he could keep his distance from the Barbican centre. He hadn't been back there since the discovery of Polly's body. He had even foregone a pre-booked trip to the theatre so he could avoid the Barbican altogether. The memory of that awful morning was seared onto his brain, just like all the other mornings when the previous victims had been discovered.

Sam turned off Old Street, which was busy with Friday night revellers, and walked down Ironmonger Row. As he neared home, he searched his pockets for his keys and checked his phone for messages. There was one from his father letting him know he had been to Sam's apartment to drop off the box of Sam's old books that he had asked for. Sam had already bought another copy of *Grimms' Fairy Tales* but was looking forward to rummaging through the box of his childhood books that had been stored in his father's musty attic for years.

Head down, reading his texts, he turned the corner by St Luke's church and ran straight into someone. Embarrassed by his self-absorption, he was halfway through an apology before he realised who it was.

"Emma." The volume of his voice was raised by both wine and excitement. "It's lovely to see you. What are you doing here?"

A light breeze ruffled her hair, a strand blowing into her eyes. The lights from the church peeped between the tall branches of the sweet chestnut trees in the graveyard, the gentle wind rustling the leaves and carrying with it the aroma of ginger and lemon grass from the nearby Thai restaurant.

Emma laughed. "It's lovely to see you, too. Although strange to run into you away from my office." She rubbed the shoulder that Sam had bumped into. "Literally."

"I'm so sorry. Are you okay?" Sam touched her shoulder before he realised that might be a little familiar. He lowered his hand and hoped the darkness hid his embarrassment. "I'm a little the worse for wine I'm afraid." He found he was struggling to reach the intimacy he'd shared with Emma in her office. Their deeper connection felt too raw for exposure out in the world. He didn't know how to behave with her now their relationship had evolved beyond therapy. He wondered whether it was even right to assume that it had.

"Or the better." Emma smiled reassuringly at him, as if she could sense his confusion. "I'm fine, don't worry. I've just been swimming the last session at Ironmonger Row, so my arms are sore anyway. Were you drinking nearby?" She brushed the hair from her face and ran her fingers through it.

Sam noticed the way the lights from the church illuminated Emma's face as if daring him to touch. He thought he could detect her perfume, something zesty and clean that reminded him of freshly cut grass drying under the sun. Perhaps a little chlorine too, smells that he associated with long, hot days that melted seamlessly into long, hot nights. It was as if Emma carried summer on her skin.

"Sam?" Emma waved her hand in front of Sam's eyes trying to attract his attention. "I asked if you were drinking somewhere close by." She laughed and pushed her hair behind her ears.

"I was," said Sam, realising he hadn't responded to Emma's question. He wondered how long he had been staring at her. "But I'm on my way home. I'm shattered. My bed is feeling very tempting right now." As if on cue he felt the beginnings of a yawn tugging at the corners of his mouth.

"It is," replied Emma. Abruptly, her smile disappeared, and her eyes widened. "Er… I meant…" She fell silent and stared at him.

Sam raised his eyebrows and the need to yawn vanished. He tried to think of something to say, but all he could manage was a grin, which made him feel silly and inadequate.

Emma stuttered. "What I meant to say is, my bed, er… my bed is tempting… For me." She laughed awkwardly and muttered something he didn't catch. She stared at the church intently and appeared to have made the decision to stop talking.

Sam laughed the moment off, an uncomfortable silence avoided, but only just. Emma was looking down at her shoes, over his shoulder, anywhere but his face. He thought he should spare her blushes, although he wanted the moment to linger.

"Sounds as if we both need to catch up on our rest, perhaps sleeping in late tomorrow?" Sam said, as he made to turn and head off.

Emma seemed relieved that Sam had broken the silence. "That would be lovely, but unfortunately I have a family therapy session at the prison first thing in the morning." She sighed. "So, I should get going." She didn't move. "I suppose."

The sound of boisterous laughter reached them from further down the street, merriment drowned out by a loud motorbike engine speeding past.

"Actually, Sam, I wondered if I might ask you a favour. It's about one of my patients. She has a…" Emma paused for a few seconds. "On second thoughts, don't worry." She shook her head. "It's not important." She smiled at him.

"Are you sure? I'm happy to help if I can," he replied.

"No, that's okay," she answered. "Thanks, though."

They stared at each other, the moment stretching out until the chiming of the church clock roused them.

"Well, I guess I'll see you back in your office." He moved around her as she mumbled goodnight and he headed towards home. As he turned the corner, he glanced over his shoulder. Emma did the same. He could see her smiling at him, the church lights making her eyes glitter. They stared back at each other for a long time, each of them seeming unsure whether to walk away, and Sam felt the exchange of intimacy after all. Eventually, she turned and walked away. He watched her leave, stared at the space under the lights long after she'd vacated it. He felt wrapped in her summer scent even though she was gone. *She looked back at me.* Her smile followed him all the way home.

Sam let himself into the main entrance of his building and emptied his mailbox before taking the lift up to his floor. The lift was one of the modern additions to the post-war warehouse but opened onto original floorboards rubbed smooth by decades of use. He unlocked his apartment and dropped his mail onto the table by the front door. The rooms were stuffy, so he opened the windows in the living room to allow a cool breeze to circulate. He dropped down onto the leather sofa, feeling sleepy but contented after seeing Emma. He knew he'd never forget the way she had looked at him before walking away. It seemed to offer such tenderness, the promise of a future. He wanted to be held under her gaze. Always.

It had been another long day, now well past midnight, and Sam kicked off his shoes and turned his attention to the cardboard box his father had dropped off. The box was years old, a relic from the long since defunct removal company that had relocated Sam and his father from the countryside of Surrey to Richmond just after Sam's mother had died. The cardboard was soft and smelt a little damp. It looked as if it would open easily – the tape holding the top closed was dry and barely sticky. But before he could open the box and embrace the rare moment of nostalgia, exhaustion and too much wine caught up with him; he gave in and stretched out on the sofa.

The sun was rising when his ringing mobile woke him, but by the time Sam found his phone on top of the pile of mail by the front door, the ringing had stopped. It was Riley. That was strange. He thought Riley would still be fast asleep. He had looked exhausted by the time they'd left the pub. He gathered his mail and took the phone into the kitchen to recharge it. He needed to return Riley's call, but he needed a drink first, the wine had left him dry-mouthed and dehydrated. He filled a glass with cold tap water, drank deeply, and then became distracted by his mail. Amongst the regular bills was a padded envelope that had no stamp. It must have been hand-delivered.

As Sam opened the envelope, what appeared to be breadcrumbs tumbled out, covering the kitchen table in small, dusty piles. Confused, Sam dumped out the remaining contents, also covered with breadcrumbs. There was a thick plait of hair, brunette and blonde woven together and held in place by an elastic band at either end. He wasn't sure what to make of it until he saw a neatly sliced section of pear, stiff but sticky to the touch. His skin went absolutely cold. The final object was a note written in a neat, flamboyant hand on white paper and placed inside a resealable plastic bag, the author obviously mindful that the ink would run if it came into contact with the pear.

Sam's hands shook as he read the letter through the plastic.

Dear Sam,
We have met only once, and yet I feel I know you so

well. I've been paying attention to you, Sam. Do you feel flattered?

I've watched you at work, tired and stressed and lost in the dark. Am I wearing you out? Will I be the death of you? I'm not allowing you much free time, am I?

It's just as well you have nobody to go home to, because you're rarely home.

I know your routines. You like your coffee strong and with a cigarette, a nasty little habit that is almost as dangerous as me – almost, but not quite. I could smell the smoke on you when we were close enough to touch.

I know where you go to pour your heart out. Do you talk about me? Is she as patient as she seems when you tell her stories about the Creeper, or do they wipe the smile from her pretty mouth? She's more than just a therapist to you, isn't she?

Do you think about me in the early hours when you walk around your flat? You really ought to try and get more sleep, Sam. Or are you too busy wondering where I am?

Sometimes I'm right where you think I am, watching the people who are supposed to be watching for me. Sometimes the Creeper is right behind you.

Now that we're friends, I'll tell you a secret, one you can share. Snow White and Goldilocks are waiting for you, sleeping the last sleep just like all the others. Their time has come. They died not so happily ever after. You are too late. A kiss won't wake them now.

They're waiting for you. Just follow the breadcrumbs to find what the Creeper has left for you this time. But it won't be the last time.

When there are eight, you will be too late.

The Creeper is going to live happily ever after. Will you?

Sam dropped the note as if it were on fire and stepped back from the table so abruptly that his sleeve caught the glass of water and sent it smashing to the floor. He swore loudly while running his hands through his hair. His breath was shallow. Adrenaline started to pump, narrowing his field of vision, and his arms and legs shook.

Riley. He needed to call Riley. He needed to call the team.

Sam ran frantically from room to room in search of his phone, but then he heard it ringing from the kitchen where he had left it charging. He ran back and grabbed it. Riley's voice was loud and urgent with the same panic Sam felt.

"There are two bodies, Sam. The Creeper has killed again, two this time," Riley shouted, his words crashing over each other.

"Where are they?" Sam asked, breathless and tense. He could hear other voices in the background, sirens and squealing tyres.

"Barnsbury Square," Riley shouted over the screaming sirens.

"Are you coming to pick me up?" Sam realised he had no shoes on, his socks turning damp as he stood in the puddle of spilled water.

"I'm five minutes away. Be waiting outside." The phone went dead.

Sam changed his socks and put on his shoes. He looked around for something to put the Creeper's letter in and grabbed a brown paper bag that he hadn't yet placed in the recycling bin. He had already contaminated the evidence when he'd opened the envelope and gone through the contents, but he used his arm to scoop the note, pear, breadcrumbs and hair into the bag. He grabbed his phone and ran to the front door, only just remembering to pick up his keys before he slammed the door behind him.

He pushed the glowing red button repeatedly to summon the lift, even though he knew that wouldn't make it come any faster. It seemed to take forever to arrive and then an eternity to reach the ground floor, Sam breathing heavily all the while and turning in small circles inside the confined space. Where could he have met the Creeper? How could he not have known it at the time? On some level he should have known who he was, should have been able to feel it. It infuriated him that the Creeper had been watching him, had intruded so far into his life that he knew all these things about him. It was far too close for comfort. The Creeper might have ridden in the very lift he was standing in, but that thought disappeared as the doors opened onto the lobby. Riley's car screeched to a stop outside. Sam ran towards the main door clutching the brown bag, his heart still thudding in his chest as he stepped out into the morning chill.

With the lights flashing, Sam and Riley drove at speed down City Road before turning off onto Upper Street in Islington. From there, it would be a short journey to Barnsbury Square. As they drove, Sam read the letter to Riley.

"Jesus Christ, Sam, this fucker knows where you live! He's been watching you, stalking you. Why has he written to you? Why has he killed two this time? It's too soon. We thought we had until September. What the fuck is he doing?"

Flashing blue lights told Sam the scene was just up ahead. The usually peaceful square was filled with police officers and homeowners who stood outside their elegant houses – hair dishevelled, faces confused, in hastily thrown-on outfits. There was fear in their eyes. Others leaned sleepy heads out of bedroom windows to see what was going on in their usually sedate neighbourhood so early on a Saturday morning. Sam used his gloved hand to push aside the metal gate on one side of the small garden square.

There were officers stationed at each of the garden's three entrances, two of whom were taking a statement from the old lady who had discovered the bodies while walking her dog just after the gates had been unlocked. Farther in, a ring of detectives stood protectively around the two bodies that had been placed in the central area of the square. As Sam and Riley followed the path into the paved, tree-enclosed circle in the middle of the gardens, Sam noticed torn pieces of white bread scattered along the path, the breadcrumbs left by a killer who wanted the police to follow them like *Hansel and Gretel*. They couldn't have been there long; surely a fox or rat would have stolen them away by now. It meant the bodies had been recently dumped. An all too familiar sense of dread descended onto Sam's shoulders as he approached the bodies, a sweet odour, jarring and out of place, was underlying the smell of damp grass.

Members of the Creeper Crew moved to one side to allow Riley and Sam access. The bodies were still warm, blood oozing into the cracks of the paving stones, glistening and reflecting the canopy of leaves above. As in the previous cases, the women's heads were missing, and they held their gelatinous hearts in their hands. Unlike the previous cases, the bodies lay in an untidy pile, thrown rather than carefully placed, the legs of both victims tangled like coils of thick rope. Only the arms were intentionally positioned so that the hearts might be neatly placed.

This time both of the victims were naked, the gaping, ragged hole in their chests making the left breast of each woman sag at an unnatural angle, the blood covering each of them like a red shroud. The women had matching tattoos of dolphins on their stomachs.

Sam pointed to them and said to Riley, "Do you think they were friends?"

"Could be," Riley said, his voice subdued.

Each body was also covered in bruises and wounds around the ankles and wrists, the same rope burns as the previous victims, but this time the wounds were still fresh and raw. Sam also thought he could see bite marks on the inner thighs of each woman, which was something new, but he couldn't be sure until the bodies had been examined more closely. He felt sick, but it was an emotional sickness as well as a physical one.

As he squatted closer to the bodies, he was overwhelmed by the warm, sickly smell of blood, sharp and metallic and underscored by a synthetic sweetness. The scene felt alive despite the presence of death, and it made Sam feel as if they had only been a little late, just a little too late to save them. These women had been alive a short time ago, and this knowledge filled Sam with a new level of despair. A powerful rage made him shake. Riley touched him gently on the shoulder.

They moved away from the bodies and sat down on one of the nearby benches, the wood chilly and damp on the back of Sam's trousers. The slimy trail of a slug glittered on the ground near his feet.

"What do you think, Sam? This scene is different. No comb, no red hat, no pears, no sign of the victim's shoes and other possessions. No careful displays. It feels like a bloody rush job. Is he losing control?"

Sam nodded. "Yes, this is far more frenzied. He was more vicious this time, took far less care with the staging. He isn't sticking to his schedule. If the hair in the package he sent me is anything to go by, then his tastes have become less particular, too."

"Meaning?" Riley sounded calmer now, focused on the job at hand.

"Meaning he's less concerned with who he kills and more concerned with the killing itself." Sam pushed his initial shock aside to make room for clarity.

213

"And the missing clues?" Riley glanced at the bodies. The grey whiskers on his face caught the light as the sun continued to climb.

"I'd say he hasn't left the usual clues because he knows he doesn't have to. He left the letter. He doesn't have to play with us anymore." Sam realised he was talking too loudly. He took a breath and continued more quietly. "The wording of the letter is also strange."

"How so?" Riley looked up as a sudden gust of warm wind moved through the trees and dislodged a few sun-dried leaves onto the ground in front of them.

"Sometimes he talks about himself in the third person, writing 'the Creeper' instead of 'I', which means he is disassociating himself on some level." The wind dried the perspiration on the back of Sam's neck, making him shiver. Both he and Riley were wearing yesterday's clothes. He wondered if he'd ever seen Riley without a tie.

Riley ran a hand through his hair. "Why, though?"

"My guess is a small part of him is ashamed of what he's doing, that he wants to remove himself from the murders. It could also mean he sees the Creeper as a different person, someone other than himself who tells him what to do. But either way, he's never been more dangerous. He's starting to panic, to evolve into someone who is more desperate to reach the magic number than remain hidden. He said when he reaches eight, I'll be too late." Sam shook his head. "Maybe this is my fault. I told you to goad him."

"There is only one person at fault here and it's not you. Besides, we haven't got time for second guessing right now." Riley squeezed his shoulder. "We have to catch him, Sam." Riley kicked at the leaves around his feet, grinding them under his heel until they were dust.

"Yes. We do. Because I think this can only end in one

of two ways: once he reaches eight, he'll disappear. He'll feel his work here is done. There'll be no reason to play with us anymore because the game will be over. If that happens, we'll never find him. He's too smart." Sam attempted to control the panic that was tightening his chest.

"And the other way?" Riley asked in a tone that made him sound unsure of wanting the answer.

"The other way is that he reaches eight and realises it isn't enough. It hasn't worked. His pain still needs an outlet. If that's the way this goes, then he'll never stop." Sam took a deep breath and hesitated. "I think it's going to be the second scenario, Albert. He won't stop killing. He stepped out of his comfort zone last night. Even if he hasn't admitted it to himself yet, deep down he knows there's no comfort to be found."

Riley appeared unsurprised by Sam's words. "Why is he letting us know he plans to kill again?" The lines on his face creased into a frown.

"Because he doesn't think we're going to catch him," Sam said. "He thinks he's smarter than we are." The tension across his shoulders was so tight that he wanted to curl into himself and just surrender.

"But he must know we'll do everything in our power to prevent him from killing his eighth victim. Is he that out of control?"

Sam couldn't help looking into the crowd of onlookers. Was he there? Right there, watching them talk about him? He shook himself back to the conversation and said, "I think it's more than that. We're dealing with a psychopath here, a narcissist who thinks he's above making mistakes. Nothing will distract him from his goal. It's similar to a bank robber who can't resist one last job because this will be the one to make his fortune. Currently, the Creeper believes victim number eight will be his last job, the one that will allow him to go out on a high, and he'll take the risk because he thinks he can get away with it." Sam felt his stomach turn as the cloying smell of the bodies reached him again. He closed his eyes and massaged his temples, trying to push away the headache that was starting to throb. He went on. "I also think this might be a mistake on the Creeper's part. He can't resist bragging. It's like he's daring us to catch him."

Riley rubbed his fists into his eyes. "Right. We need to head back to the office and plan our next move. Let the SOCOs do their job."

"We should probably wake Nina up," Sam said.

"We have to wake everybody up and get to work. He's close by. I can feel it. We can't let this bastard win. Perhaps we'll get lucky and find a clue this time. If he is losing control, then maybe he's made a mistake, left evidence behind."

"Maybe the bite marks will tell us something," Sam said.

"Maybe. In the meantime, I'm leaving the rest of the team here in case he comes back, and I'm pulling in every other officer I can find. I'll pull them off other cases if I have to. I'm also sending someone to pick up Emma Malone. If he's mentioned her in his letter, then we need to make sure she's safe. We can't afford to take any chances."

Emma. Sam turned cold and started to shake, this time with fear. He should have suggested they pick up Emma as soon as he'd read the Creeper's letter. If anything happened to her…

"Fuck!" he cried suddenly. "Jesus fucking Christ! Emma is the mistake! I think he's telling us she's going to be his next victim. He's so fucking arrogant and deluded that he thinks he can tell us what he's about to do, and we still won't catch him. We have to get to her now, Albert. She lives close by, near the Angel, I think. If we don't find her first, she won't be the Creeper's mistake – she'll be ours."

Riley barked orders at the nearest officer to find out where Emma lived and then call him with the address. He then beckoned Sam and four members of the team to follow him. As he headed towards the closest exit, Riley phoned the station and informed them he needed an armed unit ready to be dispatched to Emma's as soon as he relayed her address.

Sam followed Riley and the officers out of the square and back to the car just as a light summer shower started to fall. He glanced back at the scene in the square as the SOCOs rushed to assemble a canopy above the bodies. He turned his face upwards and allowed the cool drops to splash down onto his face, hoping they would disguise the tears welling up in his eyes.

Riley looked at him over the top of the car. "Don't worry, Sam, we'll head towards the Angel now and we'll find her. I'm sure she's okay." He opened the car door. "We're going to get this fucker."

26

This time it was a close call. Ben scrambled over the fence by a small wooden hut just as the milkman passed by the gardens, his clinking bottles disturbing the silence of the square. If he had looked more closely, he might have seen Ben, might have heard him breathing heavily from his exertions, but delivering the milk before the day started had been his priority, and the Creeper had always been good at blending into the background. He was sure nobody had seen him slipping out of his overalls and driving off. He was the Creeper after all, and he had been very quiet. The temptation to wait for Sam afterwards, to see his reaction to the latest – if slightly rushed – masterpiece, had almost made him turn around and go back, but the blank wall was a stronger temptation, and there was still so much mess to make.

The odour that was usually confined to the basement crawled up the stairs like a fat, wet earthworm emerging from a dark hole. It made its way around the old butcher shop as if purveying the meat once displayed there and then slipped under the door and up into the kitchen where it hung in the room, sweet and fetid. He inhaled deeply. The scent of fresh death was delectable, enticing. It meant two more princesses were fast asleep and awaiting their glass coffins. They were somewhat inferior to what he was used to – a little gaudy – but still too good for a sealed, dark box, especially after all that effort. They would be passable on the bottom shelf of the freezer.

He stripped off his clothes and headed down to the basement, the drop in temperature cold against his naked skin. He could hear the drone of the flies that had found their way inside, and a small cloud of them lifted from the severed heads that awaited him on the wooden table. The women smiled up at him, happy to have him home, and he kissed each of them tenderly on the lips, a thread of bloody spit stretching between his lips and the brunette's as he pulled away. A section of wall teased him with its emptiness, begging to be filled. It was one of the last spaces left. He was almost done, the stories nearly told, and yet peace seemed a long way off. He'd thought the rage would have calmed by now, but it still felt like it could erupt at the slightest provocation, like a volcano merely teasing with its silence. Where was the satisfaction he'd expected? Why did he still feel so anxious? It made his skin sensitive, as if the nerves were on the outside. He wondered if the frenzy would ever go away and leave him alone. He was so very tired. The wall would have to wait. He wouldn't allow his art to be second-rate, even if the blood was this time.

He still had an hour or so before he had to get ready for the visit. He needed to shower and scrub, scrub, scrub to make himself nice and clean. He liked to make a special effort when he saw her, and today was important. Today he needed to leave a lasting impression. He'd already laid out his smartest suit in the bedroom, ironed his shirt, polished his shoes. He felt that odd mixture of excitement and fear, dread and longing, the intensity of which hastened his journey towards his first love. He invariably arrived too early, but punctuality had been drilled into him. Punctuality and obedience were non-negotiable.

He wanted to make the most of the hour, to purge himself so he was presentable inside and out. Maybe then, she would be kind to him. Though her kindness existed under so many thick layers of bitterness, it was futile to hope for it. He needed to be prepared for that. She could be so cold and hard, her flinty edges sharp and quick to slash at what was vulnerable. Age had not withered her in the slightest. Sometimes she would pick at him as if he were a scab, caring nothing for the scars she might leave. She could still make him so angry, angry that she had so profound an effect on him. Surely, he had outgrown her by now.

He needed the blood to arm himself. The blood always made him feel better, and there was lots more this time. It was all over the floor and the table. Some of it was still wet enough to drip from the ceiling in thick, oily spools, like maple syrup. It dripped into his hair and onto his skin and into his mouth as he turned his face up to swallow it. He had almost had his fill – almost, but not quite. He was certainly less hungry, but not entirely full.

He crouched in front of the table and came face to face with Goldilocks and Snow White. This time when he smiled at them, they seemed oblivious to his presence, as if bored, which was insulting after their shared experience. He stretched out on the syrup-glazed floor, the coldness of the ground easy to ignore. Back and forth he rolled on the blanket of deep red until he was melting into the blood like wax. He rolled over onto his stomach and writhed around in the coppery sweetness until there was no separation between himself and the blood. He was the blood, and the blood was him. Then he felt the familiar, insistent demand that needed release from a bloody, well-lubricated hand. *Sometimes*, he thought, *there is peace after all*.

Afterwards, he scrubbed the piggy away until he was clean

and shiny like a star. His skin was still tender from all the scrubbing, but there was no sign of the blood anymore. He looked neat and tidy, his hair perfectly parted, just the way she liked it. His skin glowing and squeaky clean, just the way she liked it. *Like a proper little gentleman.* Her phrase in his head going round and round.

He'd bought her a basket of ripe pears, just the way she liked. She considered it bad manners to turn up empty-handed, and today there would be an extra mouth to feed. He opened the small plastic box he'd brought up from the basement and removed three hooked pork scoring blades from their padded case, as slim and sharp as scalpels. He removed the old blades and replaced them with three new ones, slotting each into its polypropylene head with a satisfying snap. It was a lightweight, highly effective tool that fitted comfortably in his hand, a little clumsy in appearance, similar to a bear's claw, but equally as sharp. It scored the flesh of pork beautifully. The flesh of princesses too. It was discreet and could be easily hidden in the basket of pears and slipped past the fat lazy prison guards transfixed by their mobile phones. They would give his usual fruit gift a customary glance, and then behind his back – as if he couldn't hear them – they would snigger at the mummy's boy and dismiss him as they always did. Familiarity breeding their contempt.

Finally, he applied the vanilla oil – he was running low after liberally coating the last two to disguise their cheap perfume – but it was a special occasion, after all. Perhaps she would be flattered that he'd gone to so much trouble. Perhaps she would be pleased to see him this time – she might behave like a proper mother towards her son – but he couldn't get his hopes up, because it hurt so much when she brought them crashing down. He tried to be a good son, but he was never good enough. *This time I am stronger, though*, he told himself.

This time I will be good enough, because her words wouldn't matter so much. They couldn't reach him. There were more princesses to stand between them.

When he looked in the mirror, his confidence increased. He felt himself at last. He looked smart and handsome – comfortable in his skin – and the Creeper was there, just behind his eyes. He wouldn't have to face Mother alone anymore. Things were different now. She would never talk to him like that again, hurt him like that again. She'd once told him he was weak and needy, that he was a leech she had never wanted, never loved. It was the cruellest she'd ever been, the day she'd finally broken him for good. When she noticed he was crying, she spat in his face and laughed as her saliva mixed with his tears and slid down his cheek. But he was a changed man, he knew who he was now. It had taken a long time, well over a year, but he was ready now. All grown up.

The Creeper would accompany him to the prison today. The Creeper would take one of her hands while he took the other. The Creeper would kiss one of her cheeks while he kissed the other. Together they would be formidable, and they'd demonstrate they were nearly finished with her because they'd almost reached eight. *When there are eight, she will be too late.* She would no longer be important. The number eight would mean the slate was wiped clean. Eight would be his then. It wouldn't spell the oncoming of loneliness and misery anymore. It wouldn't mean a broken heart and a succession of homes where he didn't belong. It would mean a brand-new beginning. Eight would be his lucky number then, not hers. It would signify the end of her, the cutting of the apron strings. "No more mummy's boy," he shouted, his voice strong and so confident he barely recognised it as his own. He liked the way those words sounded, the way they tasted as they rolled off his tongue.

He smiled as he thought about the delicious irony of it all, the twist in the plot. Mother had given him princess number eight. Her weakness, her life-sucking need for attention, had placed his princess right where he needed her. It had worked out so well. Who would love his mother then? Who would visit her in that place? She would wither and die without his attention, like a flower deprived of water. She would know she was no longer the fairest of them all. Her delusions would shatter around her feet like the mirror from the book, this time spelling her doom rather than singing her praises. He would be the one to walk away without a backwards glance.

He was still smiling when he left the house in the early morning crispness, knowing this visit would be his last. Relief crept in, just around the edges, but he had to get a hold of himself. He had to make the most of every last moment, but the feeling was hard to resist. Princess Emma had a lovely ring to it, a ring that would sound like a death knell to Sam when Ben snatched her right out of his hands. Sam would never be Prince Charming come to rescue his princess. He didn't have it in him.

Once he had Emma, he would be free at last. Free of his mother, free of the man who hunted him. Sam would be destroyed, so blinded by rage that he wouldn't be able to finish the final chapter and close the book. But for Ben, it would be a tidy ending – no loose strings.

27

The odour in the therapy room was more intense than usual. Disinfectant and a rose-scented air freshener lingered from that morning's clean – the trolly of wet mops and buckets still positioned in the corridor outside – but another fragrance was layered across it, almost strong enough to suffocate bleach, an overwhelmingly sweet top-note that turned Emma's stomach.

She studied the mother and son opposite her. They were sitting at either end of a sofa that had seen better days, the armrests frayed and the pink material shiny and thin. She could sense Annie's hostility as she yanked fibres from a small hole in the sofa, threads of cotton forming a small pile on her lap.

"Annie, aren't you going to answer Ben's question and tell him how you are? Perhaps thank him for the pears?" Emma asked, unwilling to endure the strained silence any longer. "He asked what you've been up to since he last visited."

Annie pushed a finger deeper into the sofa, the hole tearing slightly. "That is an asinine question, but I'm obviously required to answer it." She glared at Emma. "What does he think I've been up to? Hosting dinner parties or preparing to embark on a long summer cruise perhaps?"

"Could you turn and face your son, Annie?" Emma instructed. "Address him directly."

Annie sighed and adjusted her position. "I've been overwhelmed by social engagements," she said to Ben. "As have you, it seems." She leaned towards him. "You've been quite the social butterfly, haven't you, little Benny?" she laughed.

"Please don't call me that, Mother," Ben replied in a small voice as he rounded his shoulders and wrapped his arms across his body.

As Emma watched, Ben seemed to shrink in on himself. She noticed that for a tall man he was taking up very little space on the sofa. He was tucked into the corner so tightly that his movements were constricted and awkward. She wondered if he was trying to stay as far away from his mother as possible, and if what she was sensing was his fear.

It appeared Annie sensed it too. She suddenly leaned towards Ben and smiled when she saw him flinch.

"Have you been a naughty boy?" Annie wagged her finger under his nose. "Who have you been feeding off, little leech?" She licked her lips and made a sucking sound, the lines above her top lip like the wrinkles in an old, creased shirt.

This time her words made him flinch. "Please don't speak to me like that anymore," Ben whispered, as he glanced at Emma.

Emma saw that Ben's face was flushed and his eyes were wet. She couldn't let Annie continue attacking her son. She was the third side in the therapeutic triangle, and her job was to defuse the tension and act as referee in a battle that could otherwise become hostile.

"Please refrain from name-calling, Annie," she said firmly. "It's completely unnecessary and counterproductive to family therapy." She saw Annie's sneer, her thin white mouth like a well-healed scar. "Let's move on, shall we?"

"Is that what we are, Ben?" Annie asked. "Are we a family?" She moved across the sofa and put her hand on her son's upper thigh. "A little too closely knit, I think."

Emma shuddered and swallowed loudly as she glanced from Annie's hand to Ben's face. She tried to hide her extreme discomfort and adjusted her position on the chair and coughed as a sudden tightness in her throat needed to be cleared. She instinctively averted her eyes from the display of affection and immediately asked herself why she was condoning such inappropriate intimacy with her silence. Before she could intercede, a movement drew her attention back to the sofa.

Ben was stroking his mother's hand and then clasped her three middle fingers, as if his own hand were too small to accommodate any more of hers.

Emma's stomach clenched as she watched them. Ben looked like a hungry man presented with a plate of food. She saw hope in his expression, and anticipation, but in Annie's face she saw only revulsion and what she thought looked like triumph. She was certain there was no hiding the judgement in her own.

Ben glanced at Emma and seemed to understand what was going through her mind. He blushed and recoiled from his mother's touch as if burned. He slapped her hand away and abruptly stood and moved across the room, flattening himself against the wall.

Emma observed Ben as he struggled to control his breathing. She noticed the cocktail of smells had shifted and intensified in the room. It was warmer now, the air stagnant and thick with competing odours, bitter, powdery and far too sweet.

Annie laughed at Ben while digging deeper and deeper into the enlarged hole in the sofa, as if she were picking at a wound. Emma watched chunks of stuffing escape and tumble to the floor forming a multicoloured hill of foam.

Ben ran his hands through his hair, a gesture that dragged Emma's attention from Annie back to him. She saw that he was close to tears. He loosened his tie and unbuttoned the top button of his shirt, which seemed to aid his breathing, but his smart appearance was dishevelled, the dark hollows under his eyes deeper, as if the sockets were trying to swallow them. His skin so clammy it shone under the lights.

Emma thought he looked defeated. The man who'd entered the room just a short while ago and shaken her hand with confidence was no longer present. He seemed diminished, as if the wall against his back could devour him, leaving nothing but a stain on a magnolia wall.

Emma glared at Annie until she diverted her gaze back to the sofa, but not before Emma saw satisfaction in her dark eyes. She looked at Ben, and felt a surge of sympathy for him, and regret that she'd encouraged a therapy session that was clearly doing more harm than good. She stood and moved across the room towards him, her arms outstretched, an apology forming on her lips, but she was thwarted.

"This is all your fault, Emma," Ben screamed. "Pushing and meddling, trying to get to the bottom of this unfixable fucking mess. Trying to get inside my head." His hands had formed fists and a vein throbbed purple on his left temple. "There's no more room in here."

He uncurled a fist and slapped the palm of his hand against the side of his head, again and again, harder each time. "Can't you see that? Isn't that your job?"

Emma covered her mouth with her shaking hands and tried to find the right words. "I'm sorry, Ben, I'm so sorry. Please stop hitting yourself." Her voice sounded weak in her head, thin.

She moved closer to him. "Ben, please..."

"Don't come any closer, just stop talking, stop moving."

He sounded out of breath, but he stopped slapping himself and stood very still. "Please... just give me a moment." He turned his back to Emma and faced the wall. He leaned his forehead against it, his arms by his side, hands clenched tightly once more.

Emma waited, not moving, hardly daring to breathe. She could see Annie out of the corner of her eye. She was motionless on the sofa. She could hear Ben's breathing had slowed, and as she watched, he slowly uncurled his fists. She felt herself relax a little as Ben's body language changed, seemed to become looser. He turned back to Emma, but when she saw his face, her body stiffened, and she took a step back. It was like looking at a completely different man.

Any trace of distress or vulnerability was gone, the anger entirely wiped from his face, as if he'd been unmasked, his true identity revealed. *A wolf in smart clothing*, thought Emma, as she watched Ben refasten his top button and straighten his tie. She noticed his posture had changed again, his shoulders back, his spine straight, hands casually placed in his pockets; he exuded confidence rather than sweat, his face no longer shiny. She felt he was taking up more space in the room now, more than his fair share. She took another step back and glanced at the window, but the orderly must have wandered off. She turned cold as Ben moved closer.

He glanced briefly at Annie and then turned his attention back to Emma. He smiled at her calmly, a flash of steel glinting in his hand. "I'm terribly sorry for my little outburst, but I've pulled myself together. The Creeper is ready for you now, Princess."

28

Sam ran frantically from room to room inside Emma's house, his feet thundering on the floorboards of the upstairs bedrooms. "We're too late," he shouted. "She isn't here." It was the second time he'd checked the bedrooms, unwilling to trust his own eyes or those of the armed response unit that had entered first and declared the house empty. He ran back down the stairs taking them two at a time, the broad back of an officer the only thing that prevented him from falling as he reached the bottom. He ran into the kitchen again, his breath strangled by the pain in his chest, the tightness around his throat. He headed towards the back door to search the tiny garden again and collided with Riley.

"Sam, stop," Riley shouted as he stood in front of the door barring Sam's exit. "She isn't out there. She isn't here at all." He grasped Sam's shoulders. "Calm down, take a breath, and try her mobile again."

Sam knew that tone of voice. He moved away from the door and dialled Emma's phone again, but there was still no answer. He turned back to Riley, trying to hide the sense of dread that now towered over his panic, but instead he read those same emotions in Riley's face. Riley held something in his trembling hands, his eyes enlarged. It was a red hat, the same as the ones that had been left with the bodies. He gave the hat to Sam carefully, as if it were made of glass and might shatter at any moment.

"They match," Riley said, his words almost a whisper. "They fucking match! It's the same red wool." His mouth was agape.

Sam turned it over and over. It was the same design, too. The same use of the fisherman's rib stitch the expert had told them about. The quality of the work looked identical as well. He turned the hat inside out and said, "Look at this." There was a small knot inside the very top of the hat.

"It must have been knitted by the same person." Riley was now breathing rapidly, and he grabbed the back of a kitchen chair for support. "It's Red Riding Hood's hat."

Sam's fingers felt numb, uncoordinated. He dropped the hat onto the kitchen table as if scalded and leaned on the back of the chair opposite Riley. He closed his eyes as the room fell silent. It seemed as if time were standing still while it waited for Sam to collect himself. He drew from Riley's strength, absorbed it, and allowed it to replenish him. The house was eerily quiet now despite the presence of numerous police officers, as if they were all holding their breath, waiting for whatever was about to come next.

The ring of Sam's phone shattered the silence. It was Emma calling him. The sense of relief drained him so abruptly from despair that his knees buckled, and he dropped heavily into the chair. "Emma, where are you? Are you okay?"

"I have her, Sam." The words were spoken softly but triumphantly in the rhythm of a taunt.

"Who is this?" Sam stood up and kicked the chair away, sending it crashing into the front of the oven. "What have you done to Emma?" He held Riley's gaze.

"You know who this is. Emma is with the Creeper at the place where all the psychopaths stay in to play. I have two Snow Whites in the palm of my hand, one old, one new, and they're paying attention at last. My first love is going to watch my last love die. I want you to know how it feels to have your heart ripped out, so you can empathise like a good little psychologist. It's the only way this story can end." He laughed. "Your subject will be fully profiled."

"Please don't hurt her." But the phone went dead, the silence like a punch to the stomach.

"He has her, doesn't he?" Riley thumped the table when Sam nodded. "Where is she?" he asked. "Did he say?"

Sam shook his head. "He might have snatched her right from here. He might have been here, and we missed him." *We could have prevented this.*

"No," Riley said. "There were no signs of a struggle when we got here."

Sam began to pace around the kitchen. *Think, Sam, think.* He stepped around the chair. *Where is she?* There was something in the back of his mind, an idea pushing through the fog of panic. Something Emma mentioned last night.

"She's at the prison, she told me she had a session there today." Sam was aware that he was shouting; his voice sounded unrecognisable to him.

"Are you sure?" asked Riley.

Sam thought it through and nodded. *Where all the psychopaths stay in to play.* "Yes, let's go."

Riley barked orders at the team, and they hurried out of Emma's house, slamming the door behind them so loudly the windows rattled. As they made their way to the prison, he called the prison governor and briefed him on the situation.

When they finally arrived, the rusty gates of the prison yawned open with the terrible grinding sound of metal across concrete. Sam waited impatiently with Riley to drive through. It was like waiting for a drawbridge to be lowered over a moat allowing them entry into an imposing and unwelcoming fortress. With excruciating slowness, more of the prison came into view. It was an austere building, oddly beautiful, but the barred windows and coils of barbed wire revealed that the beauty was only skin deep.

As the gates finally stuttered fully open, the convoy of police vehicles drove through. Sam jumped from the car before it came to a complete stop. He followed the armed unit and Riley towards the main entrance. Behind them, the towering gates slammed closed far more quickly than they had opened, the sound deep, foreboding, and final.

The prison governor and four guards met them and led them inside in tense silence. They walked down a long, beige corridor towards the psychiatric wing where a slightly overweight orderly named Matthew nodded at them in greeting, his large hands gesturing for them to follow him. He had the cauliflower ears of a rugby player and was dressed head to toe in white. At the end of the corridor, he unlocked a door. Sam and the others followed him down another long corridor, this one painted in pale yellow. Their shoes squeaked out a quick pace on the mint-green linoleum, the smell of bleach and pine disinfectant giving the air a sharp, bitter tang. It was warm inside, and Sam's skin turned clammy as they marched one behind the other like soldiers heading into battle.

At the end of the corridor, the orderly removed a jangling bunch of keys from a clip on his belt and located the one he needed. After looking through a small, barred window to ensure a safe entry, he unlocked the heavy white door into the day room. The room was large with ornate sconces beneath vaulted ceilings, scratched parquet wooden floors and a faint smell of dampness. It reminded Sam of a church from which all the religious paraphernalia and pews had been removed. It was filled with the female patients who were stable enough to mingle with each other. If it weren't for their matching outfits and sharp, unmoderated voices, it could have been a gathering of women who had come together to gossip over knitting and painting projects.

Sam and the others must have been an alarming sight – dark-clothed police officers in body armour in place of white-clothed medical staff, led by prison guards and the orderly. As they entered, the mood in the room shifted from controlled tension to hostility and undisguised suspicion. A few inmates stood up for a closer look but were met with warning glances from the guards. Other women offered flirtatious smiles from hard faces, but their intentions seemed more aggressive than receptive, the smiles quick to disappear. Others remained oblivious, too lost in their own fog to even notice them. Some of the women stood in front of the tall windows getting a tantalising glimpse of freedom. One stood in a corner by herself, her face to the wall as she sobbed loudly. Nobody paid attention to her, even though her sobs were now the only sound in the room. The appearance of Sam and the officers had silenced the shrill voices. Sam was relieved when the orderly unlocked another door allowing them to escape, but he was dreading what they would find behind it.

They were now approaching the therapy area, a collection of rooms with large windows that enabled the orderlies to keep a close watch over what went on. It was here that the less dangerous inmates underwent therapy in surroundings that attempted to be welcoming and soothing. The rooms lined both sides of a small, brightly lit corridor, the persistent hum of the fluorescent lights the only sound. Somebody had tried to disguise the ever-present smell of disinfectant with air freshener, but the result was a stifling chemical mix that smelled sickly sweet. Riley glanced over his shoulder at Sam with an expression that told him their long journey was almost at an end.

The governor came to a stop and faced the group. His cheeks were flushed, and he was a little out of breath. "They're in the last room on the left," he said in a quiet voice. He gestured towards the other end of the corridor. "The medical staff have been briefed and told to keep away for now, but as requested, there are orderlies and guards on standby in the rooms on either side of Emma, the patient and her son." He turned to Riley. "The patient's name is Annie."

"And her son?" Riley asked.

"Ben Shaw," the governor replied.

Sam exchanged a brief glance with Riley. They finally had a name, but there was no time to acknowledge the unveiling of the man they'd been hunting for over a year.

"How do you want to proceed, Chief Inspector?" asked the governor. The sweat on his forehead slid down the sides of his face.

"Sir, you and your staff need to wait in one of the rooms until the situation is under control," Riley said.

The governor nodded and moved off, looking relieved to be out of the way.

Riley seemed remarkably calm and looked very much in control as he turned and faced his team. "Remember, this is first and foremost a hostage situation, and Sam and I will be taking control of the negotiations. Our objective, however, is a peaceful resolution." He turned to the pair of officers closest to him. "You two will go in first and stand on either side of the door. Your primary focus is the Creeper. I want him to see your weapons. He has to know we're in control now, but keep them down unless this whole thing goes to shit."

The officers nodded. Their faces serious with concentration.

They looked imposing in their black body armour, as if they had doubled in size when they'd suited up.

Riley then addressed two other officers. "You two position yourselves behind me and Sam after we go in. Emma and Annie are your primary focus. As soon as they're safe, arrest that fucking psycho. Once the situation is under control, hand Annie off to the orderlies next door."

Riley eyed Sam with unease. "Are you certain you're ready for this? I know you think it's the right thing to do, and the Creeper has pretty much requested your presence, but I have concerns. You're the one he's chosen to fixate on. Aren't we playing into his hands by allowing him to call the shots?"

"Look, Albert, we went through this on the way over here," Sam replied, sounding far braver than he felt. "He used Emma's phone to call me because he wants me to watch him finish the story, and he is calling the shots because he has Emma, so I don't see that I have a choice." He suddenly felt cold, and yet his hands were clammy. "Let me help."

Riley looked only slightly more convinced. "Alright, listen. I've been in this type of situation before. He's going to be focused on you and that might work to our advantage, and we have to use any advantage we can get right now. It gives us a greater opportunity to get Emma and Annie out of there safely."

Sam wondered if he was right to enter the room, but there was no time for second-guessing now.

"Stay close to the officers who go in first," Riley said, "and stay close to me. The other two will be right behind us. We need to get this over with as quickly as possible, so let me do the talking." He ran a finger across his top lip and wiped away the sweat that had collected there. "Are we clear?"

Sam nodded, his stomach clenched with nerves, his throat dry. "Remember to use his name. We know who he is now.

Call him Ben. He'll feel disempowered if he can't hide behind the Creeper anymore." His words were sticking to the roof of his mouth.

Riley turned to the others. "Remember, everyone, peaceful resolution is our objective. We're about to close the book on Ben Shaw. The Creeper is finished." The team members each gave a brief nod as they headed towards the therapy room.

There wasn't far to walk, but it was one of the longest walks of Sam's life – and yet also not long enough. As he moved, he had a sudden flashback to his childhood. He remembered shuffling towards the end of a high diving board above a swimming pool that seemed a long way down and far too small. As he neared the end of the board, it flexed and vibrated beneath him, turning his legs to jelly. When he risked peeking over the edge, the pool rushed up at him as if trying to pull him off the board and suck him under the water. He froze for what felt like an eternity before finally turning around and inching his way back along the unstable board until he could climb down. The same paralysing fear gripped him now – but this time, he'd have to jump.

As he neared the window to the therapy room, Sam could sense the adrenaline coursing through Riley and the team like an electric current. The armed officers positioned themselves outside the door and waited for permission to enter. Riley and Sam turned and looked through the window, a chorus of heavy, accelerated breathing keeping tempo with the flickering lights.

Emma and her patient, Annie, sat next to each other on a threadbare pink sofa facing the window. Annie had squeezed herself into the corner of the sofa as though she couldn't bear to be that close to Emma. Her arms were folded, and her lips were so tightly pinched they had turned white, as if she were digesting something bitter. There was stuffing erupting from a large hole in the sofa, a pile scattered on the floor by her feet. She glared at her son, her face devoid of any emotion resembling warmth.

This was the Creeper's mother?

Something… there was something familiar about her. It played at the edges of Sam's thoughts, but he couldn't pin it down. His eyes wouldn't leave her face.

Riley put a hand on his arm, startling him. "You sure you're alright?"

He nodded absently.

Emma had her back pressed against the sofa, her cheeks glistening, talking to the man sitting opposite her on an armchair. While she didn't look outwardly panicked, there was something about the rigid way she held herself that told Sam she was already aware of the danger.

A small, wooden table sat between them on which was a box of tissues and a small woven basket of pears with a red ribbon tied around the handle. Ben Shaw, the Creeper, had his back to the window and didn't see Sam, but Annie did. A confused look crossed her face, the beginnings of a smile returning colour into her clenched mouth. Riley nodded at the armed officers who opened the door and rushed inside, followed by Riley and Sam.

"Sam!" Emma's eyes darted around at all the officers in the room.

Ben wheeled around to face Sam, a look of surprise on his face that was swiftly replaced with a smile. He bolted from his chair, leapt towards Emma, and grabbed her from behind as she tried to run towards Sam. He pulled her against him in a tight embrace. Something in his hand glinted as it caught the light, and he held it against Emma's throat. It was some kind of knife. She froze in his arms and didn't make a sound, her eyes fixed on Sam.

The officers drew their weapons while Sam stood paralysed near the doorway.

"Put it down, Ben," Riley said calmly. "Put it down and let her go."

"I told you," Ben said, but he wasn't speaking to Riley. He was speaking to Sam. "Now you'll see how it feels."

"Ben, you don't have to do this," Riley said. His voice was placating as he continued to speak.

Sam was busy putting together the pieces of a puzzle. He recognised this man. He'd met him. It was the man who repaired toys in the museum.

Suddenly he became aware of another pair of eyes fixed on him – those of the older woman, Annie.

"I know you," she said.

"Mother!" Ben shouted. "Be quiet."

It felt like the shift of a child's kaleidoscope, everything suddenly slipping into place. Yes. Yes, Sam knew her, too. It was a face he clearly remembered, despite not having seen it for a long time. The years had stretched out and fallen away, reducing memories into faded snatches of hazy recollections. But there was no mistaking her.

Annie rose from her chair awkwardly, an uncertain smile on her face.

"Sit down!" Ben shouted.

"Mum?" Sam said in a strangled tone. The word felt awkward in his mouth. He'd thought his mother was long dead, but there was no question: this was her. Sam's reality shattered, taking with it everything he knew to be true. He held the wall to keep himself upright.

Annie came towards him, but he was unable to move, as if his feet were cemented into place. "Is it really you?" she asked.

Sam knew the voice, even though it had been silent for most of his life.

"For fuck's sake, Mother, what are you talking about? Get away from him!" Ben cried.

"It is you, isn't it?" Annie said. "He made me leave you, but now you've come back to me. My darling son, my little boy."

Sam struggled with too many powerful emotions. Riley was still speaking to Ben, the officers with their guns trained on him. Sam's eyes were now fixed on Emma, but his senses were overwhelmed by Annie's perfume, the unmistakable intensity of vanilla oil wrapped around coal tar soap, enclosing him in an unbearable cloud. The smell that had evaded him for years confronted him now, bringing with it long-buried memories. These hands that now held him in a motherly embrace were the hands that had searched aggressively for places they shouldn't have been looking for. They were the hands that had held him underwater during bath time when he'd tried to push her away. The hands that had crept under the bed covers and were always reaching, clawing, invading. They were the hands of the woman he used to fear so much he would hide from her at the top of a tree despite the terrifying, lonely darkness of night. The woman who always found him. She had followed him into his dreams and turned them into nightmares – the same nightmares that troubled him still. She had filled those nightmares with her insistent grasping and vanilla perfume, always that smell.

Instinctively Sam pushed her away, feeling like a terrified boy once more, and as he did so he became aware of Ben. A new thought came to him with terrifying clarity. The killer he'd been looking for, thinking about for so long that he had become a part of him, was his brother – the brother he didn't know he had.

Sam collapsed against the side of the sofa. He reached uselessly for Emma, his hands grasping air. His legs felt unstable. He felt unstable.

Everything happened very quickly after that. Ben pushed

Emma away and stepped over her as she fell heavily onto the floor, and then he screamed. It was a cry of terrible pain, of years of anguish and unbearable anger. He grabbed his mother and drew her tightly against his body, her back against his chest, and held his weapon under her chin. Sam saw the flash of metal blades as they pushed into the folds of his mother's neck, but her whimpering was engulfed by her son's screams.

"I had a brother! All this time, I had someone. I wasn't alone. I had a family." Ben gasped for breath. "I never had anyone. I've always been so alone. Nobody ever wanted to be close to me. It was like I had a smell about me that warned people off, and that smell was you. Your breath, your blood, the stink of you inside me that kept people away. You destroyed me, Mother. You broke me. You broke everything." Ben's voice was quieter now, but the control merely underlined the intensity of his emotions, the weight of consuming anger that must have lived inside him ever since he was a boy. He started to sob, his body swaying and vibrating as he leaned against his mother, as if he were trying to hug her while she turned her back on him. "I didn't need to be so alone, but all I had was you, and then you were gone. I wanted a new voice in my head."

Annie barked with laughter, a spray of spit landing on her son's arm. "I'm the only voice you'll ever hear, you insignificant little worm."

Emma struggled to her knees. "Ben, if you keep listening to her voice, you'll never hear your own."

Ben glanced at Emma and the anger in his face fell away like he was shedding skin. He grasped Annie's hair, nestled against her cheek briefly and then pulled her head back, exposing her thin, white neck. In a quick movement, he drew the blades across her throat, covering them both in a spray of warm blood. Annie collapsed onto the floor, her weight dragging Ben down with her. An awful, gurgling noise came from her, like water escaping down a drain, and blood bubbled from her sagging mouth.

A single shot exploded, startlingly loud in the small room. Emma cried out as the armed officers shouted commands at Ben.

Blood poured from the bullet wound in Ben's shoulder, but it seemed to have no effect on him. "You are number eight, you evil bitch. You are number eight." Ben screamed the words over and over again as he stabbed at Annie's throat, her face, her chest, not stopping even though his own hand was ragged and torn. Not stopping even though she was dead. Nobody had heard Annie take her last breath.

Sam looked on at the unfolding horror, his eyes wide, his mouth hanging open in a silent scream. Suddenly the armed officers pushed him to one side and piled on top of Ben. Riley was speaking to him, but he couldn't focus on the words. How long had he been on the floor? He wrapped his arms around himself as two officers lifted Ben from the ground.

Ben was laughing hysterically, his face bloody and wild. "Visiting hours are over, Mother," he shouted down at her body. Then he turned to Sam. "I was right, wasn't I? When there are eight, you will be too late."

A second before they dragged Ben from the room, Sam looked into his eyes. He wanted to believe an exchange had taken place – a recognition of mutual pain and a silent offering of gratitude. Could he have stopped Ben from killing the mother who had abused them both? Had he even wanted to?

Sam brought his knees to his chest and buried his face in his lap. Shock travelled through his body, making him shiver. They'd caught the Grimm Creeper. The long search was finally over. But there wasn't room inside him for relief. Only one emotion consumed him, taking him completely by surprise. Empathy moved through him without warning and with such intensity that it took his breath away. Empathy for a killer. It made him sob with the pain that exploded and burned inside him. The empathy didn't reach his mother, however, it could never stretch that far.

29

Sam rested his head on Emma's lap, and she stroked the back of his neck. The hospital blanket was rough against his cheek, but her soothing touch was like a healing balm. The shock was leaving his body, but in its place was an incoming tide of exhaustion determined to carry him towards sleep.

"How long are they keeping you in?" he asked, his skin tingling under her touch.

"Just tonight for observation," Emma said. "They want to rule out a concussion. I hit my head quite hard when I fell, and I've got a pretty big lump, but I feel okay, considering." She exhaled loudly, her breath shuddering. "Although I won't be working at a prison any time soon."

"What happened?" Sam lifted his head. "Before we came in? What did he say to you?"

She interlaced her fingers with his. "He told me his mother was a stain that needed to be washed away, and that killing me would make him clean again. I told him killing me would make no difference, because she wasn't a stain. She was a scar. I think my challenge gave him pause." She squeezed his fingers. "But I didn't think it would make him kill her. I'm so sorry." She looked flushed and tearful.

Sam shook his head. "Your challenge saved your life. It made him realise he would never have a clean slate. It was always going to end that way. You have nothing to be sorry for." He wiped a tear from her cheek and smiled. "I thought I would be the hero and come and save you, but you saved yourself." He adjusted the blankets to cover Emma's exposed feet. She looked cold.

"I'm not a princess, Sam. I don't need saving." Emma smiled and leaned back against the pillows.

"Maybe I'm the one who needs saving." Sam stood up, his body weary and reluctant to move, but he had one more thing to do before his long day was finally over. He leaned towards Emma and kissed her gently on the forehead. "I'll see you soon. Get some rest."

She reached up and clasped the back of Sam's neck so that the kiss might linger a little longer and leaned into him. She seemed to breathe him in, as if she were inhaling his scent, and then closed her eyes.

$$*$$

Still feeling Emma's caress on the back of his neck, Sam drove with Riley down the deserted street. Riley looked pale. The watery sunlight caught his greying whiskers. The furrow between his eyebrows now seemed permanent. Sam wondered if the affectionate nickname of Smiley Riley would ever fit again.

"How're you doing, Albert?" he asked as they came to a stop at a red light.

Riley yawned loudly. "Bloody shattered, but that bastard is on his way to prison, and the job is done – well, almost. I might finally get a good night's sleep." He turned to Sam, took a breath, paused. "I'm not sure what to say to you. Sorry about your mum. Sorry your brother is a fucking whack job. I mean, what does one say in a situation like this?"

Sam burst into laughter, the sound explosive in the quiet car. "How about, sorry the brother you didn't know you had killed the mother you thought was dead? That should cover it."

Riley looked at him in surprise and then added his laughter to Sam's. "That's a fucked-up family dynamic." He pulled away from the lights. "You might need a good therapist."

Sam savoured the moment. He had put the smile back on Riley's face. But it fell away again as they turned the corner into the Creeper's neighbourhood. The street felt utterly abandoned, as if all the inhabitants had rushed to escape a natural disaster – or an unnatural one. Georgian houses were dilapidated shells, only a hint of their former grandeur visible beneath the encroachment of Mother Nature. The few signs promising forthcoming modern homes and regeneration projects were graffitied and rusty. It was an eerie place, devoid of the life that existed just a few streets away. It seemed forgotten and pitiful, soulless. As if the marching of time had overlooked it and marched right by.

"This is the perfect place for a serial killer," said Sam. "He must have been able to come and go without ever being seen."

"There's nobody around *to* see him, Sam," replied Riley. "This street is perfect for keeping secrets – but not for much longer." He pointed as he slowed the car. "The SOCOs are already here."

Riley pulled up in front of a row of empty shops. Ben Shaw – Sam's brother – had lived in an old, neglected butcher shop. Sam surveyed the run-down exterior, the tattered remnants of an awning, the colours rendered pale by the passing years. He thought how fitting a place it was for a killer and dreaded confronting the nightmare they might find inside. Once he entered that place, nothing would ever be the same again. He would never be the same.

Riley turned to him, his face set in the mask he always wore at crime scenes, as if he had to close down a part of himself in preparation for the horror laid bare. "Are you ready for this, Sam? I don't think it's going to be pretty in there." There was no trace of a smile left on his face.

Sam nodded as they got out of the car. He searched for the right words to break the tension, but there were none. He felt sure that Riley could hear his heart pounding as they walked towards the shop. The back of Sam's neck was stiff with tension. The same tightness across his shoulders made it awkward to duck under the blue and white crime scene tape stretched across the entrance to the flat. He attempted to smile at the officer guarding the entrance, but the smile wouldn't come. It felt as if he had forgotten how to form one.

As the officer moved aside and allowed them to pass, he grabbed Riley's arm. "Prepare yourself, sir – although I'm not sure how you can prepare for something like that." He glanced at Sam. "It's a hellhole inside. Unbelievable. I've never seen anything like it." He shook his head as he handed them protective gloves and shoe coverings before he stepped outside and made three attempts to light a cigarette with a shaking hand.

Time seemed to pass in slow motion as Sam followed Riley up the steep staircase and stepped over what remained of a smashed front door. The smell inside the flat hit him first and made him gag. It was so overpowering and thick, it felt like he might push it aside, like curtains. Instead, it clawed at him with a sticky persistence and grew more determined as he and Riley headed towards the voices that were coming from downstairs. Fat black flies bombarded their faces. Halfway down, Riley was nearly knocked over by a young officer running up the stairs with one hand across his mouth, trying to leave the crime scene before vomiting and contaminating it. With his other hand he attempted to wipe away tears. He looked deeply shocked. Concerned, Riley turned and followed the officer, and Sam moved to one side to allow them to pass. His stomach lurched again. The smell intensified as it climbed the stairs to greet him.

Sam followed the voices, moving into what appeared to be the storage rooms behind the shop. There he saw two SOCOs standing in front of a large, glass-fronted freezer. They turned as Sam approached and moved aside, but they said nothing. There was nothing they could say. Five heads sat on the shelves, each under a glass dome. It took his brain a while to process what he was seeing, as if it wanted to shut down and spare him too shocking a reality. Sam knew each face so well, he had lost count of the hours he'd spent committing them to memory, but all those memories would be replaced by how the faces looked now. Their skin sagged around the cheekbones and hung from the jaw in loose folds. The grey and pale blue pallor of the skin was a stark contrast to the red lipstick smeared across stretched lips. Each mouth hung open as if fighting for air, and as Sam drew closer, he could see something yellow lying on each of the victims' dark, swollen tongues. He would have to wait for the SOCOs to examine the scene before he could be sure, but he suspected they were slices of pear taken from the fruit the Creeper had left with the bodies.

Ice crystals glittered in their hair and eyelashes like tiny diamonds. Each victim seemed to be looking at Sam through cloudy eyes that offered up a plea – one he was too late to hear. The heads seemed almost unreal, wax models in a display case at a museum, or the heads from mannequins awaiting a body. If he hadn't known the birthmarks and scars so well, he might have convinced himself these women were strangers to him, but they had grown too intimate over time for so easy a dismissal. Instead, it was like looking at the faces of loved ones he had failed to protect. His chest tightened and tears formed in his eyes, but he had to get a firm grip on his emotions before they overwhelmed him and left him incapable of completing a full and coherent profile, or from ever doing his job again. As he turned away from the freezer, it felt like he was turning his back on the victims, but there was more to see. He wasn't turning his back on them for good, and that was what he whispered to them over his shoulder as he moved away.

Other officers were moving about below him, so he followed the sound to a small staircase and headed down to the basement. As he entered the large, dimly lit room, he instinctively put his hand over his mouth, but he didn't know if that was a reaction to the unbearable smell or the unbearable sight. Everywhere he looked there was blood. Blood had been used as ink to write across the walls in sweeping lines and curling tendrils like ivy on a garden wall. A bloody, evil hand had tainted the fairy tales of *Snow White*, *Little Red Riding Hood* and *Rapunzel*. Glass coffins, red hats, a tower and a wolf with bloody jowls leaving his pawprints among the words. Sam was more convinced than ever that Ben Shaw had been stuck inside an infantile psyche, one that had broken him. As he surveyed the room, he wondered about his mother: what had she done to her young son to turn him into the kind of monster that cut off women's heads and decorated walls with their blood? And what might she have done to him?

He noticed an untouched section of wall, pristine and China white. He doubled over and sobbed as he realised it must have been waiting for Emma. His breathing accelerated, the dread of what might have been too much to confront. He pushed thoughts of her away; he wouldn't allow her into this room, this evil place. With a struggle, he managed to pull himself together.

When Sam turned from the walls and looked behind him, a moan escaped his lips: two heads sat on top of a large, wooden table. There was nothing of the mannequin about these ones. They were fresh, the wounds still shiny and wet. These were two faces Sam didn't know but knew he would never forget. They hadn't been made presentable yet. Both faces were puffy and bruised and smeared with blood, lips pulled back behind teeth in a grimace that could almost be mistaken for a smile. On one, the matted, blonde hair looked closer to brown as the blood dried in thick clumps. One eye was purple and swollen shut, her nose smashed and crooked – evidence of the fight she had put up. The brunette was missing some of her hair, bald patches of white scalp peeping through what remained, her two front teeth jagged and broken.

Sam couldn't be in that room anymore. He couldn't look at the faces that showed him all too clearly what their fate had been. The smell had moved inside him and coated the back of his throat. He couldn't breathe it in anymore. He ran from the room on legs that felt too weak to hold him, climbed the stairs that seemed far steeper this time and stumbled down another flight of stairs that never seemed to end, until he finally made it outside where he doubled over and was violently sick.

He thought he would pass out. The corners of his vision turned black, and he sank to the ground, caring nothing for the dirty pavement – only that it felt stable enough to hold him. He tried to take deep breaths, but his chest felt constricted, so all he could manage were shallow rasping sounds that made him shiver. He felt Riley's hand on the back of his neck. How long ago it seemed that Emma's hand had rested there.

30

Sam stared out of the large windows in the living room of his flat. The smell of the coffee his dad was brewing was beginning to reach him. Below him, the streets of London flowed and stretched towards the horizon, where they fell away like water over a waterfall and disappeared from view. The city was a little safer now.

It was the morning after the Grimm Creeper's reign had ended, and yet the city continued on as if it hadn't been divided into a 'before' and 'after' by the presence of a killer walking its streets. This was how it should be – life would carry on regardless, scars forming over the wounds. Sam's wounds were deeper and would take far longer to heal. Part of the healing would involve accepting a changed personal history that would eventually solidify into a new reality. He couldn't face that reality, though, not until he felt emotionally strong enough to make sense of it. When he felt strong enough to visit the Creeper in prison and acknowledge that he so easily could've had a childhood like Ben's. It was a day that had to come.

His dad poured the coffee, the steam rising and forming a temporary veil that almost obscured his strained expression.

"This is a story I hoped never to tell you, Sam. I thought you would be better off not knowing." He stirred sugar into both of their cups. "But I suppose I'm forced to tell you now."

Sam nodded as he finished rolling a cigarette. "I'm sorry we have to talk about this, but I think we have to if we want to move on." He lit his cigarette, glanced at his dad, and waited for the customary frown of disapproval at his smoking.

"Can you roll me one of those?" his dad asked. "It's been a long time, but I think I need one."

Sam raised his eyebrows, handed him the one he was smoking, and rolled himself another.

"Thanks." His dad inhaled deeply, coughed, and then sighed with relief. For a while, they were both silent. And then he spoke. "I came home from work early one day and found that woman abusing you in the bath. You were six years old." The words rushed from his mouth as if he had expelled something deeply unpalatable. "She protested her innocence, but there was no mistaking her actions." He studied Sam's face closely, and then continued more slowly. "I threw her out of the house that day, told her to disappear and never come back or I would call the police, but I didn't know she was pregnant with my second son." His last words were almost swallowed by a sob.

Sam moved towards him. "Dad, I'm sorry. We can do this another time."

His dad waved him away. "It's okay. Just let me get through this." He took a couple of puffs on the cigarette. "If I had known that she later gave birth to Ben, I would have done everything I could to track her down and save him." He placed the cigarette on the side of the ashtray, watching it smoulder. "I told you she was dead because I didn't want that woman in your life. I didn't want you to ever see her again. Killing her off was the best way I knew to make that happen." He put his head into his hands and started to cry. "I should have killed her for what she did to you. I'm so sorry, Sam. I'm so sorry."

Sam kneeled on the floor in front of his dad and removed his hands from his face. "If you had killed her, you would have gone to prison, and I would have lost you. You saved me from her." He lifted his dad's head so he could see his eyes. "Saving me like you did means that your voice is the only one that has been inside my head throughout my life. I've never heard hers." He hugged his dad and held him close, the smell of cigarette smoke on his clothes strange but comforting as it mixed with the familiar smell of his soap.

"I wish I could have saved you both." His dad buried himself in his son's neck, stubble tickling the side of his face. They held each other for a long time.

His father spent the day with him. After he left, Sam stood at the windows and watched the streets empty, the full moon glittering on the Barbican towers. Feeling as if he could finally sleep, he turned from the city below and noticed the cardboard box his dad had dropped off containing his old books. He decided to have a quick look before he went to bed.

As he removed old football manuals and books about dinosaurs, their pages yellowed and mottled with age, the sweet vanilla scent of his mother invaded the room like a bad feeling. At the bottom of the box was a large book wrapped in a red scarf, the material silken and soft. Inside was Sam's old copy of *Grimms' Fairy Tales*, a damp mustiness clinging to its pages. The book fell open to the story of *Snow White*, a faded photograph of his mother like a bookmark halfway through the story. He hadn't seen the photograph before, or the inscription on the back: *Remember, I was your first love, Sam. Don't forget me.*

Sam didn't hesitate before ripping the photograph into eight pieces, which seemed only fitting, and throwing them in the ashtray. He lit a match and allowed the flame to caress each piece, watching as his mother curled up and disappeared into a pile of blackened ash.

As the flames died down, Sam carried the ashtray across the room and opened a window. He dumped the ashtray upside down and let the ashes of his mother blow away on a cleansing current of air. The sky was a dark indigo blue and completely clear. Tomorrow would be a beautiful day. He headed towards his bed, secure in the knowledge that his nightmare would trouble him no longer, that sleep would now be the refuge that healed him and made him feel new again. That perhaps, after all, he could live happily ever after.

Acknowledgements

I would like to thank the team at Troubador for bringing my book out into the world.

Thanks also to the wonderful editor Michelle Barker at The Darling Axe for her enthusiasm and encouragement in the early days of this book.

I'm grateful to author Amanda Reynolds for mentoring me in the developmental stage, and to Claire Dyer, Guy Hale and Colette Dartford for generously sharing their knowledge.

Special thanks to Gylda who read this book countless times and offered so much feedback.

Huge thanks to my mum and dad who gave me my first book and so much more. My path is easier to tread because of their support and love.

For my brother, Adam, who has walked the path with me and always laughs at the same things. The roots run deep.

For Molly, Maisy and Maudy, much-loved distractions.

The biggest thanks of all go to my incredible super-hero husband. For his endless reading, encouragement and tireless support of this book. Without him, this book wouldn't exist. Without him the sun would always be behind a cloud.